COMICS SQUAD
DETENTION!

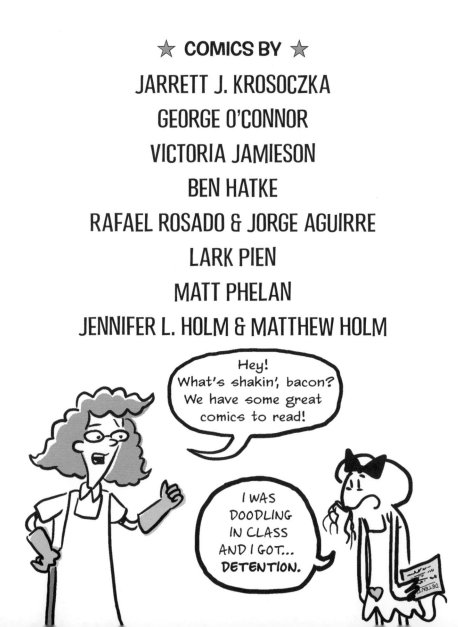

★ **COMICS BY** ★

JARRETT J. KROSOCZKA

GEORGE O'CONNOR

VICTORIA JAMIESON

BEN HATKE

RAFAEL ROSADO & JORGE AGUIRRE

LARK PIEN

MATT PHELAN

JENNIFER L. HOLM & MATTHEW HOLM

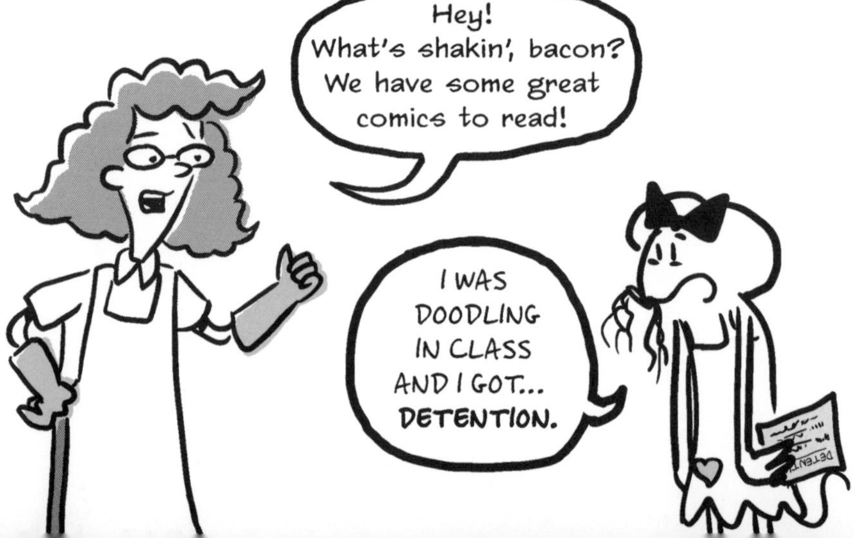
Hey! What's shakin', bacon? We have some great comics to read!
I WAS DOODLING IN CLASS AND I GOT... DETENTION.

COMICS SQUAD

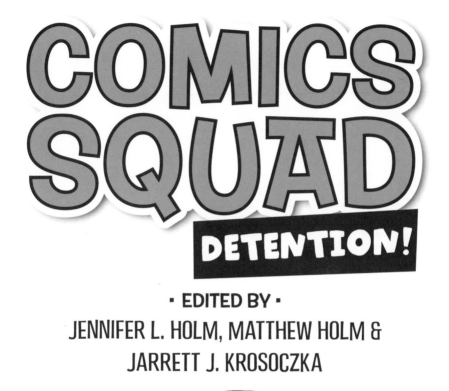

DETENTION!

· EDITED BY ·

JENNIFER L. HOLM, MATTHEW HOLM &
JARRETT J. KROSOCZKA

Oh no! Here. Take a cookie.
NO CUPCAKES?

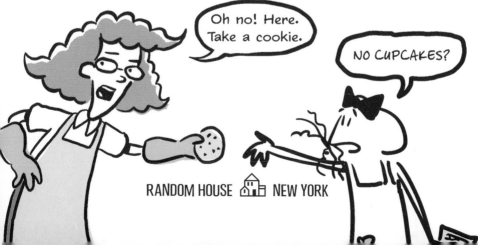

RANDOM HOUSE NEW YORK

Compilation copyright © 2017 by Jennifer L. Holm, Matthew Holm, and Jarrett J. Krosoczka

"The Breakfast Bunch in . . . Detention Disaster" copyright © 2017 by Jarrett J. Krosoczka. "Cheating Death w/ Sisyphus" copyright © 2017 by George O'Connor. "Worse Than Detention" copyright © 2017 by Victoria Jamieson. "Milo's Journey" copyright © 2017 by Ben Hatke. "Too Nice!" copyright © 2017 by Rafael Rosado and Jorge Aguirre. "Cyclopean Kid: Detention Is Forever!" copyright © 2017 by Lark Pien. "Think About What You've Done!" copyright © 2017 by Matt Phelan. "Squish: Leave No Cell Behind!" copyright © 2017 by Jennifer L. Holm and Matthew Holm.

Cover art copyright © 2017 by Jennifer L. Holm and Matthew Holm, Jarrett J. Krosoczka, George O'Connor, Victoria Jamieson, Ben Hatke, Rafael Rosado, Jorge Aguirre, Lark Pien, and Matt Phelan.

All rights reserved. Published in the United States by Random House Children's Books, a division of Penguin Random House LLC, New York.

Random House and the colophon are registered trademarks of Penguin Random House LLC.

Visit us on the Web! randomhousekids.com

Educators and librarians, for a variety of teaching tools, visit us at RHTeachersLibrarians.com

Library of Congress Cataloging-in-Publication Data is available upon request.

ISBN 978-0-553-51267-0 (tr. pbk.) — ISBN 978-0-553-51268-7 (lib. bdg.) — ISBN 978-0-553-51269-4 (ebook)

MANUFACTURED IN CHINA

10 9 8 7 6 5 4 3 2 1

First Edition

★ CONTENTS ★

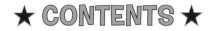

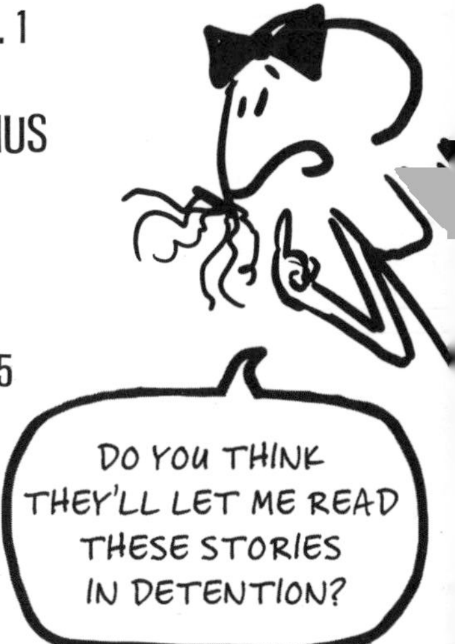
DO YOU THINK THEY'LL LET ME READ THESE STORIES IN DETENTION?

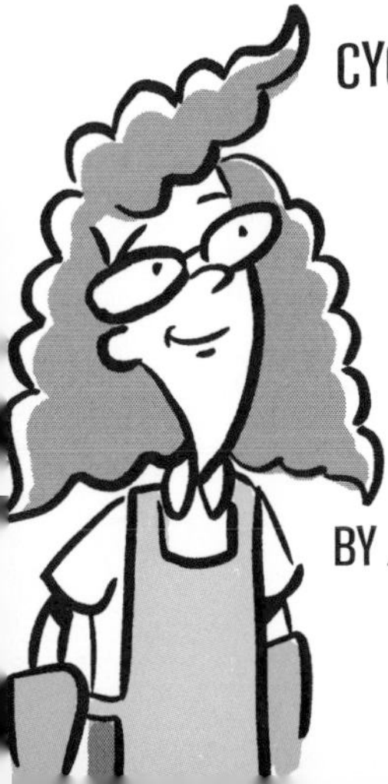

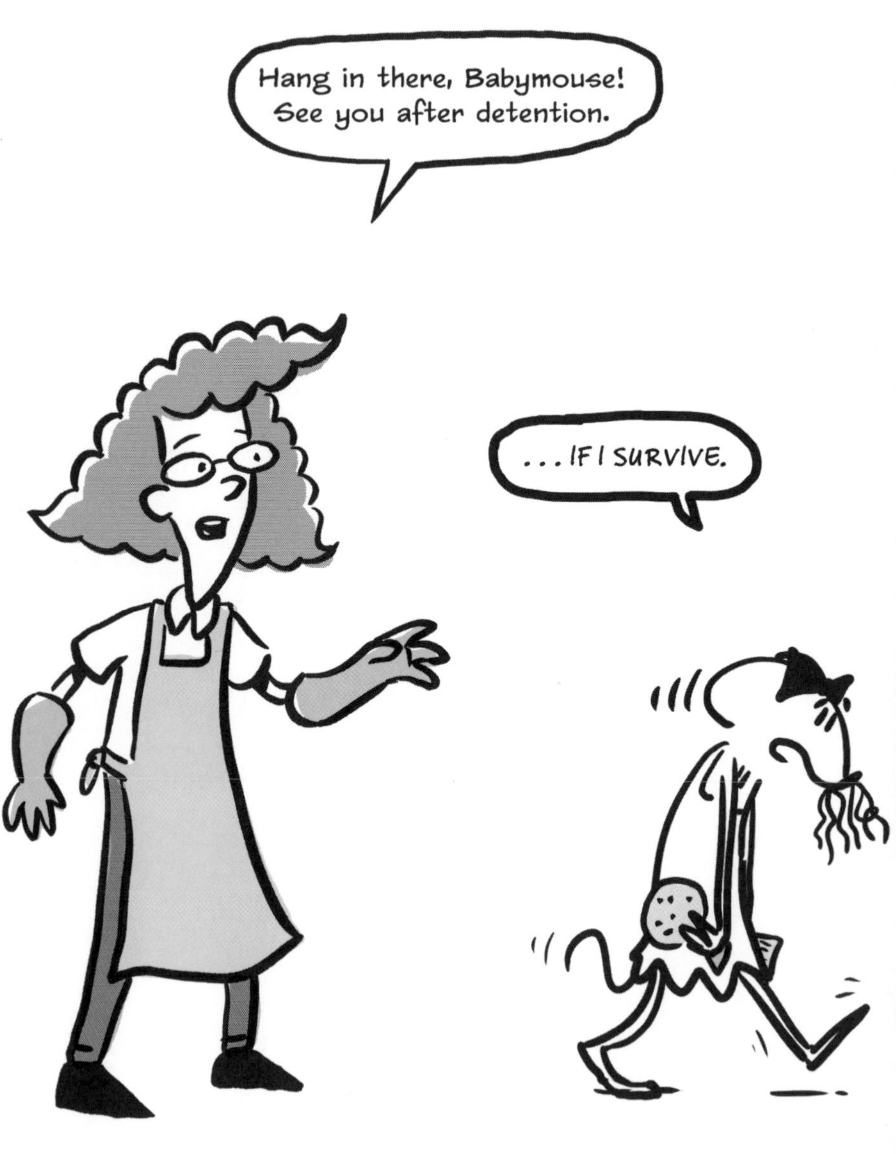
Hang in there, Babymouse! See you after detention.
. . . IF I SURVIVE.

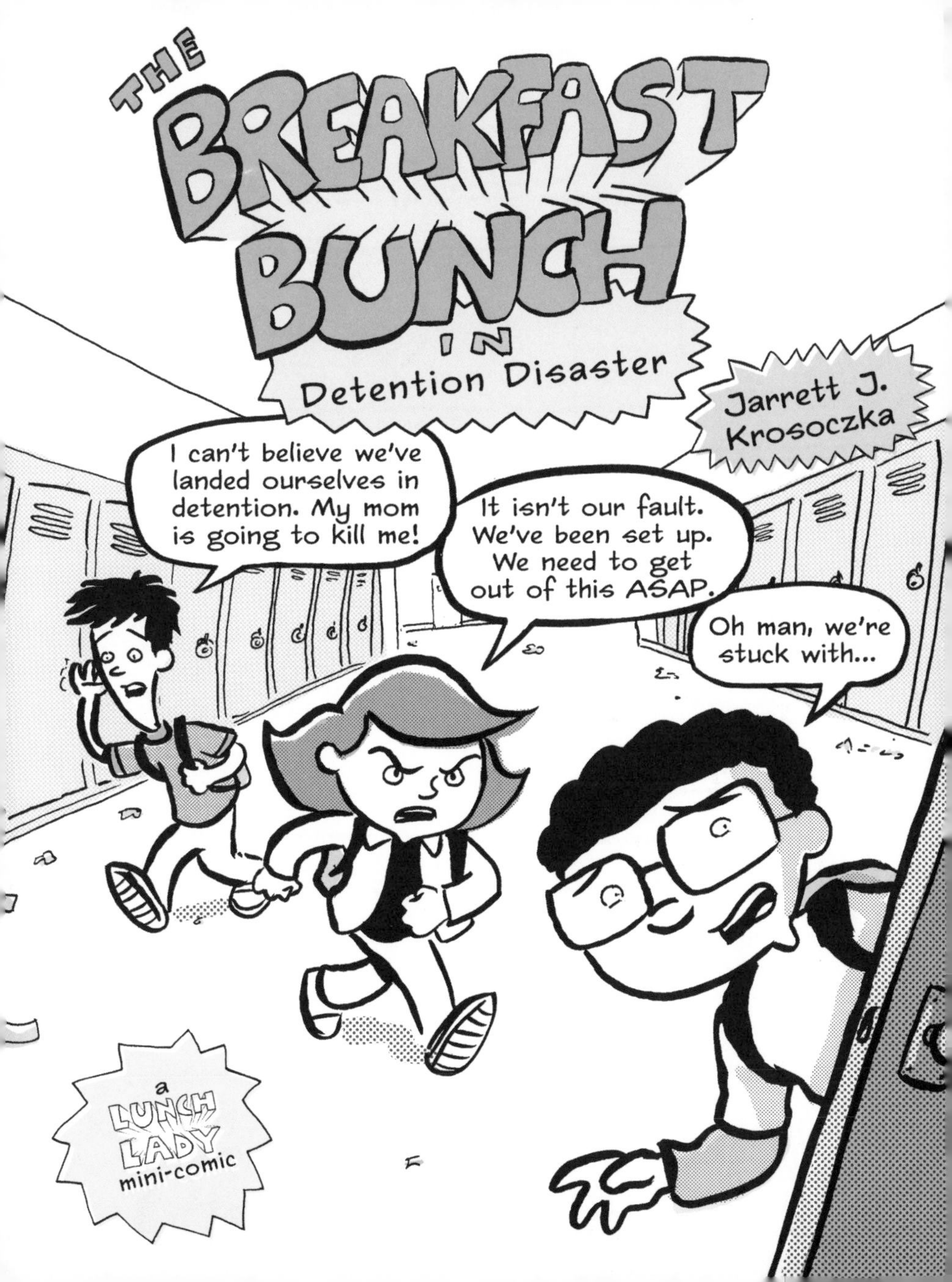
THE BREAKFAST BUNCH IN
Detention Disaster
Jarrett J. Krosoczka
I can't believe we've landed ourselves in detention. My mom is going to kill me!
It isn't our fault. We've been set up. We need to get out of this ASAP.
Oh man, we're stuck with...
a LUNCH LADY mini-comic

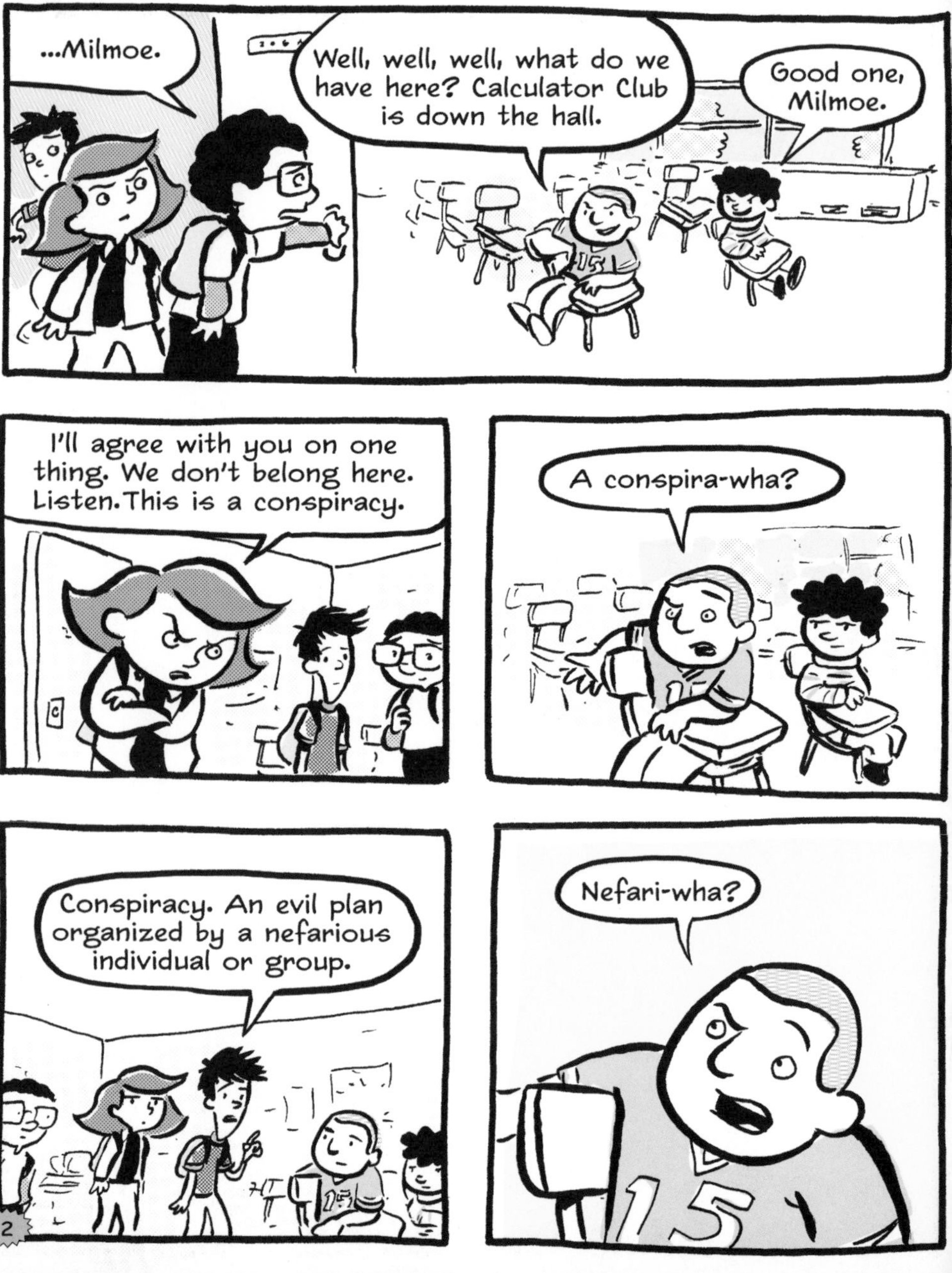
...Milmoe.
Well, well, well, what do we have here? Calculator Club is down the hall.
Good one, Milmoe.
I'll agree with you on one thing. We don't belong here. Listen. This is a conspiracy.
A conspira-wha?
Conspiracy. An evil plan organized by a nefarious individual or group.
Nefari-wha?

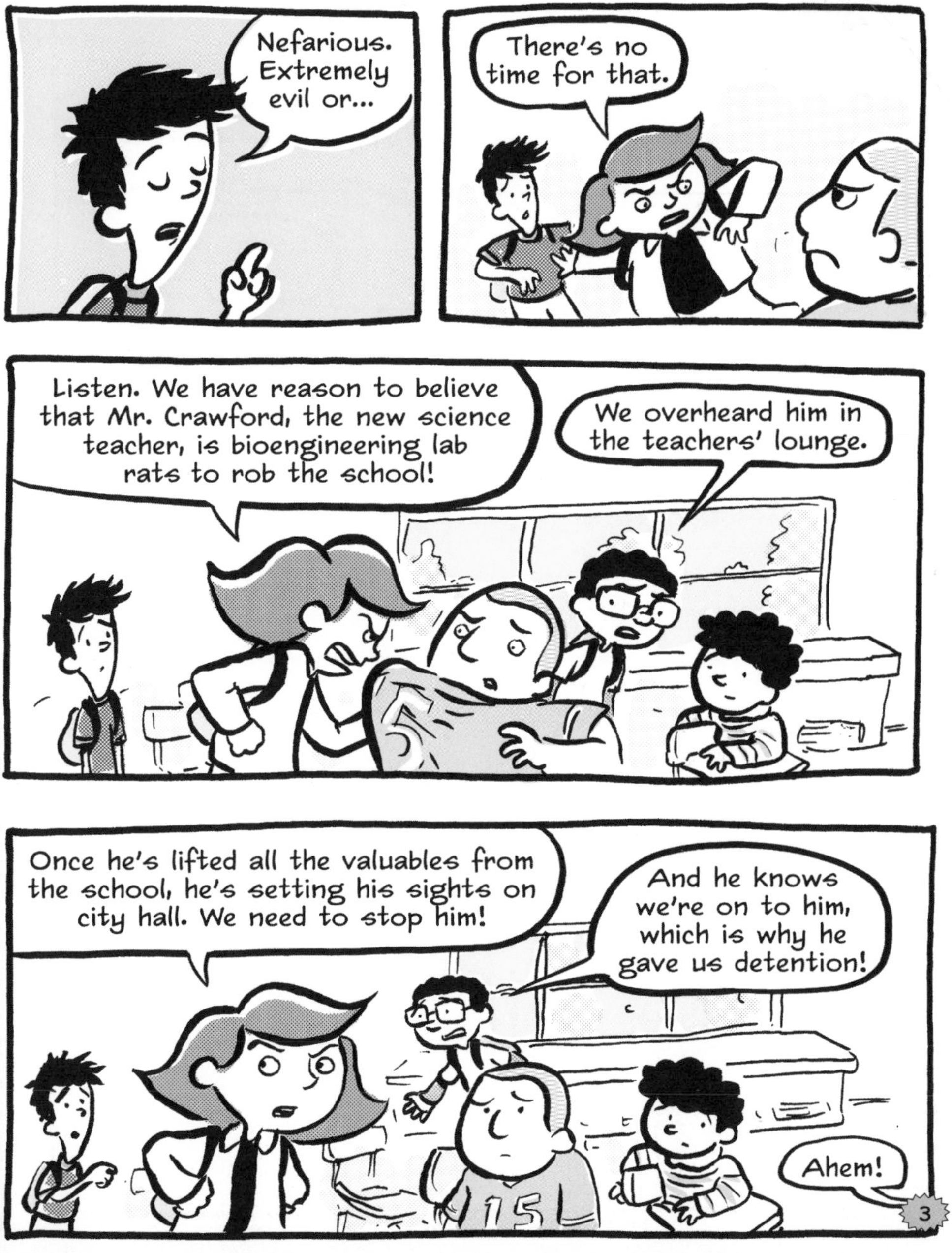
Nefarious. Extremely evil or...
There's no time for that.
Listen. We have reason to believe that Mr. Crawford, the new science teacher, is bioengineering lab rats to rob the school!
We overheard him in the teachers' lounge.
Once he's lifted all the valuables from the school, he's setting his sights on city hall. We need to stop him!
And he knows we're on to him, which is why he gave us detention!
Ahem!

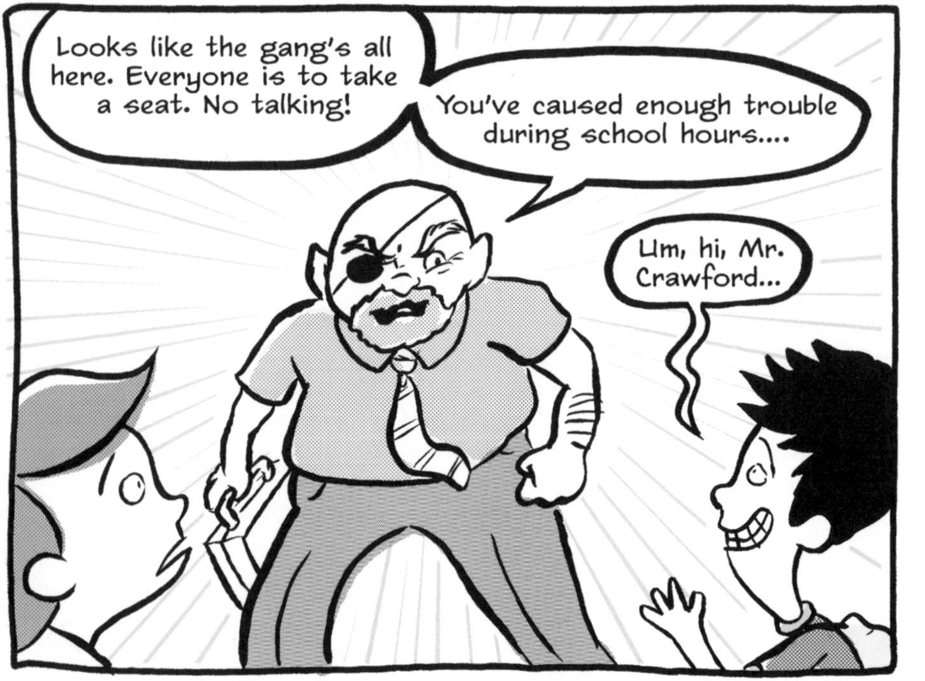
Looks like the gang's all here. Everyone is to take a seat. No talking!
You've caused enough trouble during school hours....
Um, hi, Mr. Crawford...

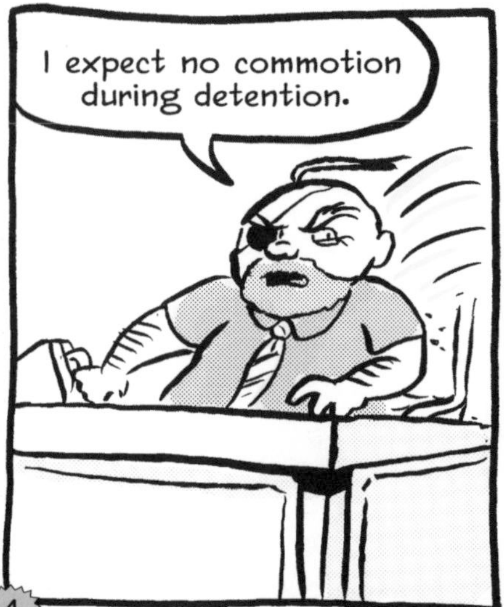
I expect no commotion during detention.

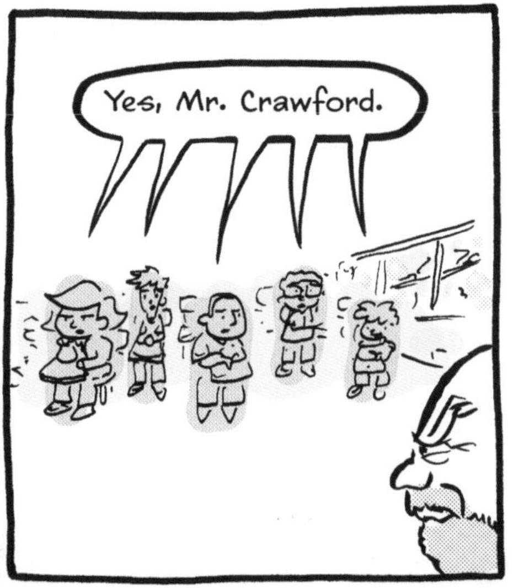
Yes, Mr. Crawford.

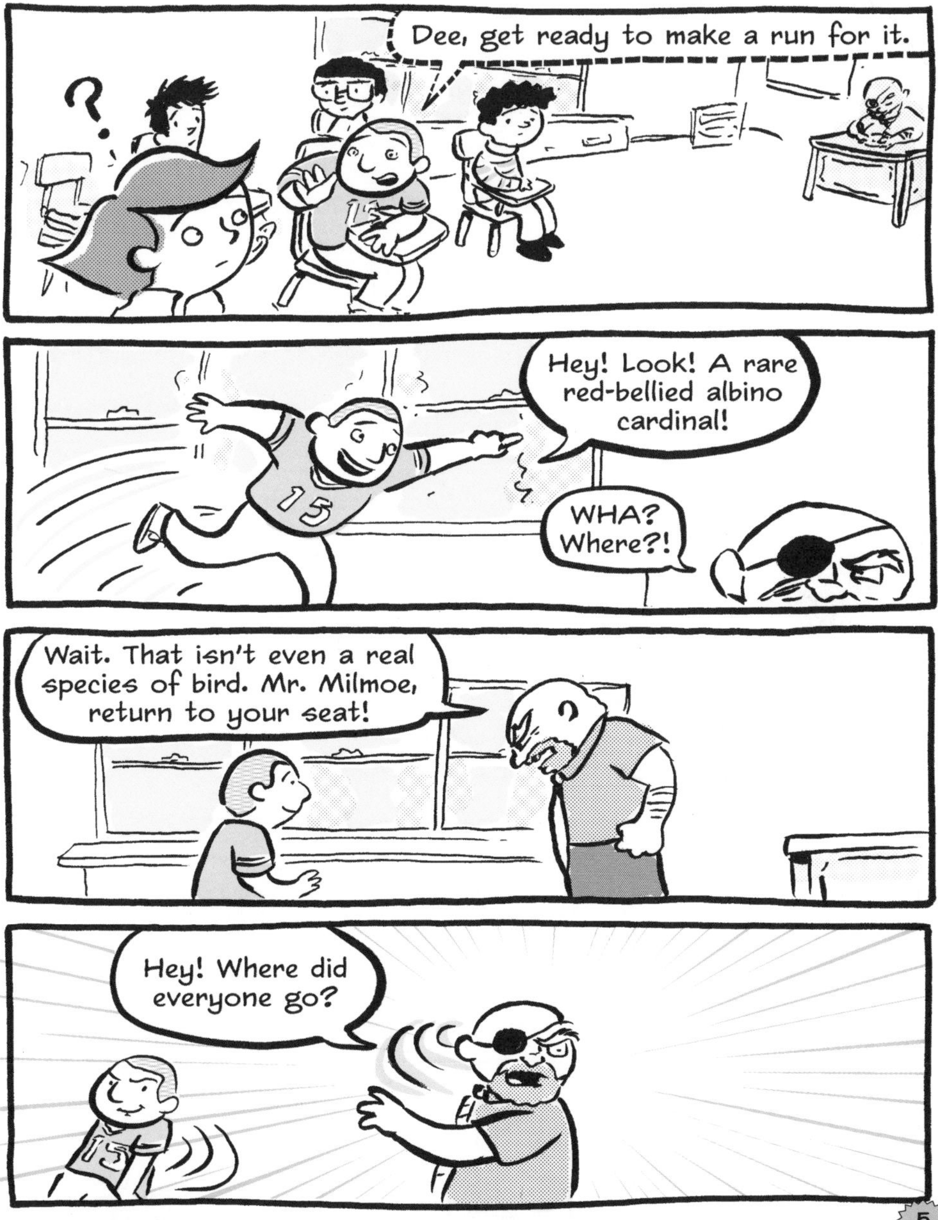
?
Dee, get ready to make a run for it.
Hey! Look! A rare red-bellied albino cardinal!
WHA? Where?!
Wait. That isn't even a real species of bird. Mr. Milmoe, return to your seat!
Hey! Where did everyone go?

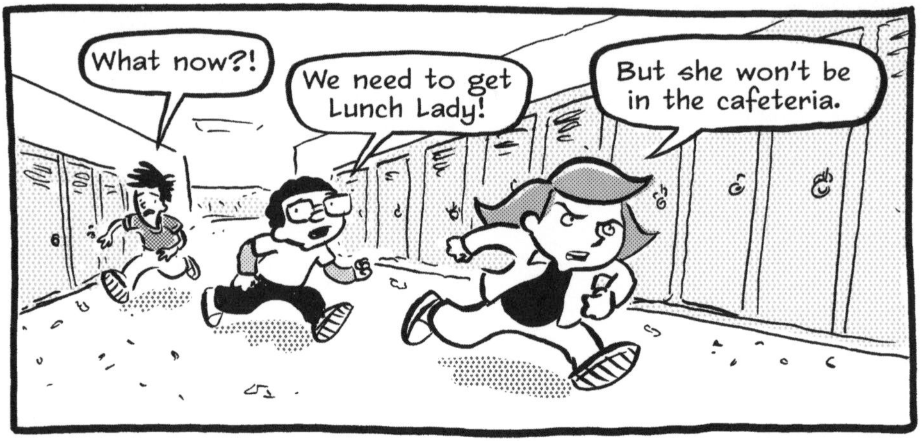
What now?!
We need to get Lunch Lady!
But she won't be in the cafeteria.

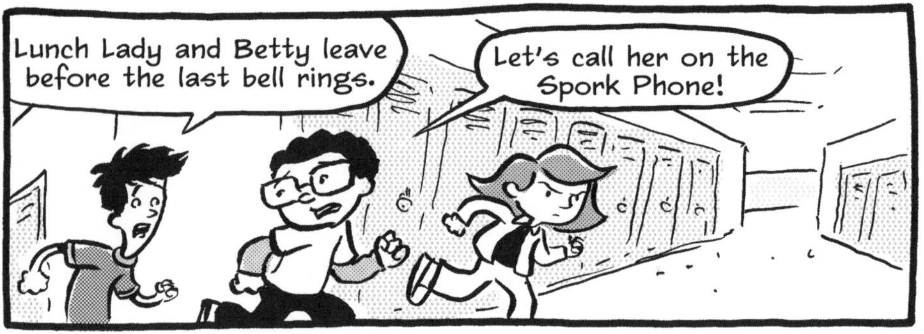
Lunch Lady and Betty leave before the last bell rings.
Let's call her on the Spork Phone!

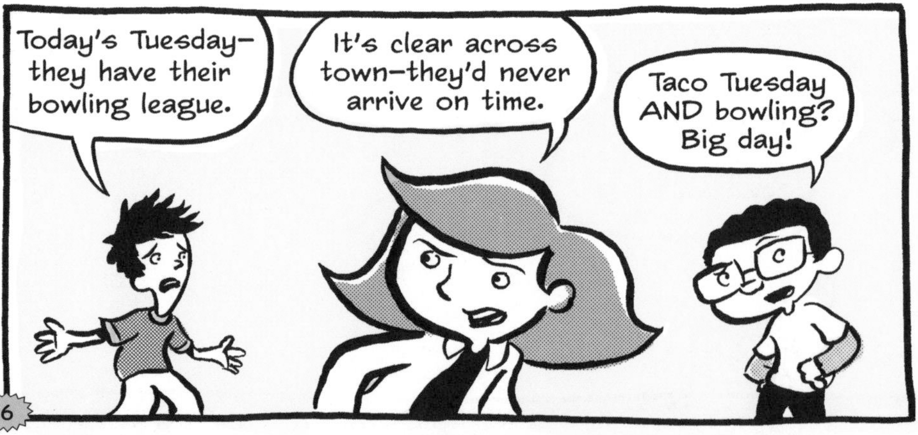
Today's Tuesday—they have their bowling league.
It's clear across town—they'd never arrive on time.
Taco Tuesday AND bowling? Big day!

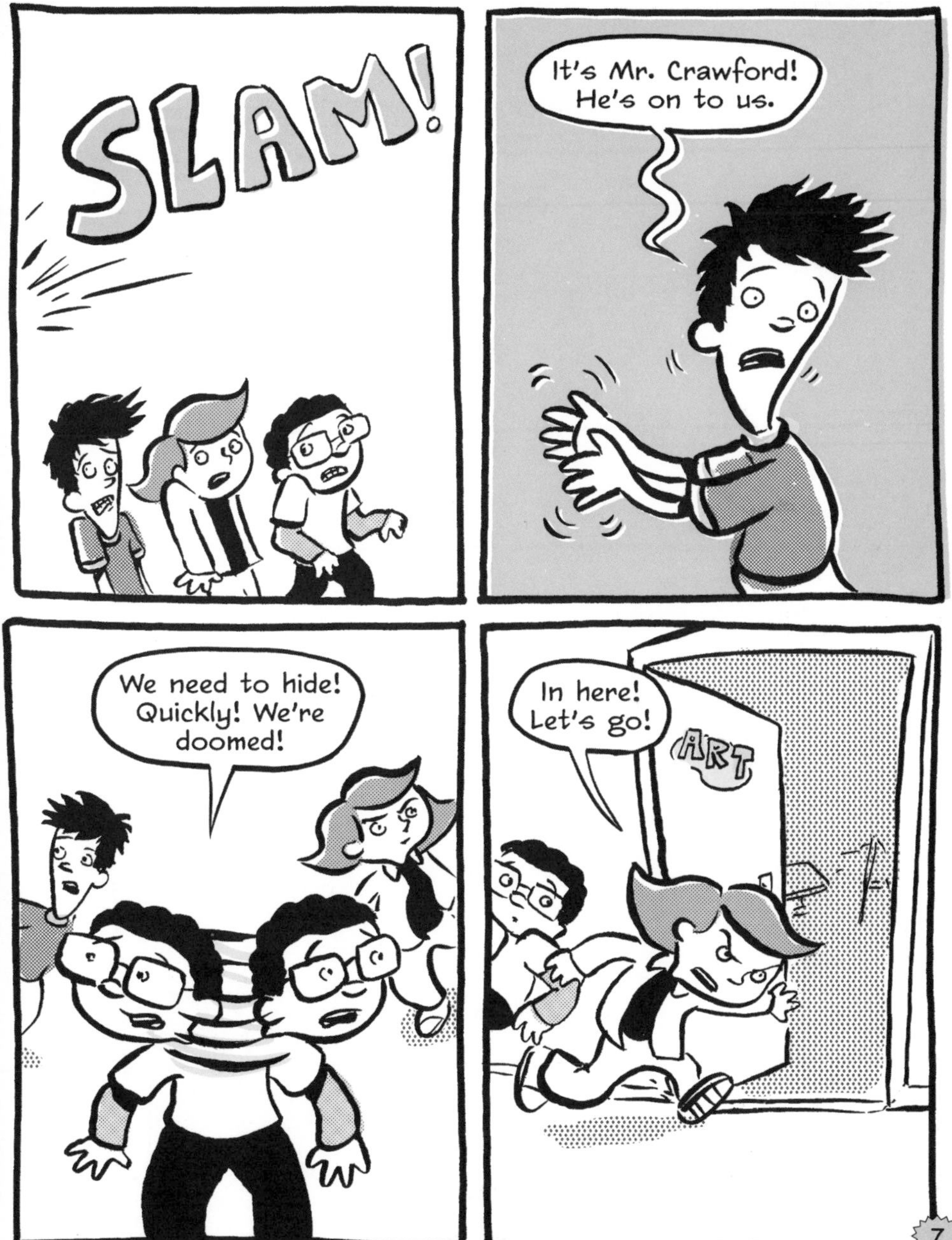
SLAM!
It's Mr. Crawford! He's on to us.
We need to hide! Quickly! We're doomed!
In here! Let's go!
ART

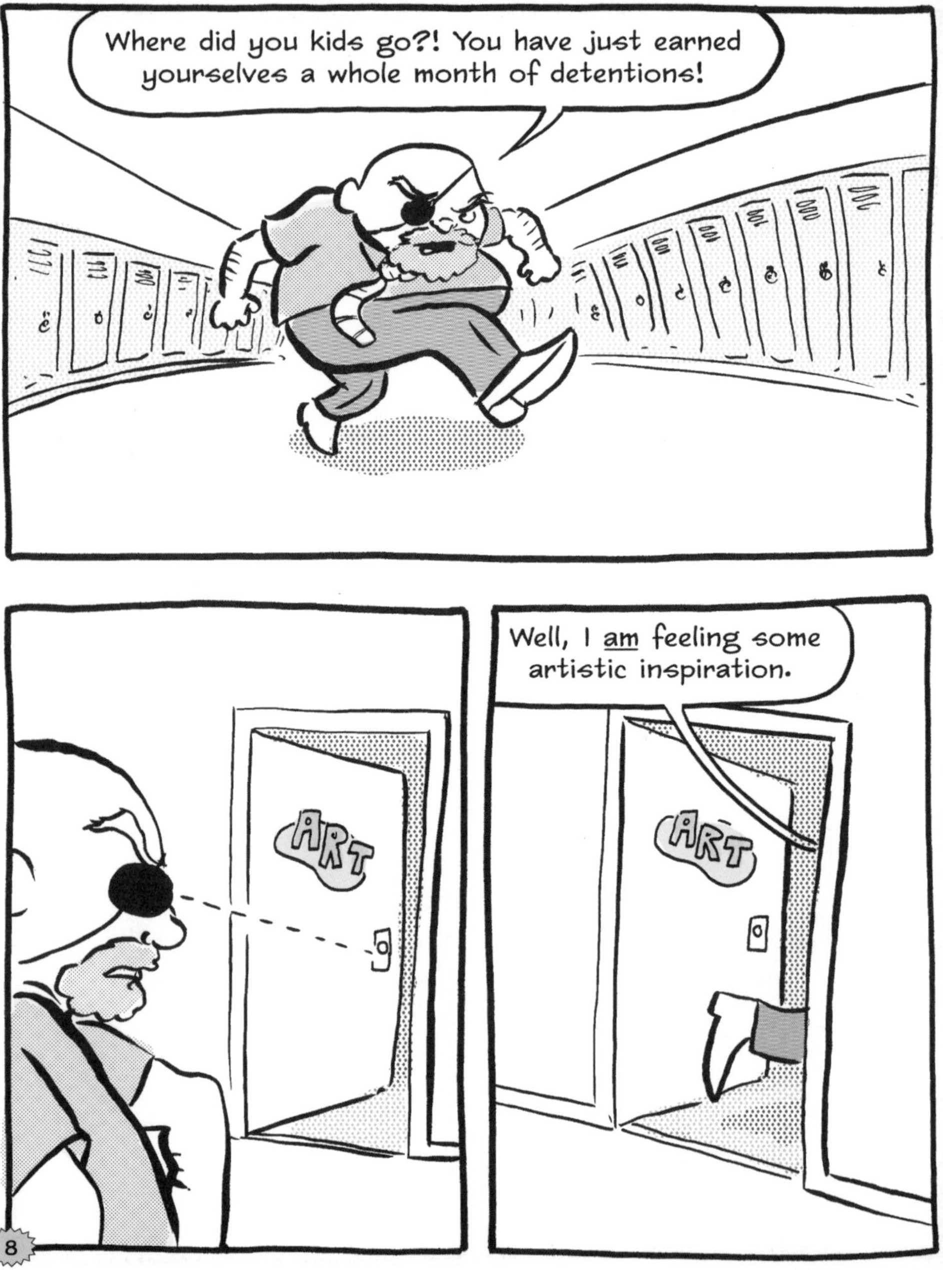
Where did you kids go?! You have just earned yourselves a whole month of detentions!
ART
ART
Well, I am feeling some artistic inspiration.

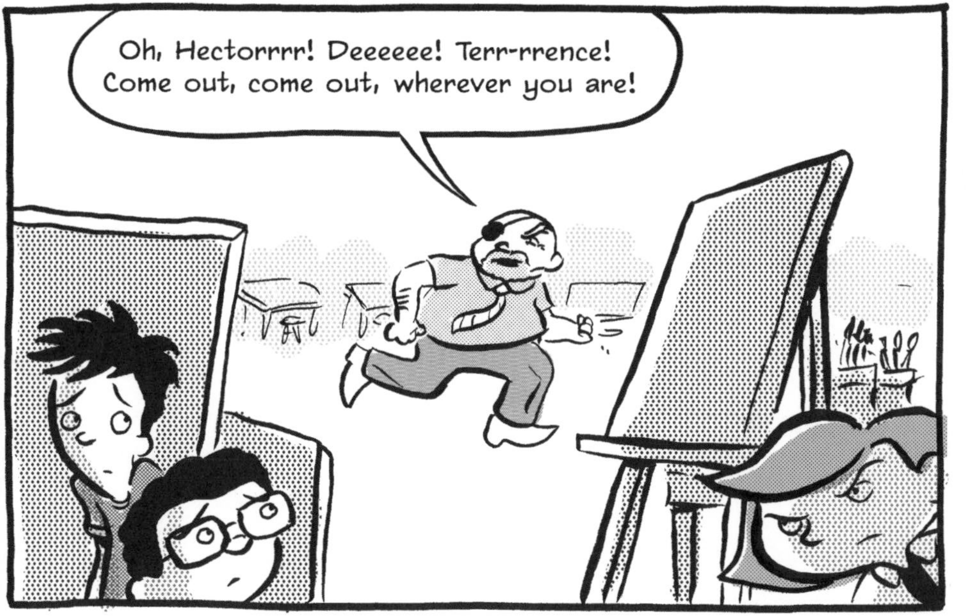
Oh, Hectorrrr! Deeeeee! Terr-rrence! Come out, come out, wherever you are!

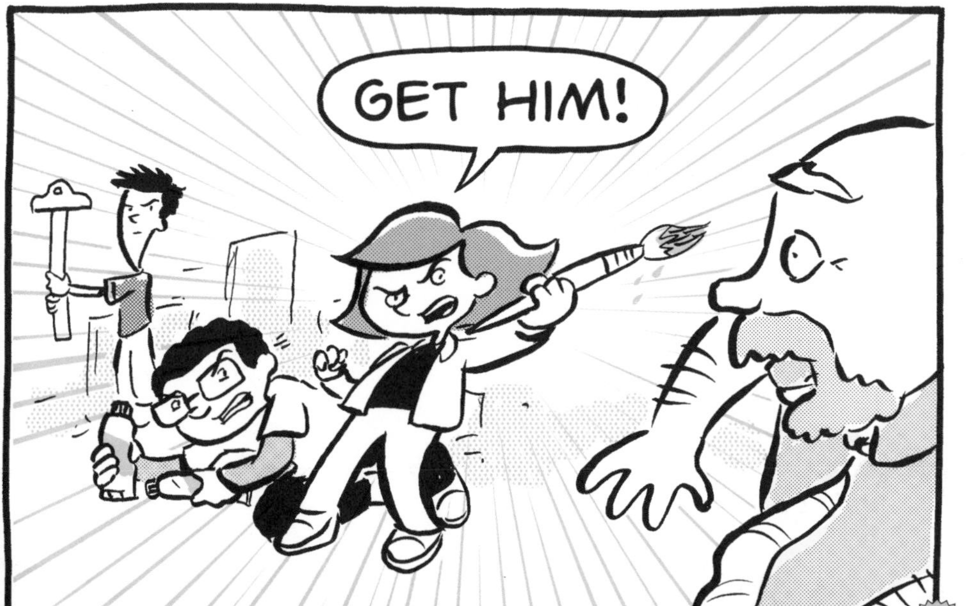
GET HIM!

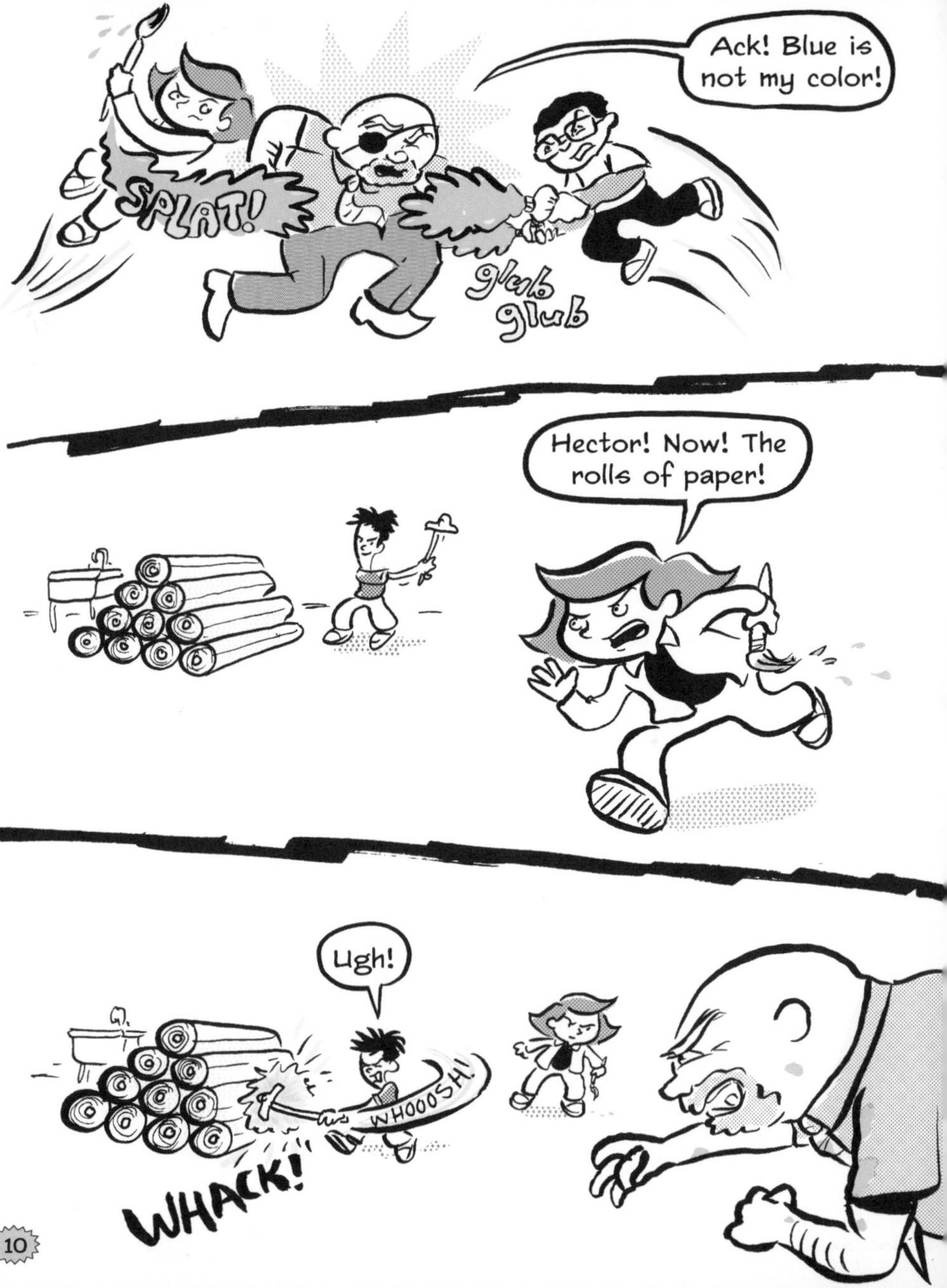
Ack! Blue is not my color!
SPLAT!
glub glub
Hector! Now! The rolls of paper!
Ugh!
WHOOOSH!
WHACK!

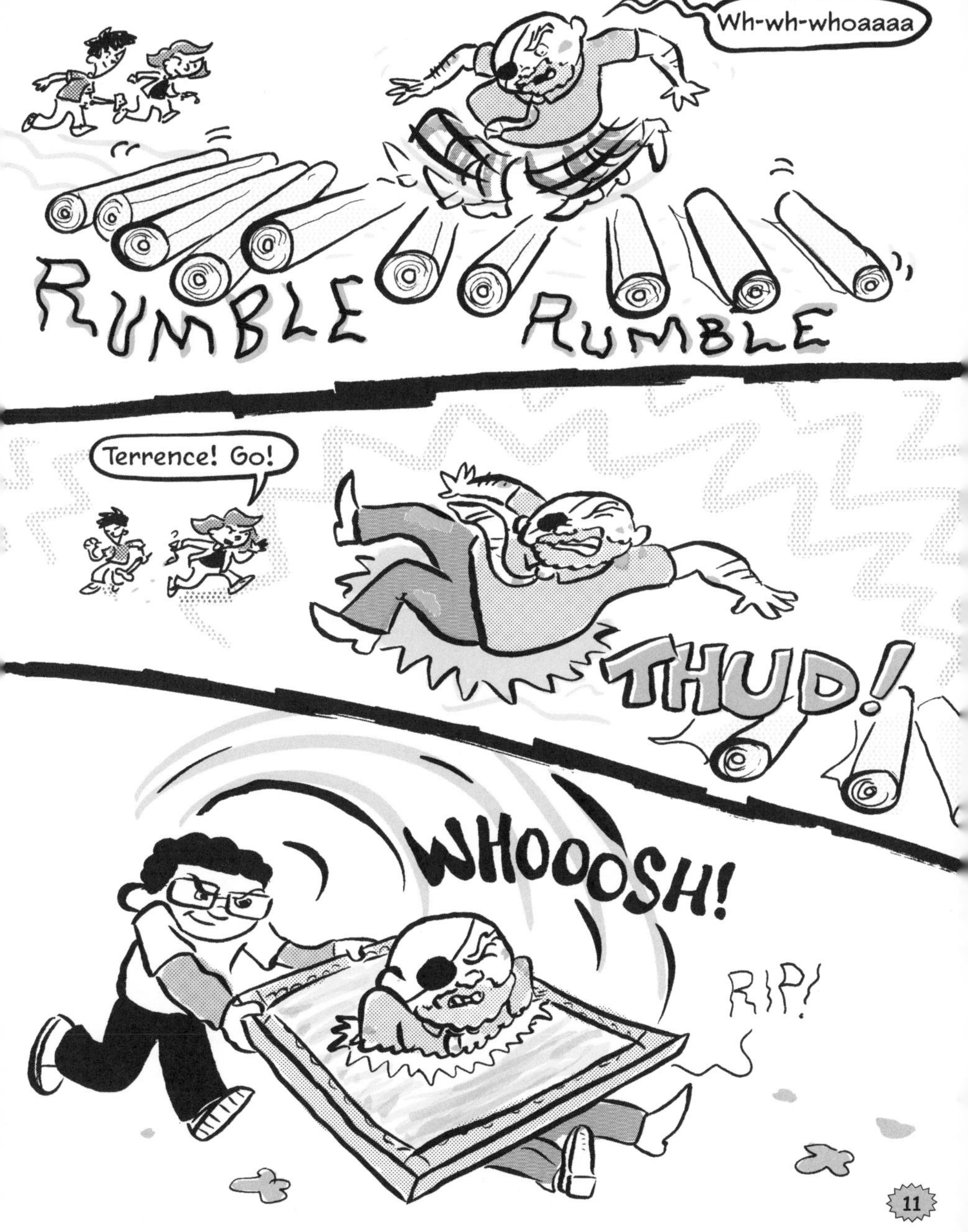
Wh-wh-whoaaaa
RUMBLE
RUMBLE
Terrence! Go!
THUD!
WHOOOSH!
RIP!

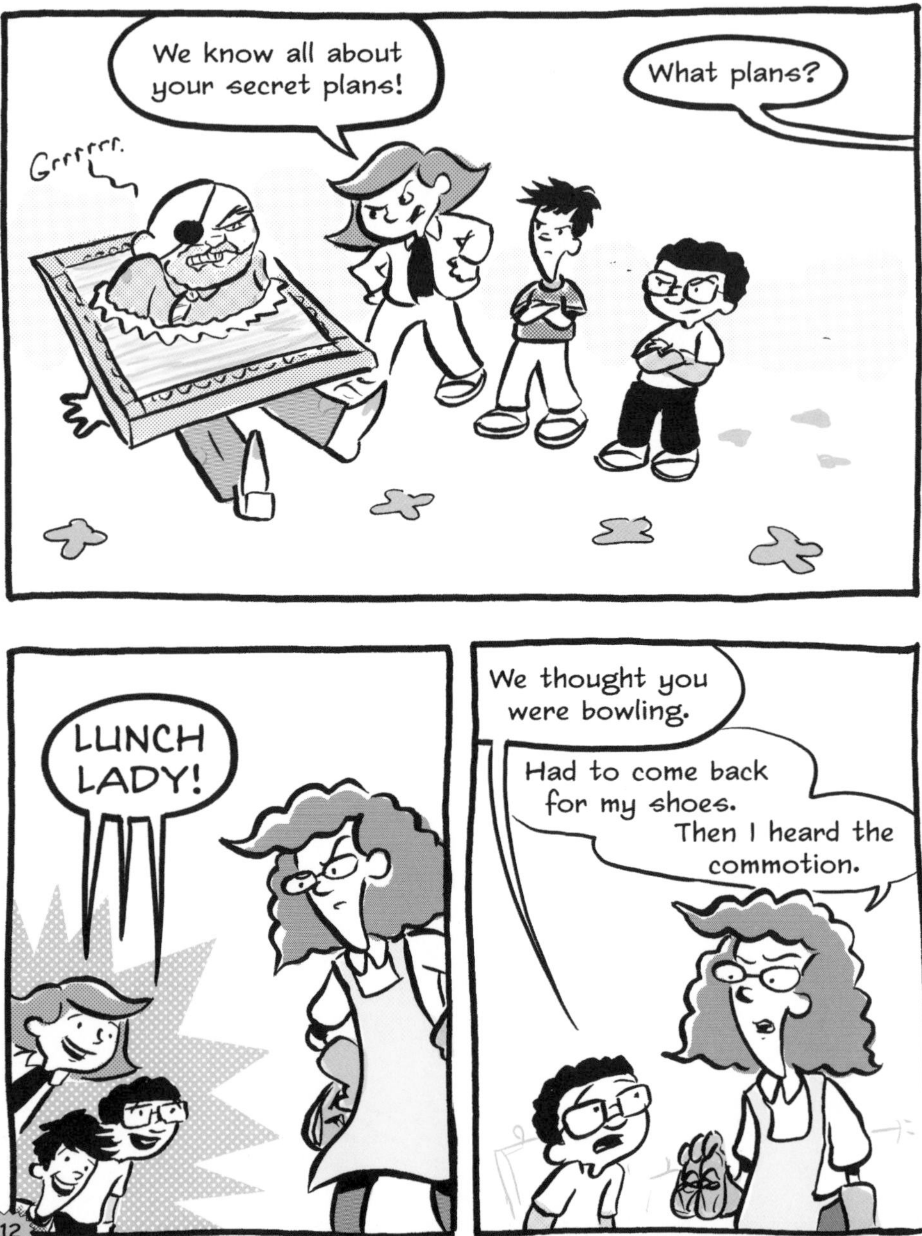
We know all about your secret plans!
What plans?
Grrrrrr.
LUNCH LADY!
We thought you were bowling.
Had to come back for my shoes.
Then I heard the commotion.

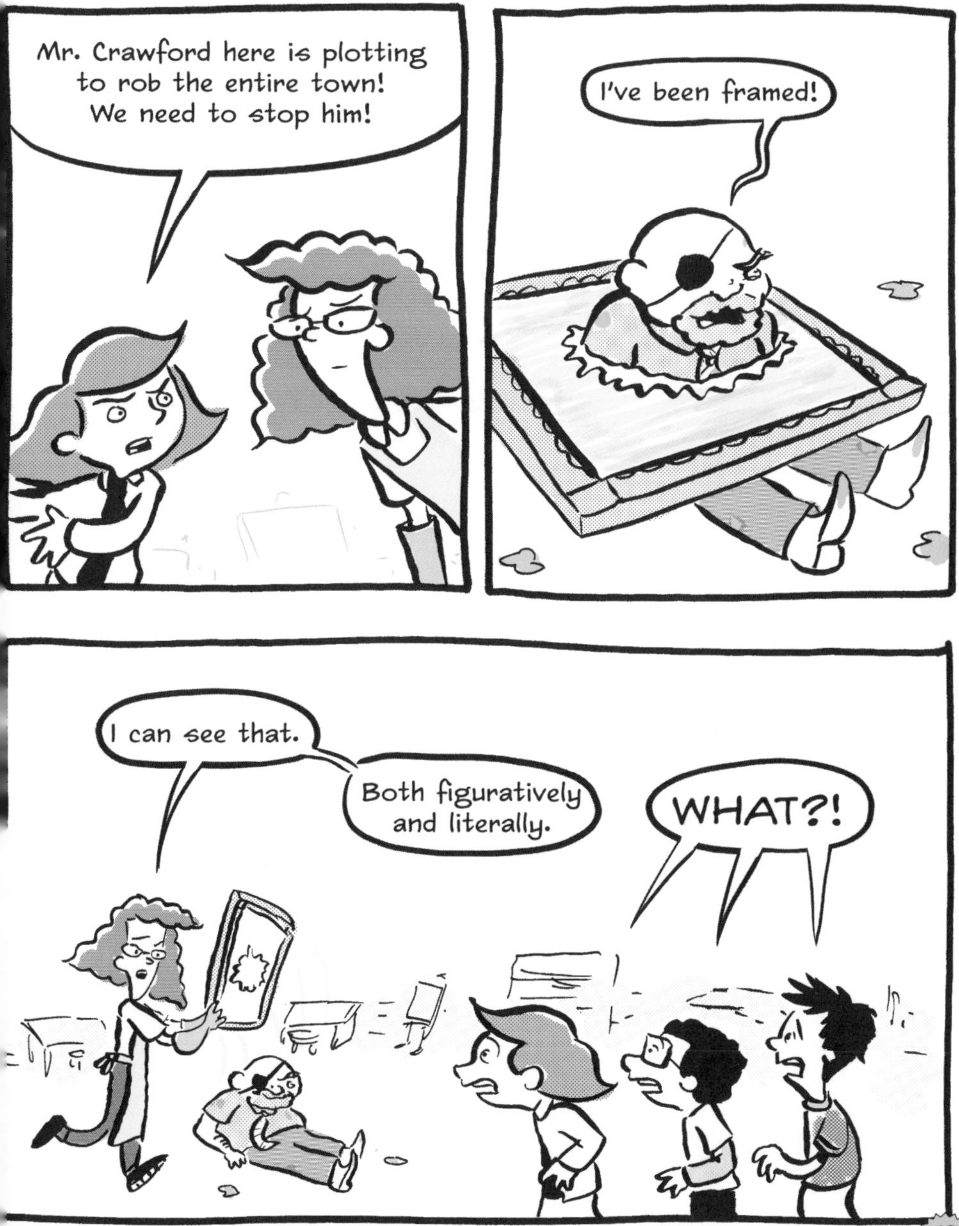
Mr. Crawford here is plotting to rob the entire town! We need to stop him!
I've been framed!
I can see that.
Both figuratively and literally.
WHAT?!

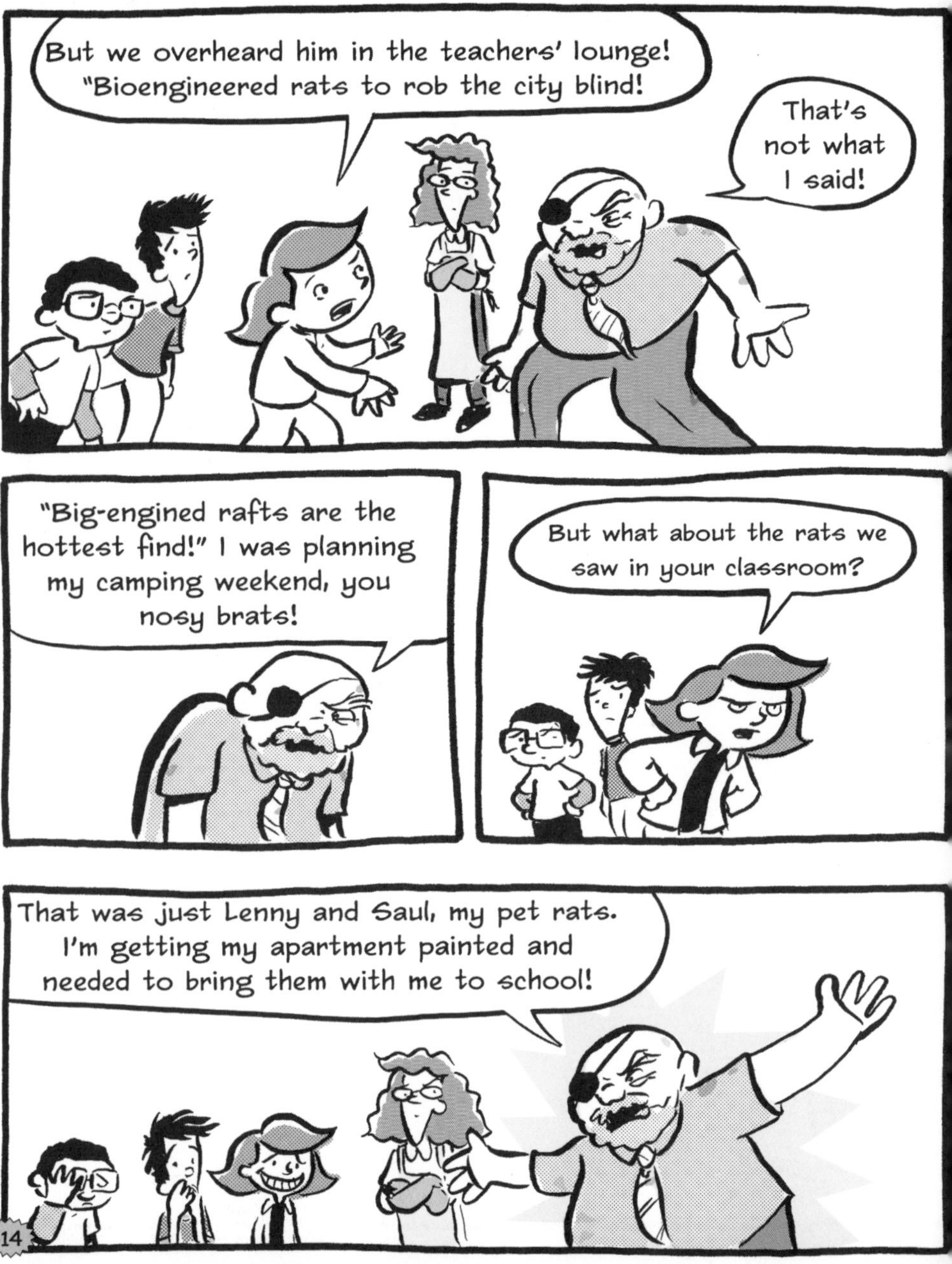

But we overheard him in the teachers' lounge! "Bioengineered rats to rob the city blind!
That's not what I said!
"Big-engined rafts are the hottest find!" I was planning my camping weekend, you nosy brats!
But what about the rats we saw in your classroom?
That was just Lenny and Saul, my pet rats. I'm getting my apartment painted and needed to bring them with me to school!

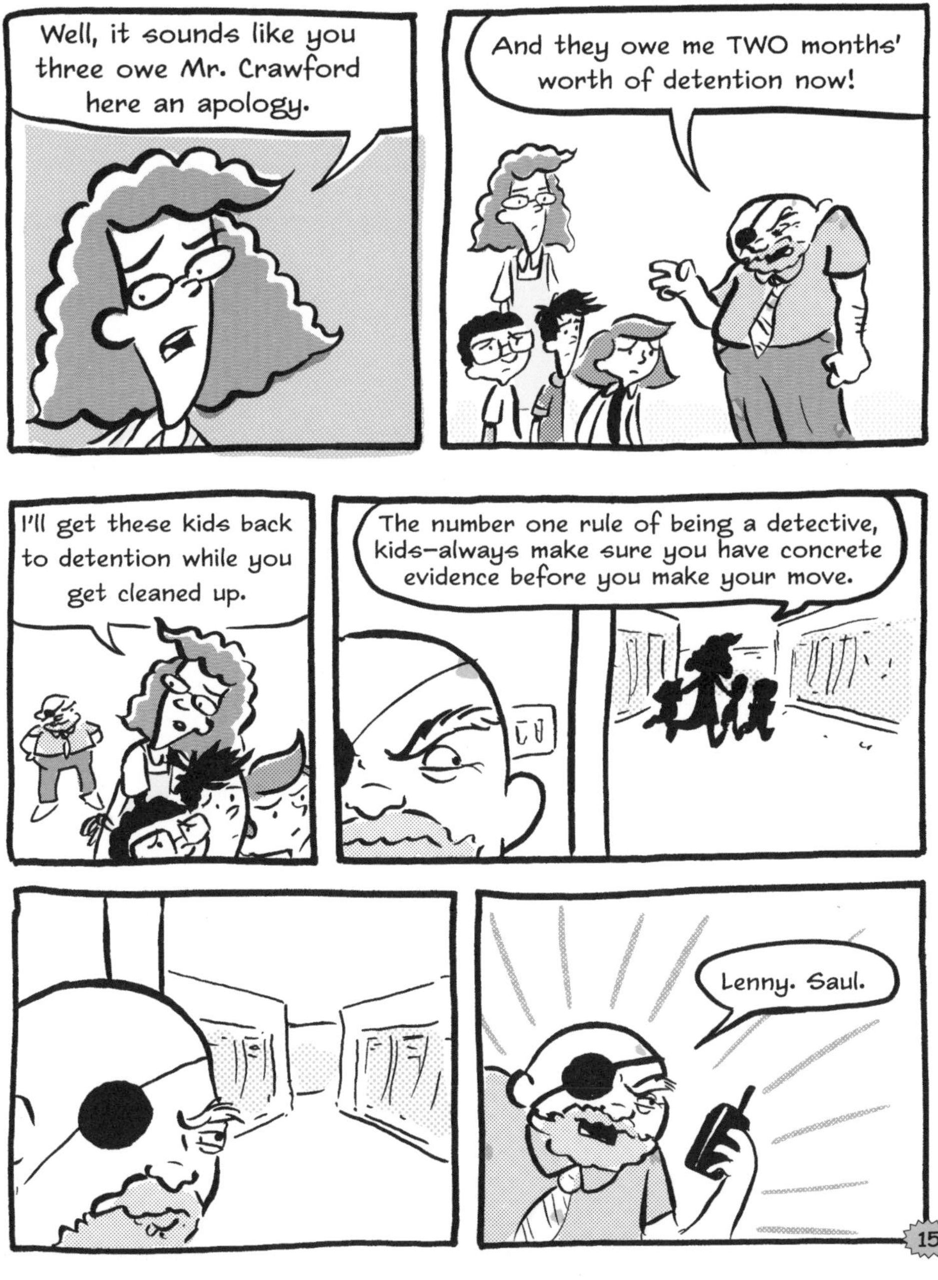
Well, it sounds like you three owe Mr. Crawford here an apology.
And they owe me TWO months' worth of detention now!
I'll get these kids back to detention while you get cleaned up.
The number one rule of being a detective, kids—always make sure you have concrete evidence before you make your move.
Lenny. Saul.

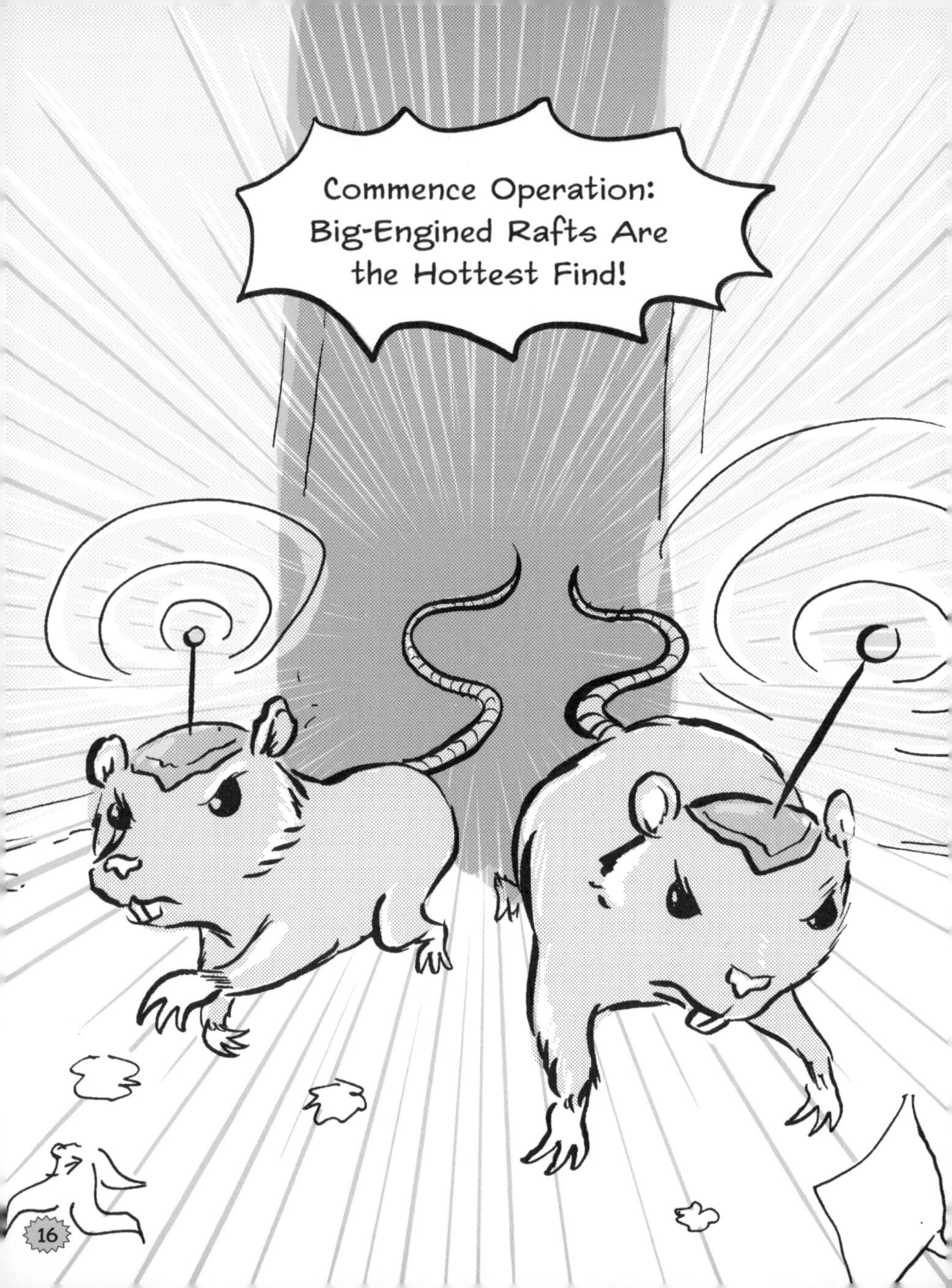
Commence Operation: Big-Engined Rafts Are the Hottest Find!

How I Draw Lunch Lady
by Jarrett J. Krosoczka

When I draw my comics, I sketch with a non-photo blue pencil and draw the final artwork with a brush dipped in India ink.

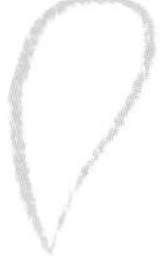

1) I draw an upside-down teardrop.

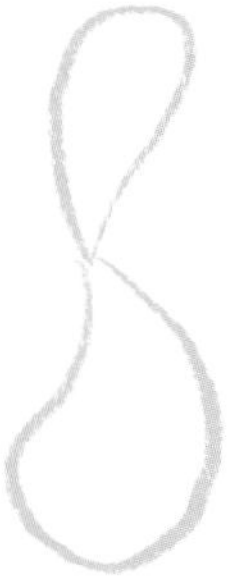

2) I draw a regular teardrop.

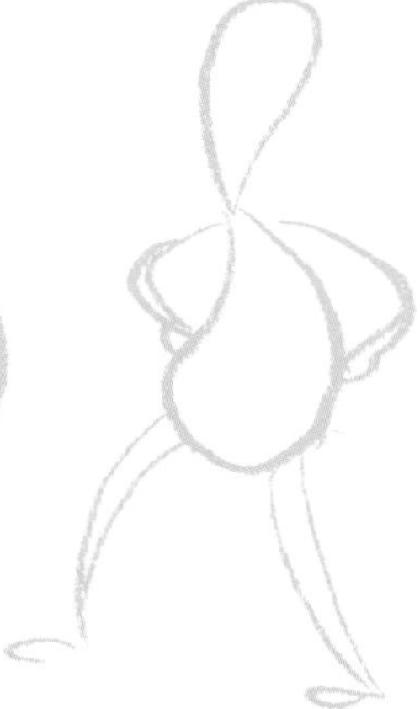

3) I sketch out her arms and legs.

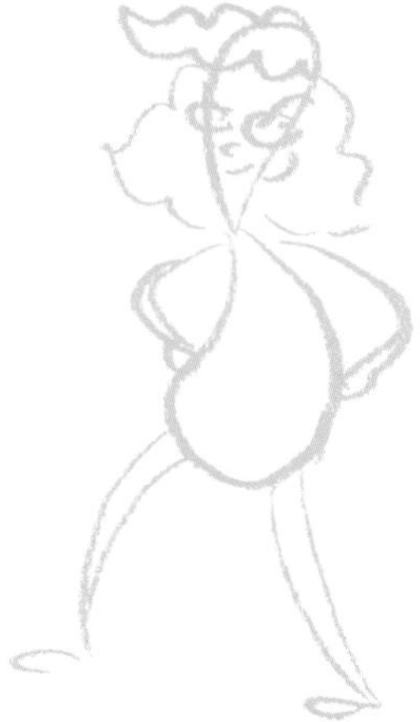

4) I draw her perm and facial features.

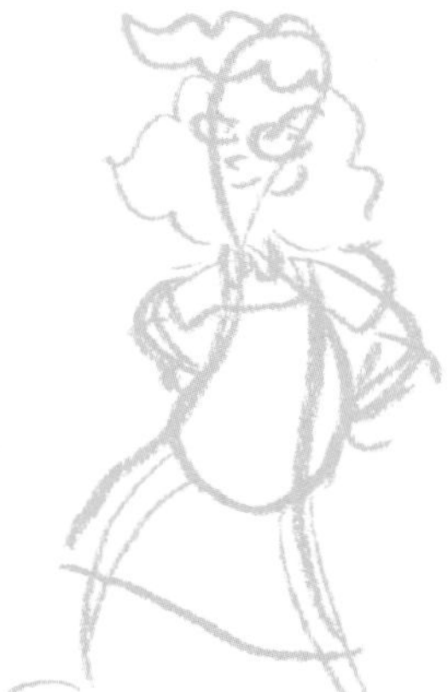

5) I sketch out her apron, gloves and clothes.

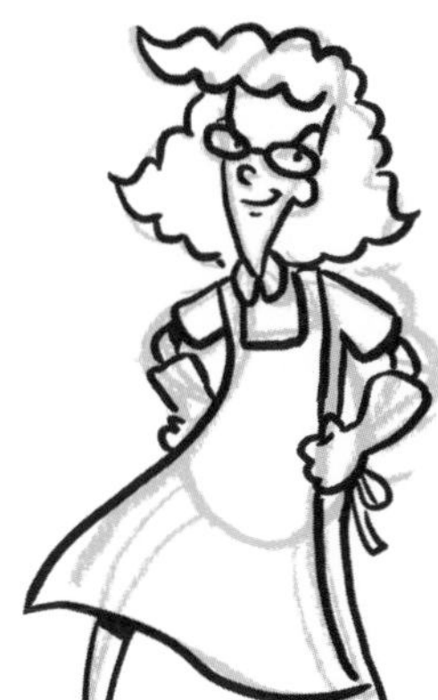

6) I go over the pencil sketch with ink.

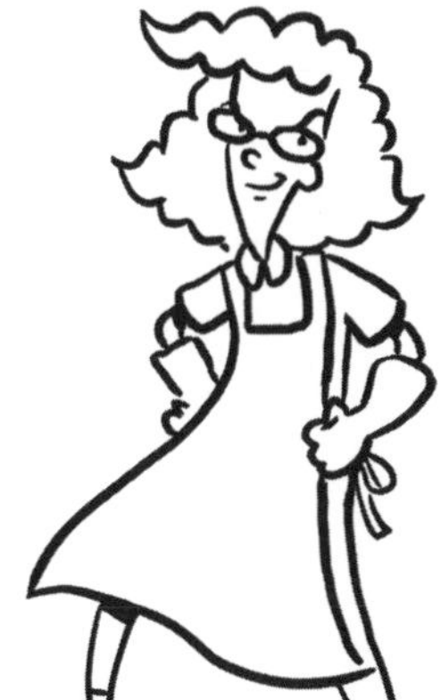

7) Then I scan in the artwork as black-and-white.
(The computer can't see the non-photo blue color.)

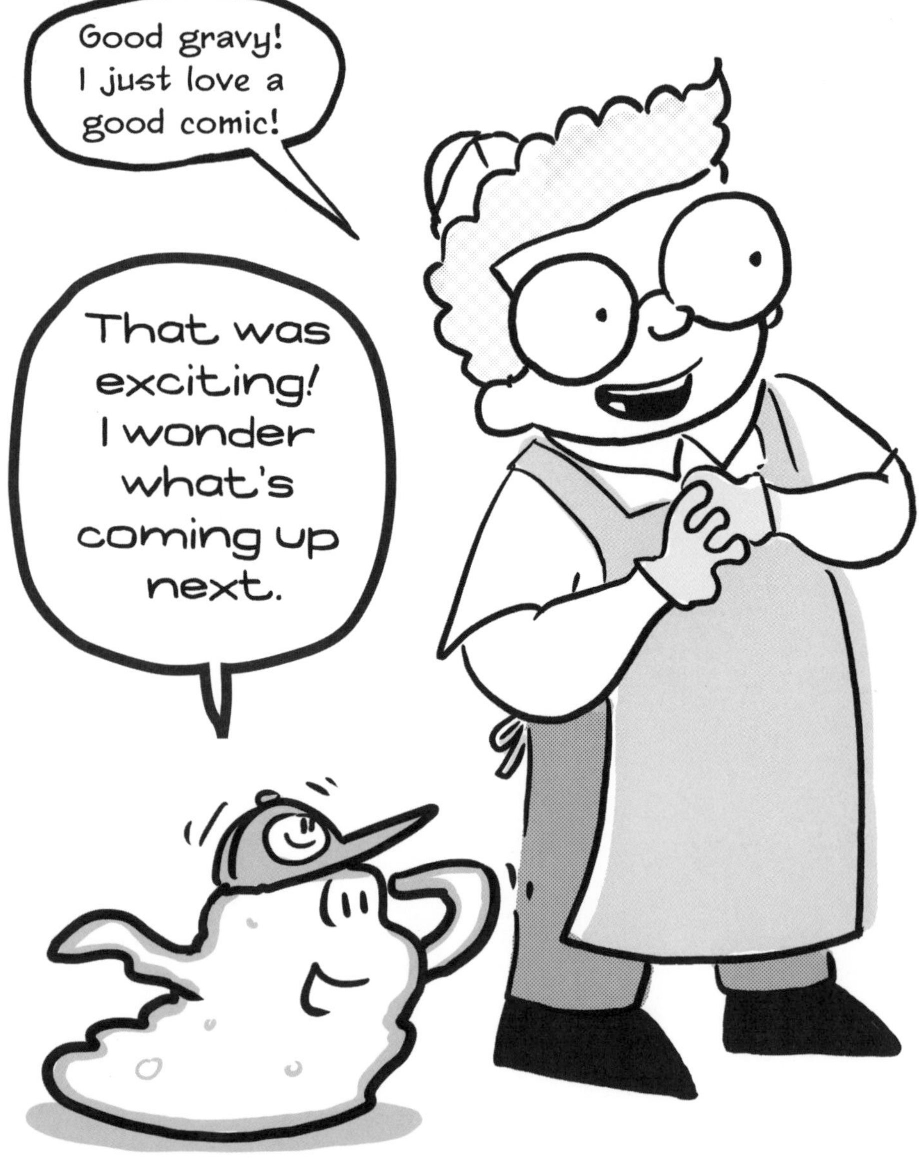
Good gravy! I just love a good comic!
That was exciting! I wonder what's coming up next.

CHEATING DEATH W/ SISYPHUS

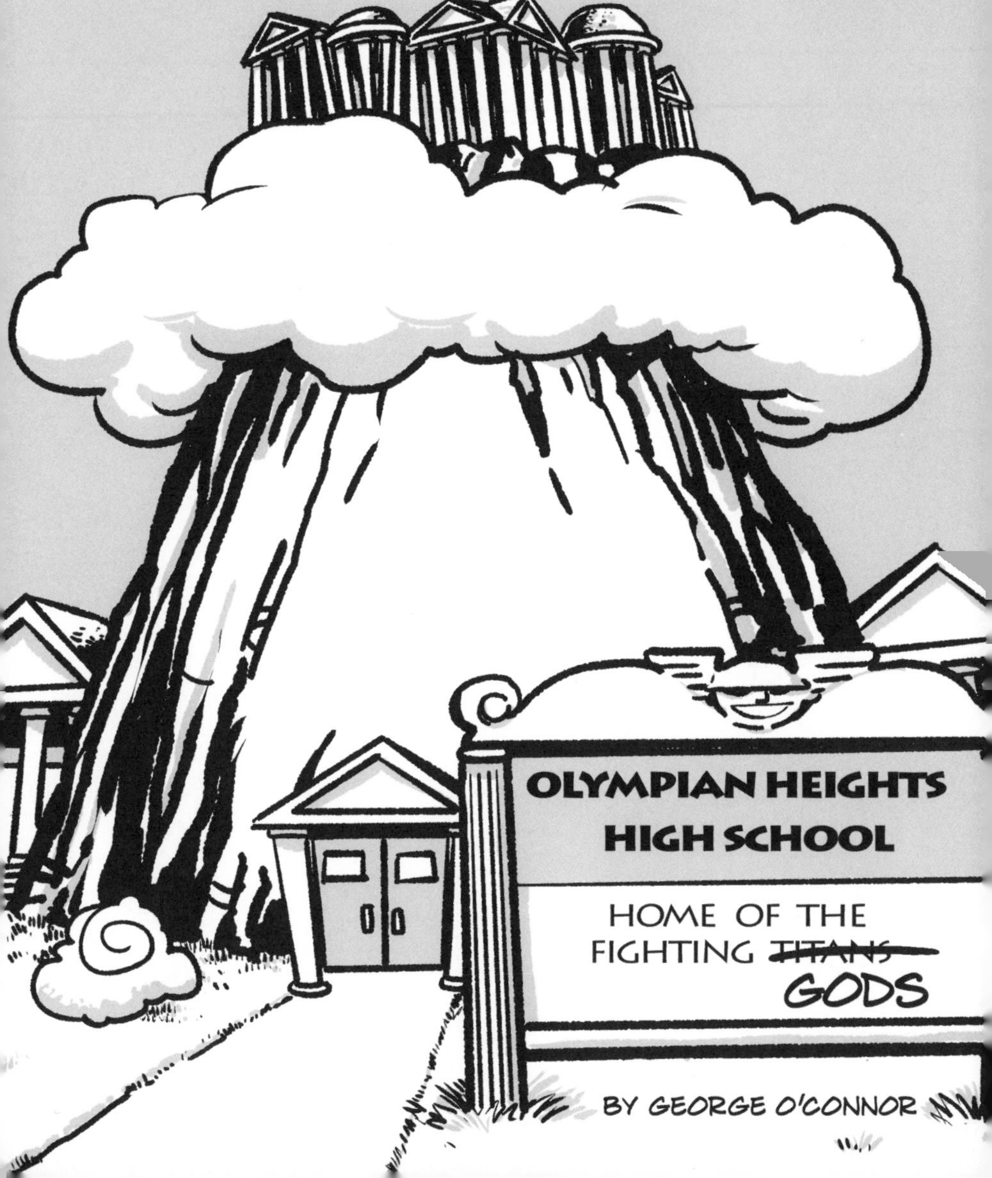

OLYMPIAN HEIGHTS
HIGH SCHOOL
HOME OF THE
FIGHTING ~~TITANS~~
GODS

BY GEORGE O'CONNOR

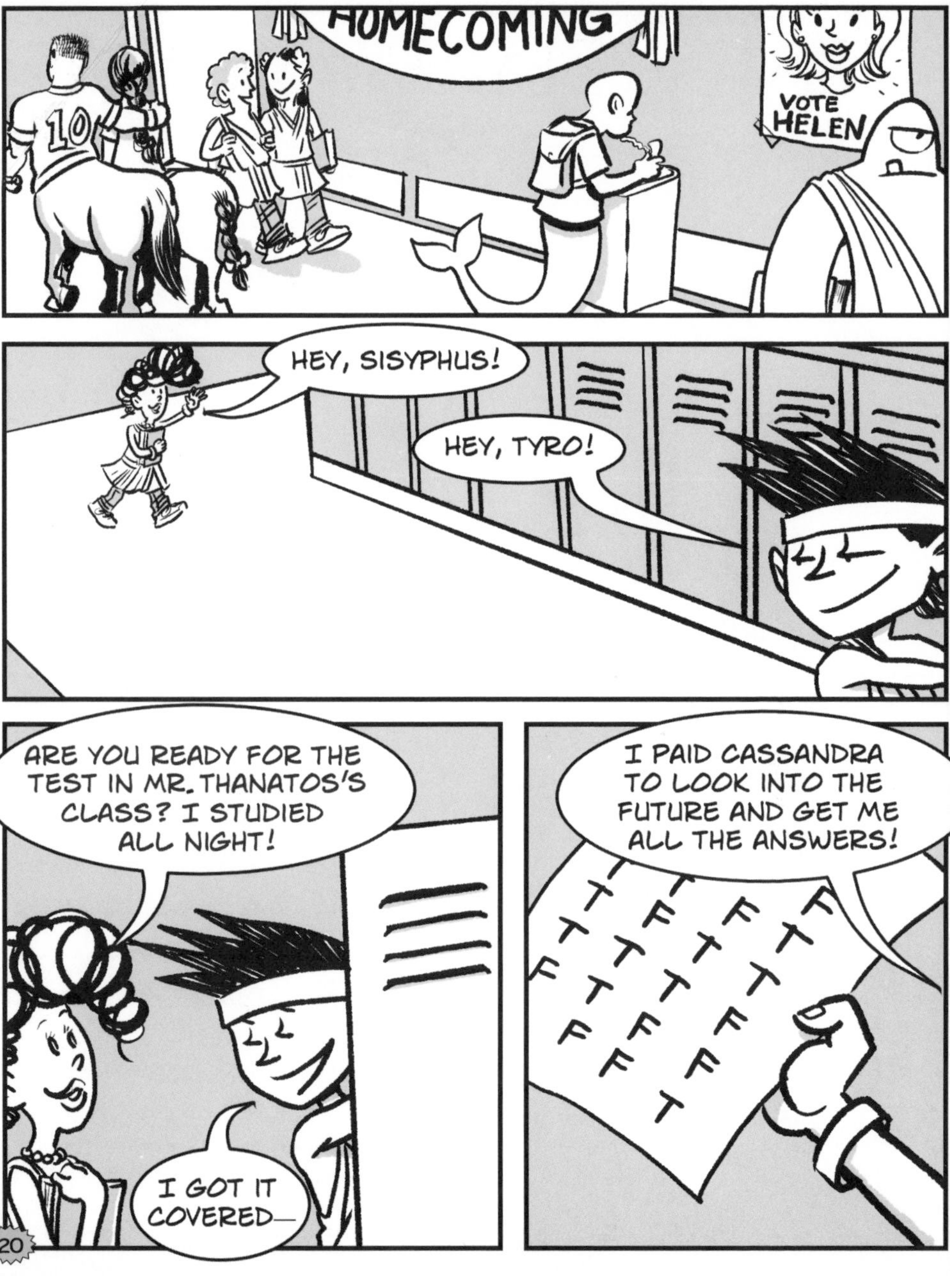
HOMECOMING
VOTE HELEN
HEY, SISYPHUS!
HEY, TYRO!
ARE YOU READY FOR THE TEST IN MR. THANATOS'S CLASS? I STUDIED ALL NIGHT!
I GOT IT COVERED—
I PAID CASSANDRA TO LOOK INTO THE FUTURE AND GET ME ALL THE ANSWERS!

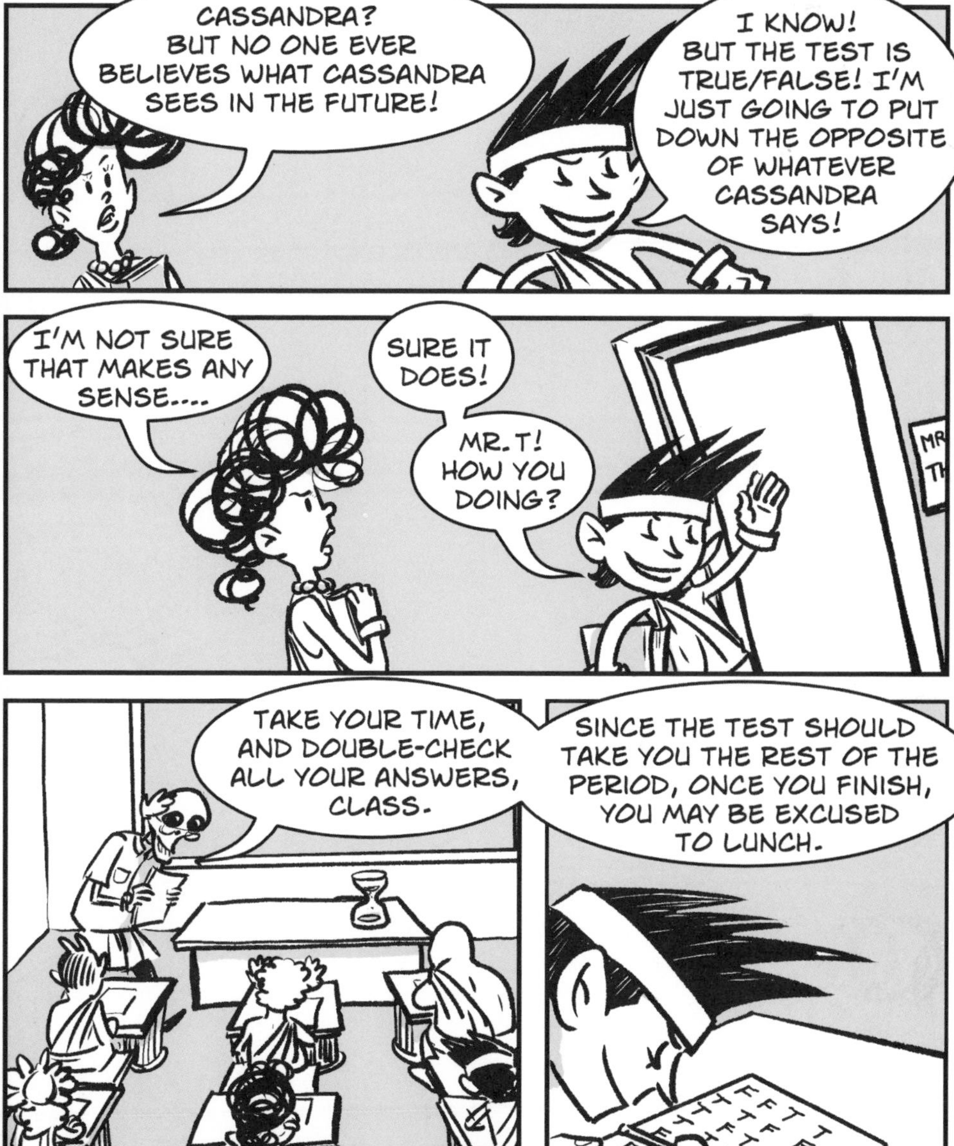
CASSANDRA? BUT NO ONE EVER BELIEVES WHAT CASSANDRA SEES IN THE FUTURE!
I KNOW! BUT THE TEST IS TRUE/FALSE! I'M JUST GOING TO PUT DOWN THE OPPOSITE OF WHATEVER CASSANDRA SAYS!
I'M NOT SURE THAT MAKES ANY SENSE....
SURE IT DOES!
MR. T! HOW YOU DOING?
TAKE YOUR TIME, AND DOUBLE-CHECK ALL YOUR ANSWERS, CLASS.
SINCE THE TEST SHOULD TAKE YOU THE REST OF THE PERIOD, ONCE YOU FINISH, YOU MAY BE EXCUSED TO LUNCH.

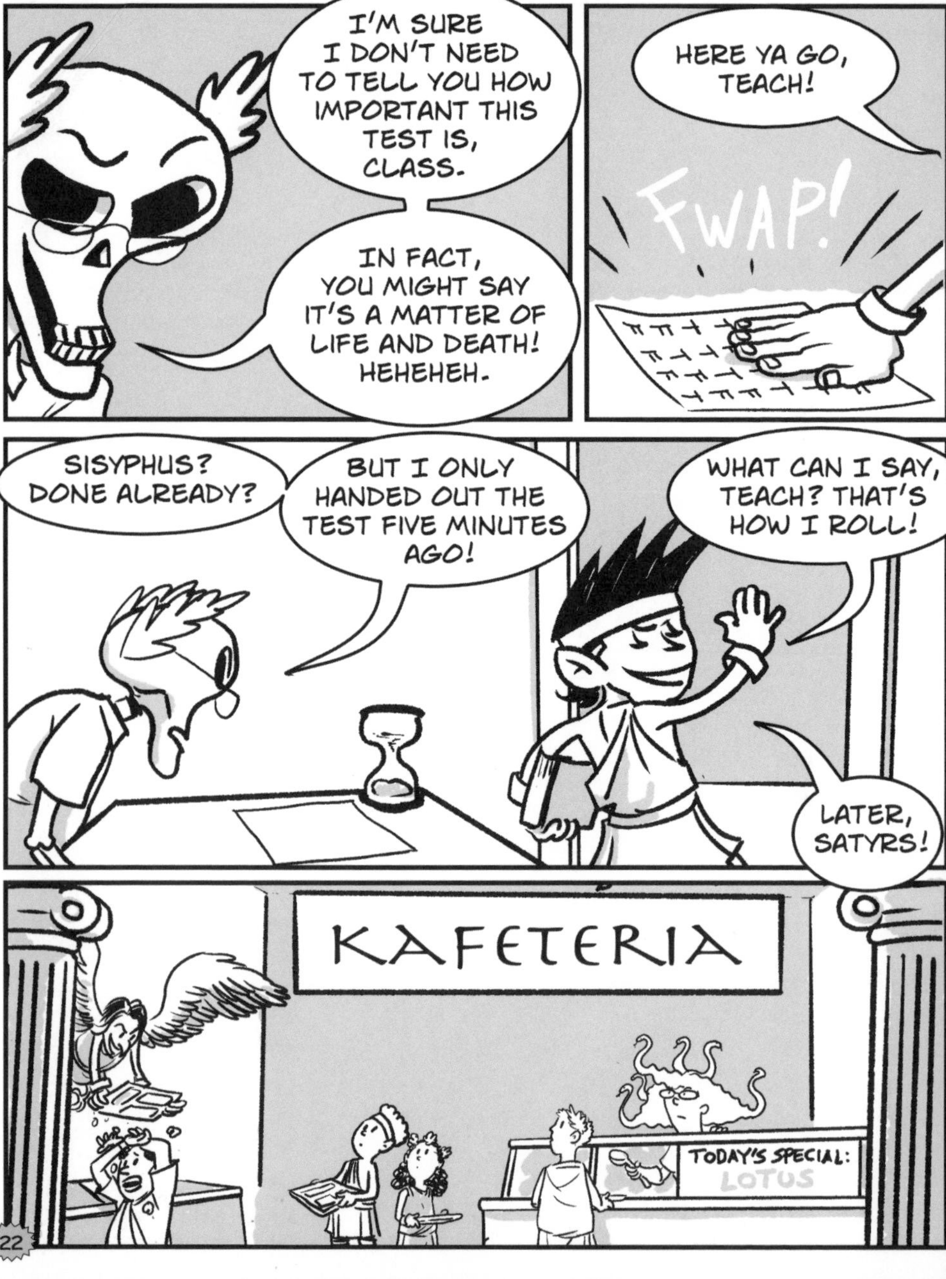
I'M SURE I DON'T NEED TO TELL YOU HOW IMPORTANT THIS TEST IS, CLASS.
IN FACT, YOU MIGHT SAY IT'S A MATTER OF LIFE AND DEATH! HEHEHEH.
HERE YA GO, TEACH!
FWAP!
SISYPHUS? DONE ALREADY?
BUT I ONLY HANDED OUT THE TEST FIVE MINUTES AGO!
WHAT CAN I SAY, TEACH? THAT'S HOW I ROLL!
LATER, SATYRS!
KAFETERIA
TODAY'S SPECIAL:
LOTUS

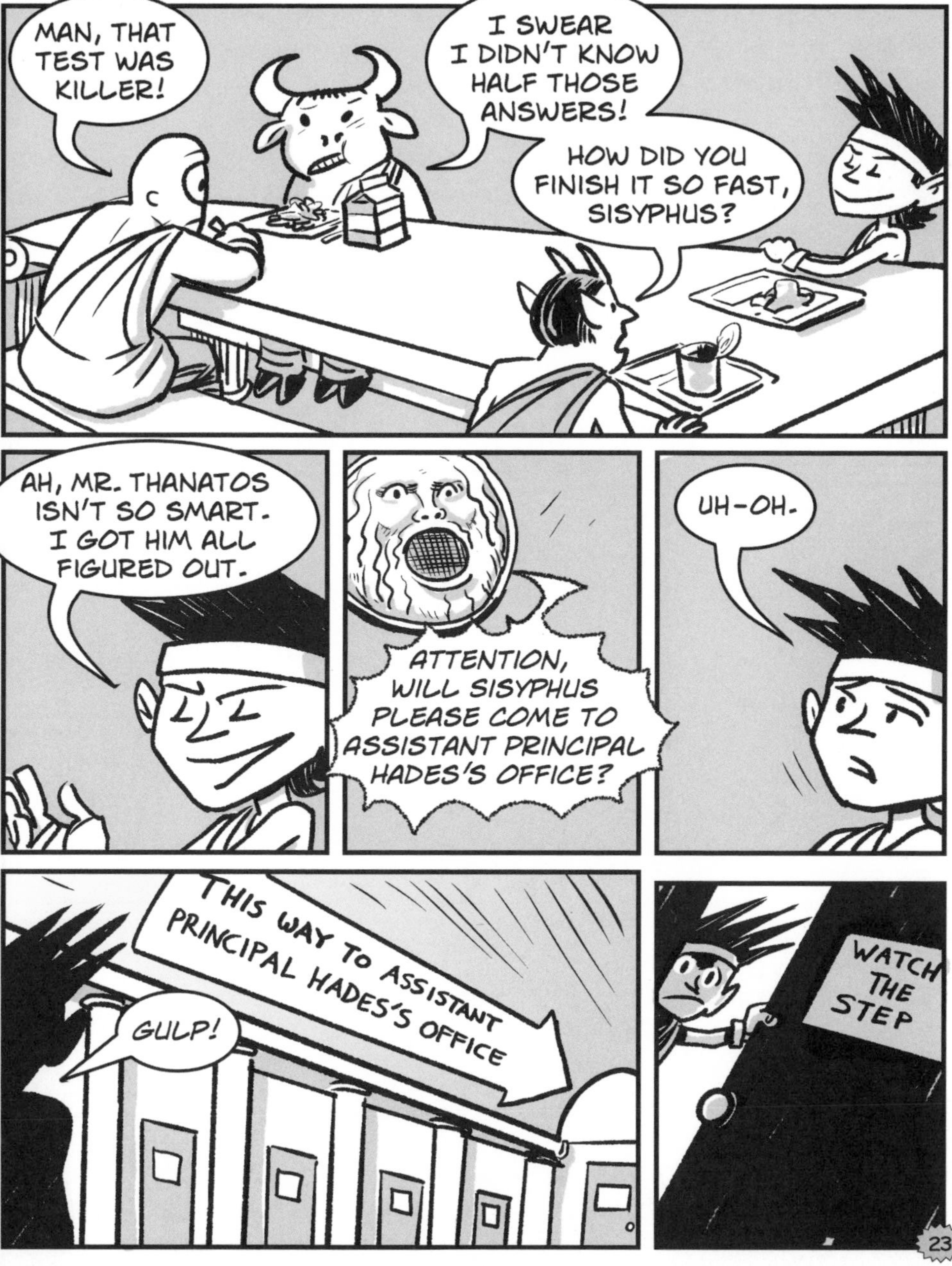
MAN, THAT TEST WAS KILLER!
I SWEAR I DIDN'T KNOW HALF THOSE ANSWERS!
HOW DID YOU FINISH IT SO FAST, SISYPHUS?
AH, MR. THANATOS ISN'T SO SMART. I GOT HIM ALL FIGURED OUT.
ATTENTION, WILL SISYPHUS PLEASE COME TO ASSISTANT PRINCIPAL HADES'S OFFICE?
UH-OH.
THIS WAY TO ASSISTANT PRINCIPAL HADES'S OFFICE
GULP!
WATCH THE STEP

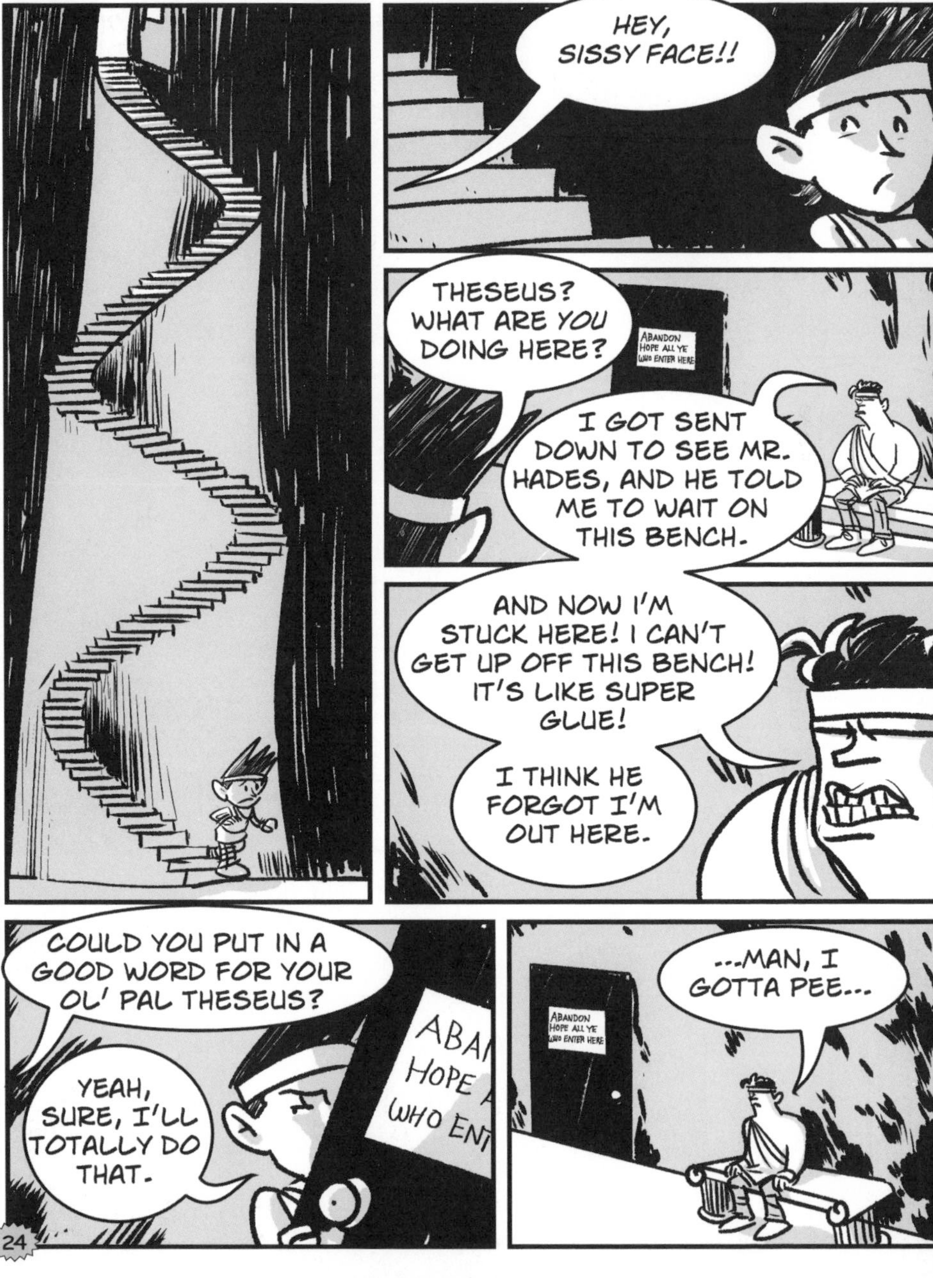
HEY, SISSY FACE!!
THESEUS? WHAT ARE YOU DOING HERE?
ABANDON HOPE ALL YE WHO ENTER HERE
I GOT SENT DOWN TO SEE MR. HADES, AND HE TOLD ME TO WAIT ON THIS BENCH.
AND NOW I'M STUCK HERE! I CAN'T GET UP OFF THIS BENCH! IT'S LIKE SUPER GLUE!
I THINK HE FORGOT I'M OUT HERE.
COULD YOU PUT IN A GOOD WORD FOR YOUR OL' PAL THESEUS?
YEAH, SURE, I'LL TOTALLY DO THAT.
ABANDON HOPE ALL YE WHO ENTER HERE
...MAN, I GOTTA PEE...

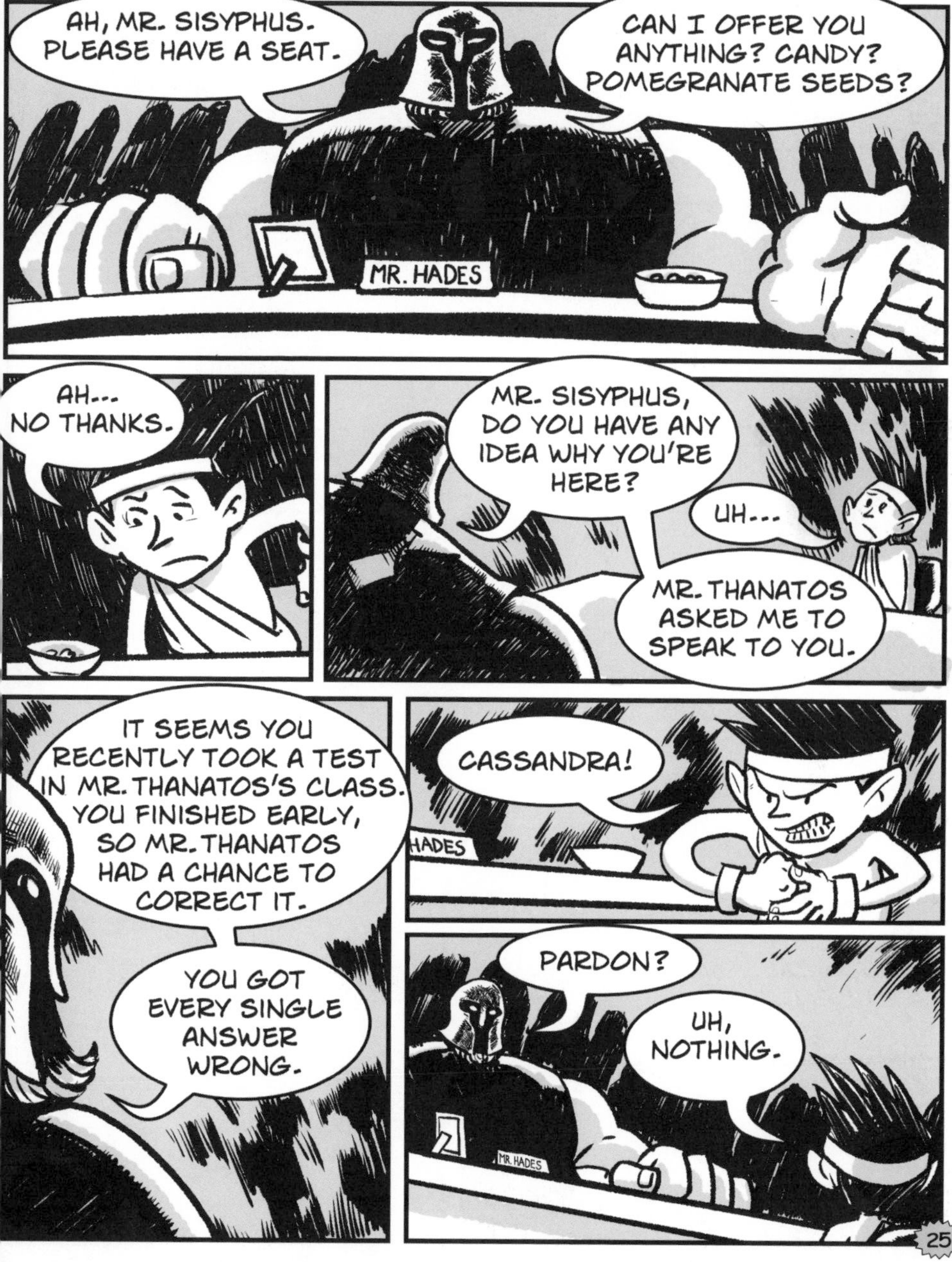
AH, MR. SISYPHUS. PLEASE HAVE A SEAT.
CAN I OFFER YOU ANYTHING? CANDY? POMEGRANATE SEEDS?
MR. HADES
AH... NO THANKS.
MR. SISYPHUS, DO YOU HAVE ANY IDEA WHY YOU'RE HERE?
UH...
MR. THANATOS ASKED ME TO SPEAK TO YOU.
IT SEEMS YOU RECENTLY TOOK A TEST IN MR. THANATOS'S CLASS. YOU FINISHED EARLY, SO MR. THANATOS HAD A CHANCE TO CORRECT IT.
YOU GOT EVERY SINGLE ANSWER WRONG.
CASSANDRA!
HADES
PARDON?
UH, NOTHING.
MR. HADES

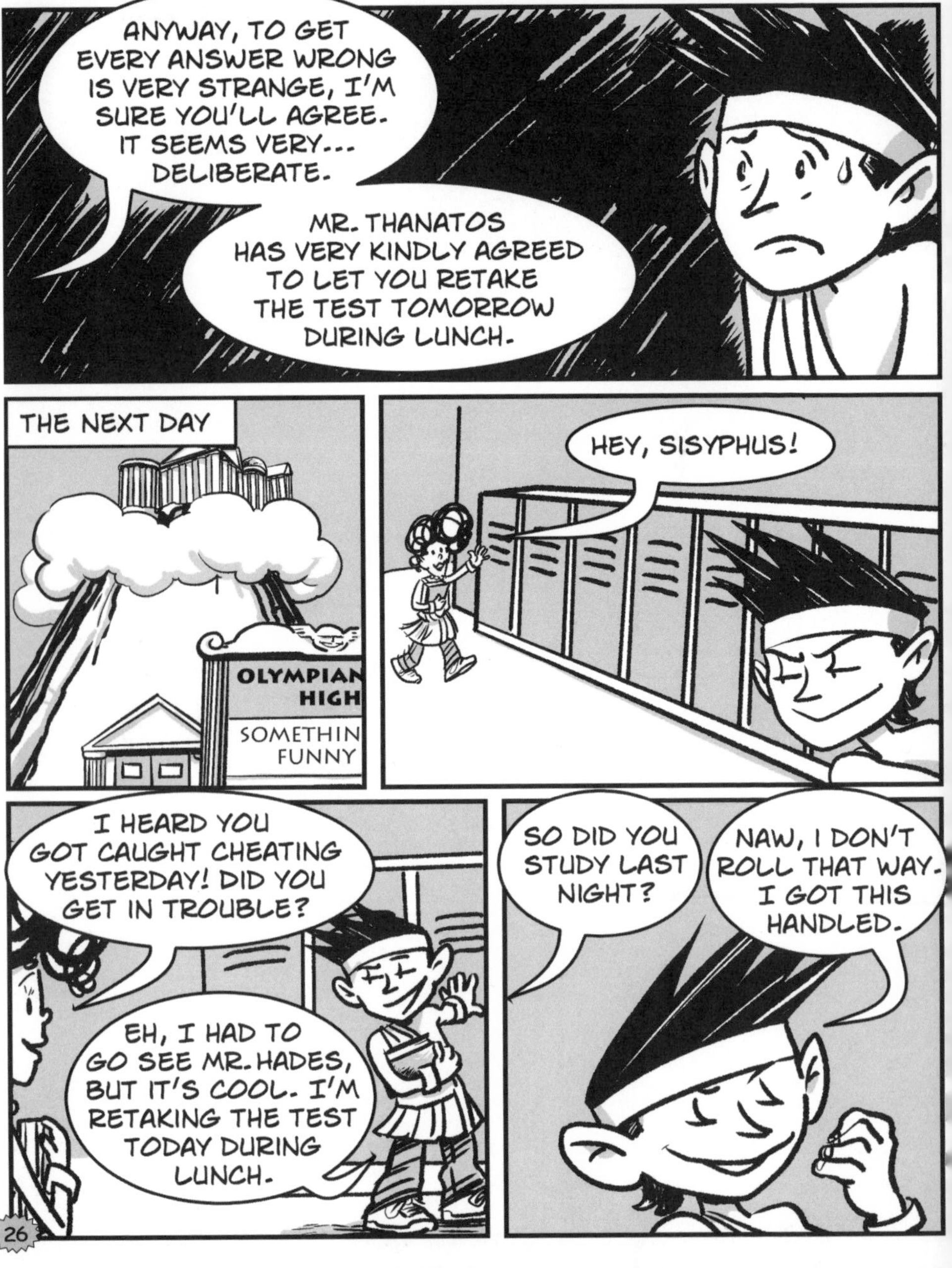
ANYWAY, TO GET EVERY ANSWER WRONG IS VERY STRANGE, I'M SURE YOU'LL AGREE. IT SEEMS VERY... DELIBERATE.
MR. THANATOS HAS VERY KINDLY AGREED TO LET YOU RETAKE THE TEST TOMORROW DURING LUNCH.
THE NEXT DAY
OLYMPIAN HIGH
SOMETHIN FUNNY
HEY, SISYPHUS!
I HEARD YOU GOT CAUGHT CHEATING YESTERDAY! DID YOU GET IN TROUBLE?
EH, I HAD TO GO SEE MR. HADES, BUT IT'S COOL. I'M RETAKING THE TEST TODAY DURING LUNCH.
SO DID YOU STUDY LAST NIGHT?
NAW, I DON'T ROLL THAT WAY. I GOT THIS HANDLED.

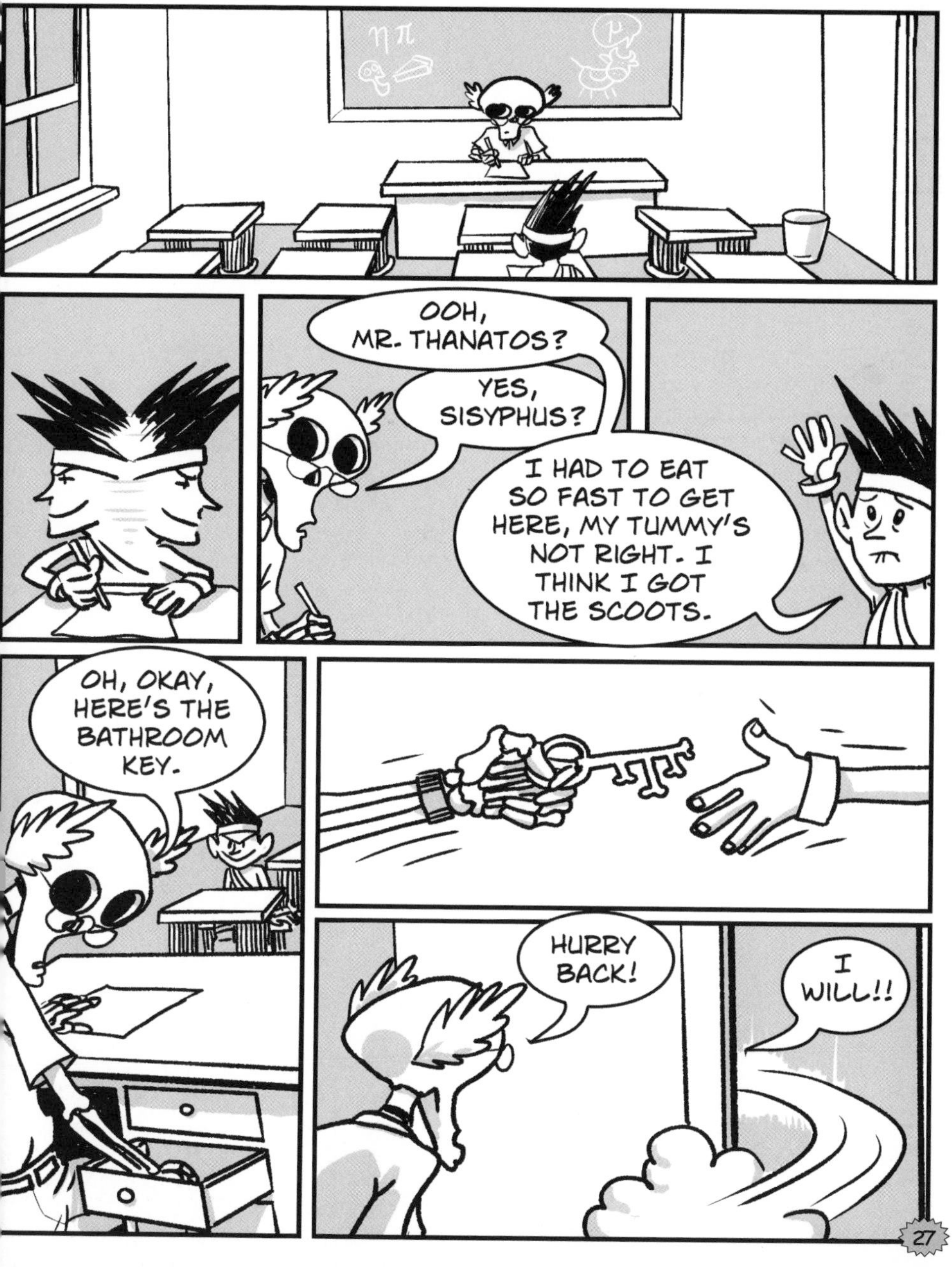
OOH, MR. THANATOS?
YES, SISYPHUS?
I HAD TO EAT SO FAST TO GET HERE, MY TUMMY'S NOT RIGHT. I THINK I GOT THE SCOOTS.
OH, OKAY, HERE'S THE BATHROOM KEY.
HURRY BACK!
I WILL!!

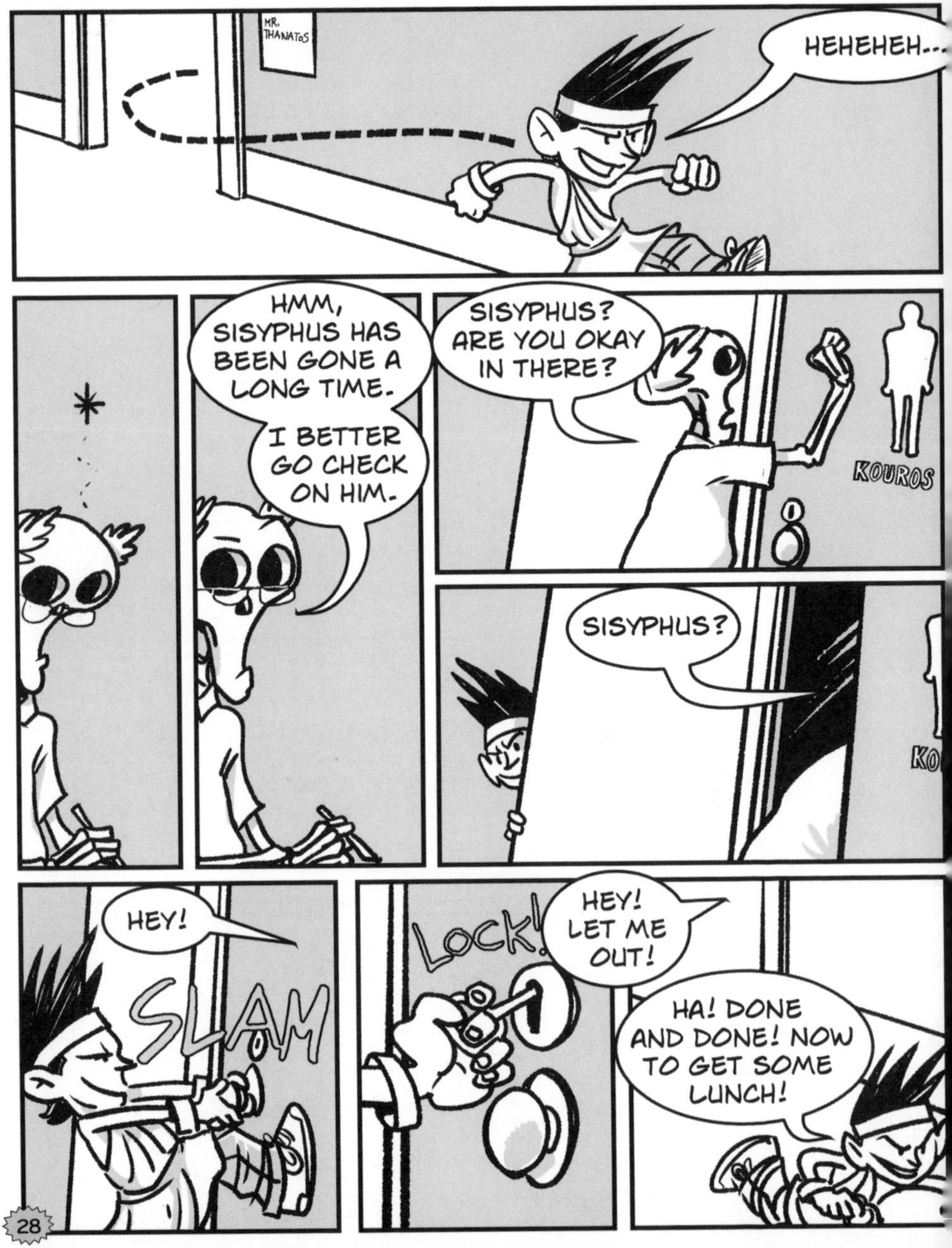
MR. THANATOS
HEHEHEH...
HMM, SISYPHUS HAS BEEN GONE A LONG TIME.
I BETTER GO CHECK ON HIM.
SISYPHUS? ARE YOU OKAY IN THERE?
KOUROS
SISYPHUS?
HEY!
SLAM
LOCK!
HEY! LET ME OUT!
HA! DONE AND DONE! NOW TO GET SOME LUNCH!

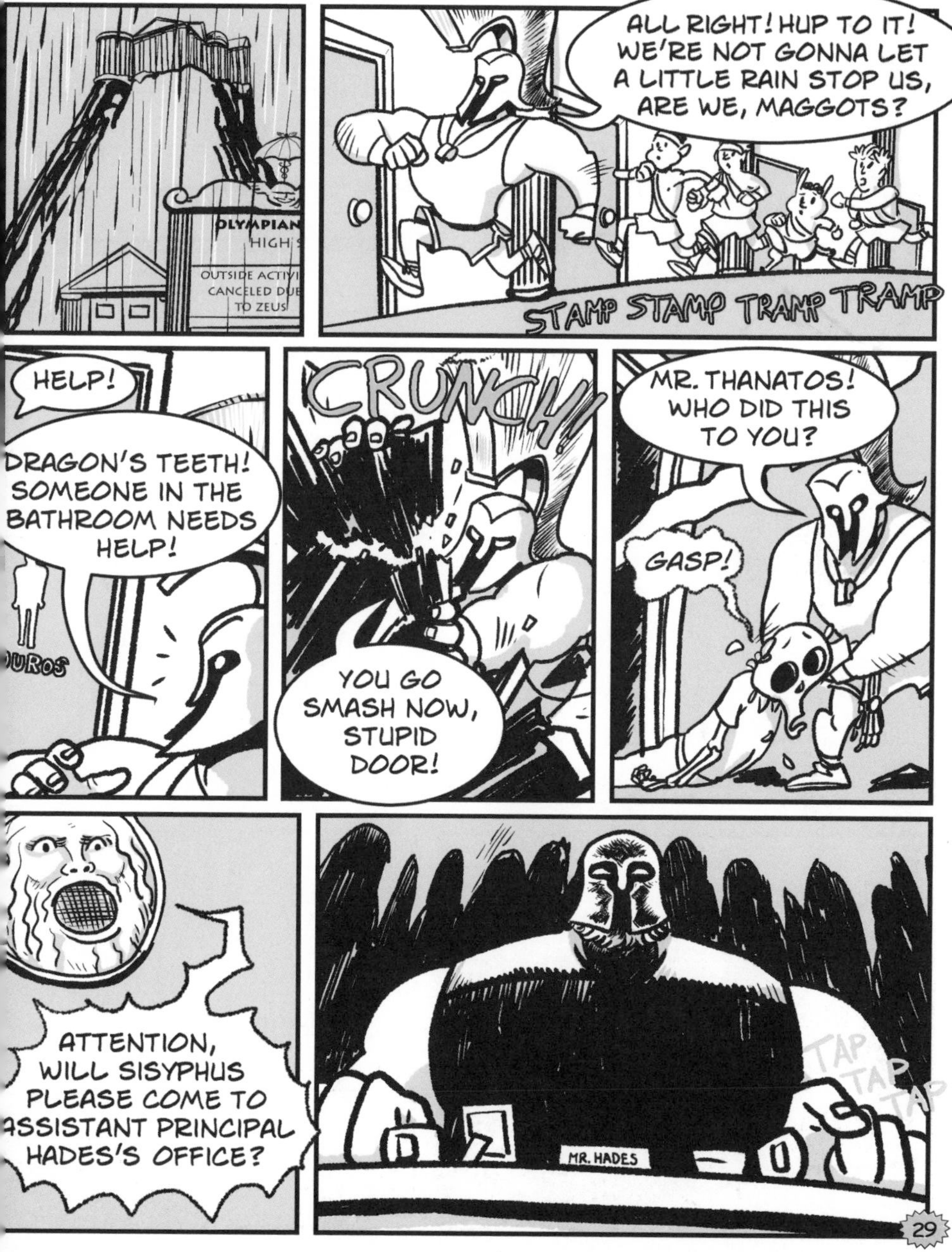
OLYMPIAN HIGH S
OUTSIDE ACTIVI CANCELED DUE TO ZEUS
ALL RIGHT! HUP TO IT! WE'RE NOT GONNA LET A LITTLE RAIN STOP US, ARE WE, MAGGOTS?
STAMP STAMP TRAMP TRAMP
HELP!
DRAGON'S TEETH! SOMEONE IN THE BATHROOM NEEDS HELP!
CRUNCH!
YOU GO SMASH NOW, STUPID DOOR!
MR. THANATOS! WHO DID THIS TO YOU?
GASP!
ATTENTION, WILL SISYPHUS PLEASE COME TO ASSISTANT PRINCIPAL HADES'S OFFICE?
TAP TAP TAP
MR. HADES

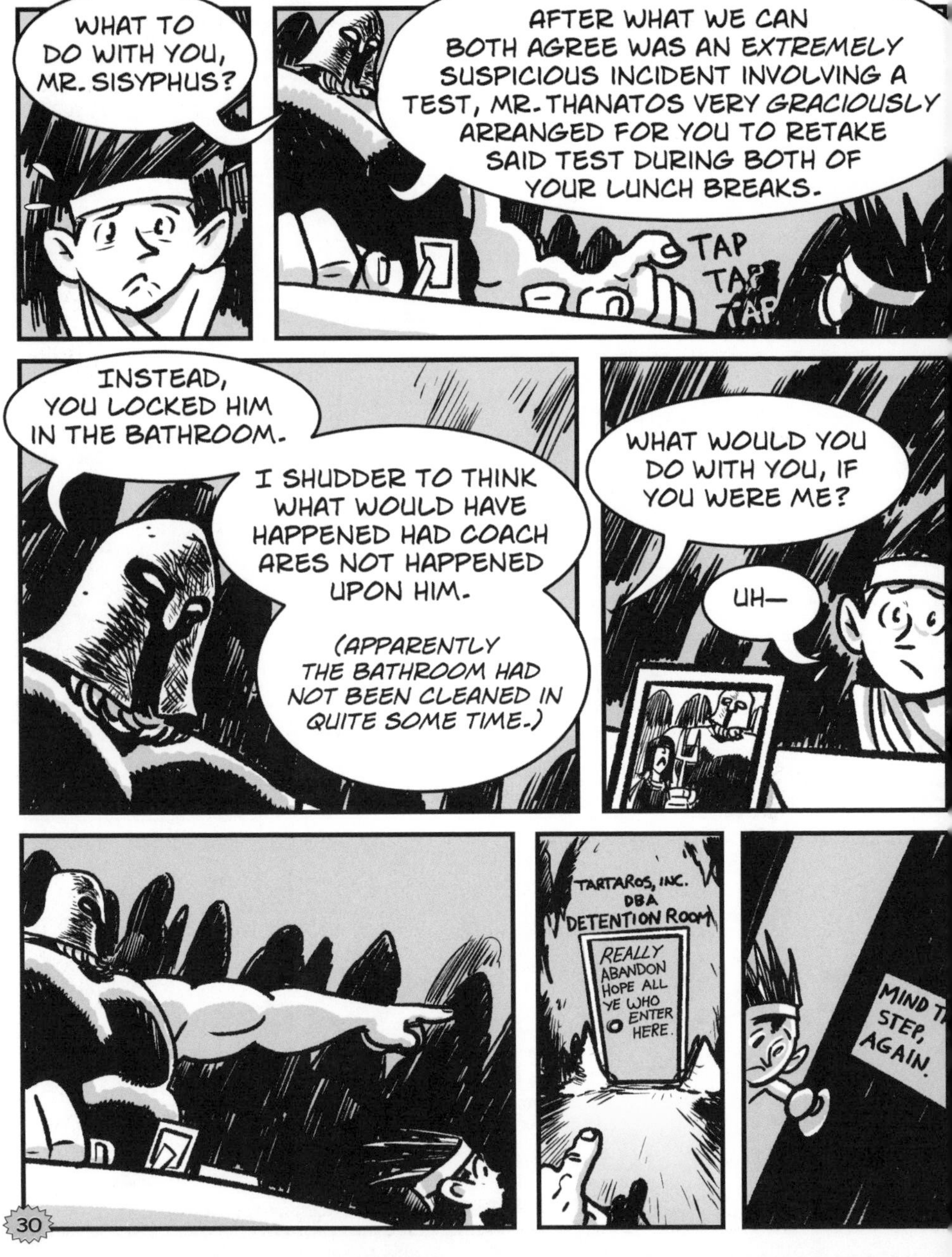
WHAT TO DO WITH YOU, MR. SISYPHUS?
AFTER WHAT WE CAN BOTH AGREE WAS AN EXTREMELY SUSPICIOUS INCIDENT INVOLVING A TEST, MR. THANATOS VERY GRACIOUSLY ARRANGED FOR YOU TO RETAKE SAID TEST DURING BOTH OF YOUR LUNCH BREAKS.
TAP TAP TAP
INSTEAD, YOU LOCKED HIM IN THE BATHROOM.
I SHUDDER TO THINK WHAT WOULD HAVE HAPPENED HAD COACH ARES NOT HAPPENED UPON HIM.
(APPARENTLY THE BATHROOM HAD NOT BEEN CLEANED IN QUITE SOME TIME.)
WHAT WOULD YOU DO WITH YOU, IF YOU WERE ME?
UH—
TARTAROS, INC. DBA DETENTION ROOM
REALLY ABANDON HOPE ALL YE WHO ENTER HERE.
MIND THE STEP, AGAIN.

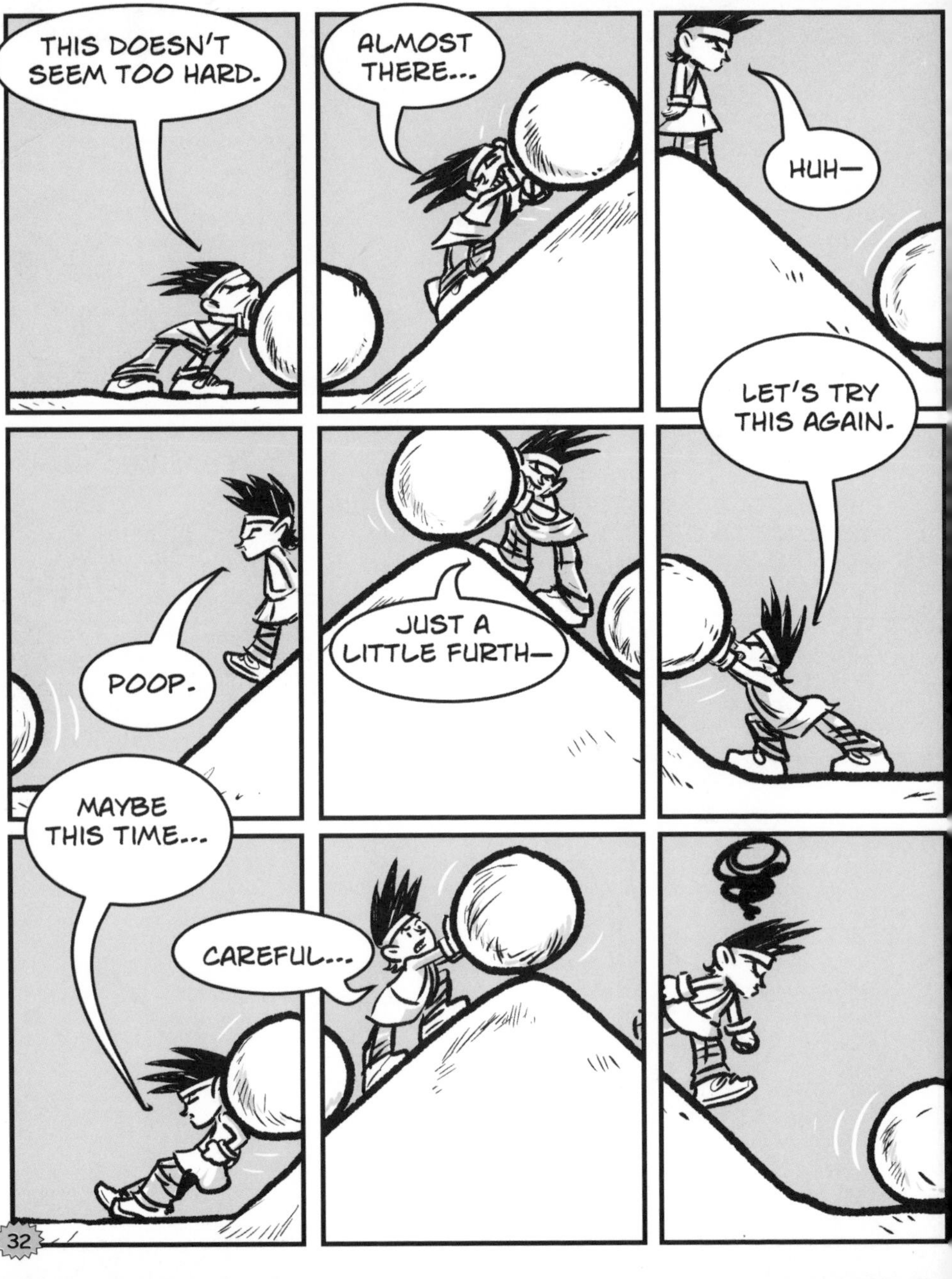
THIS DOESN'T SEEM TOO HARD.
ALMOST THERE...
HUH—
LET'S TRY THIS AGAIN.
POOP.
JUST A LITTLE FURTH—
MAYBE THIS TIME...
CAREFUL...

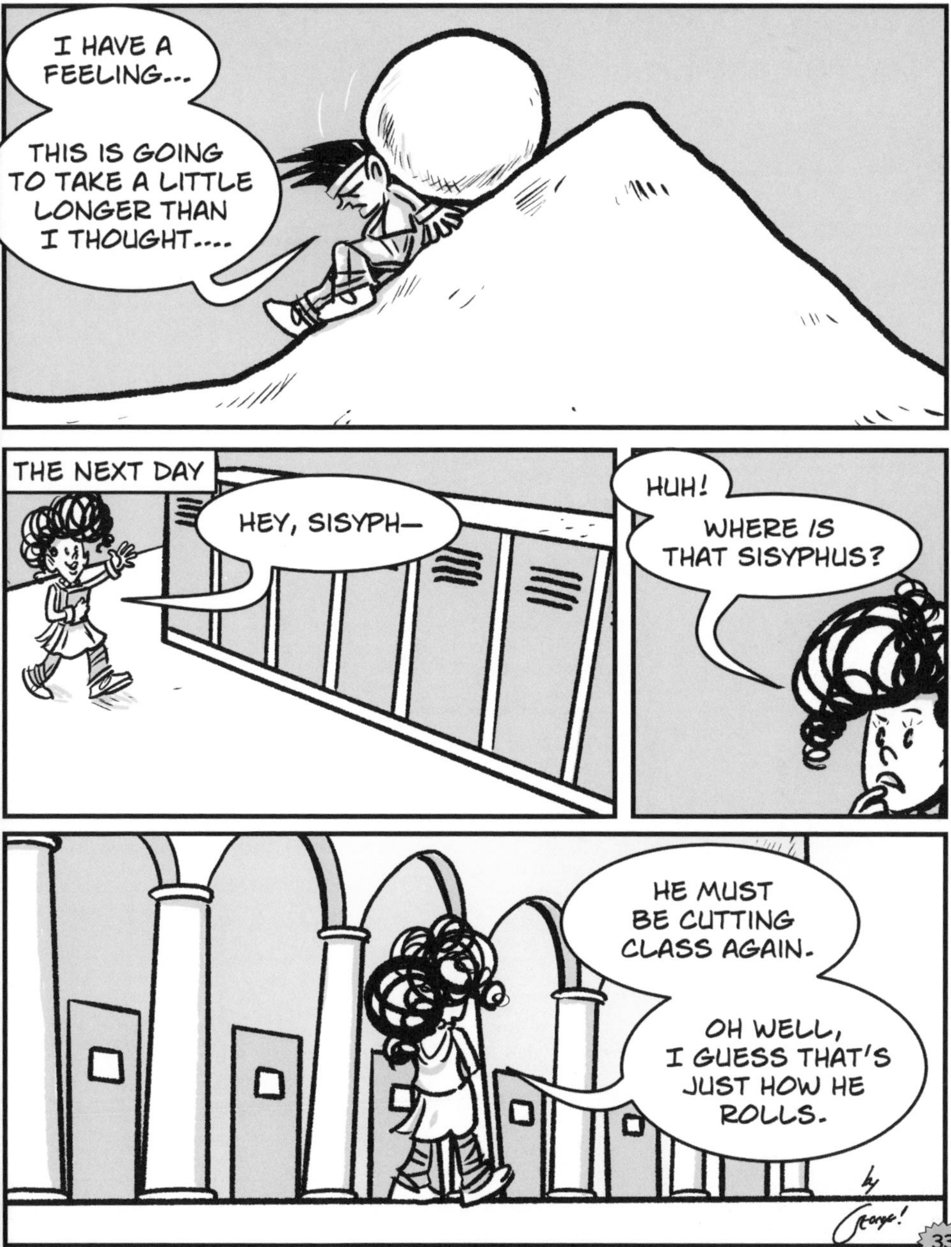
I HAVE A FEELING...
THIS IS GOING TO TAKE A LITTLE LONGER THAN I THOUGHT....
THE NEXT DAY
HEY, SISYPH—
HUH!
WHERE IS THAT SISYPHUS?
HE MUST BE CUTTING CLASS AGAIN.
OH WELL, I GUESS THAT'S JUST HOW HE ROLLS.
by
George!

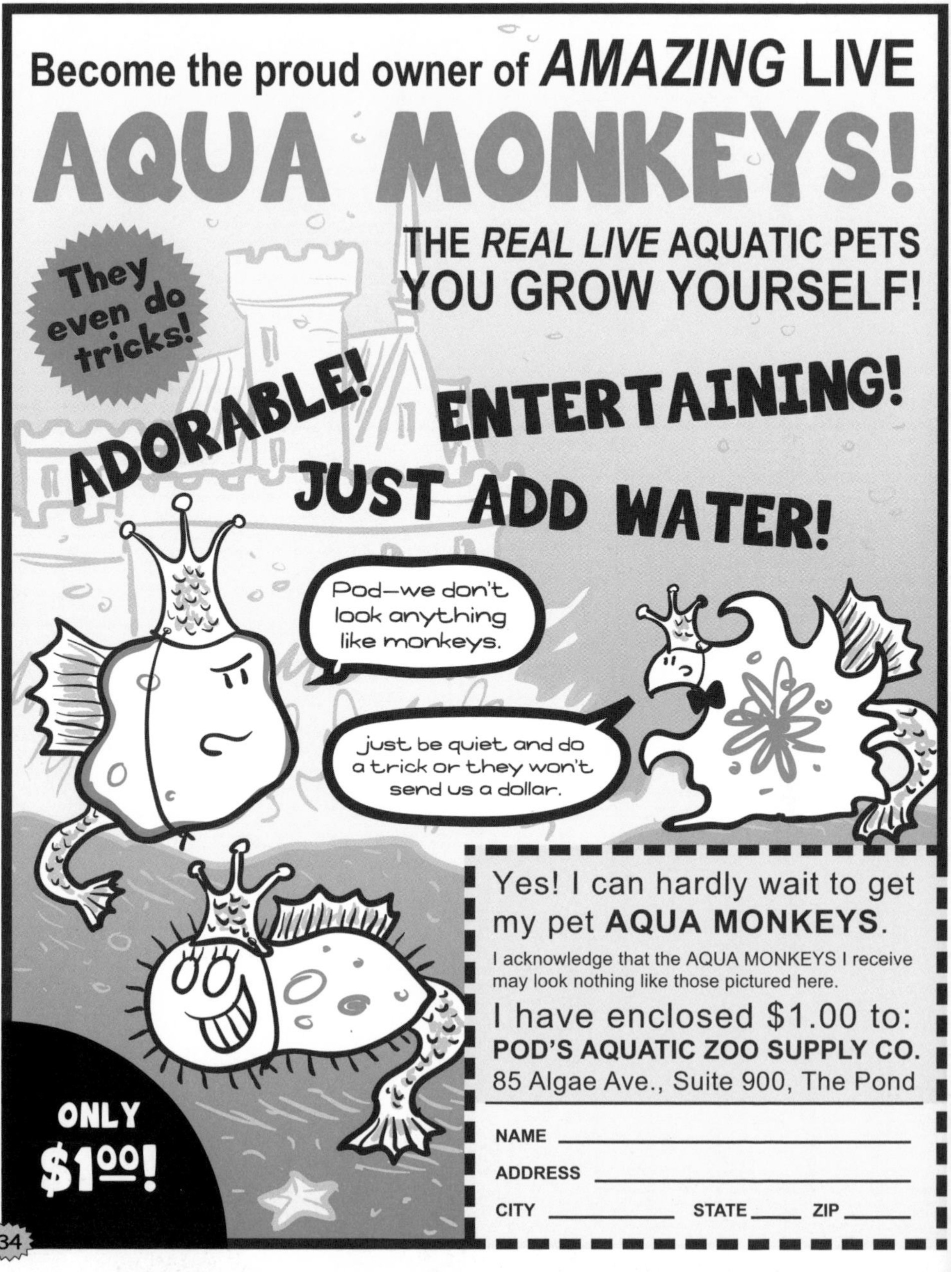
Become the proud owner of AMAZING LIVE
AQUA MONKEYS!
THE REAL LIVE AQUATIC PETS YOU GROW YOURSELF!
They even do tricks!
ADORABLE!
ENTERTAINING!
JUST ADD WATER!
Pod—we don't look anything like monkeys.
just be quiet and do a trick or they won't send us a dollar.
Yes! I can hardly wait to get my pet AQUA MONKEYS.
I acknowledge that the AQUA MONKEYS I receive may look nothing like those pictured here.
I have enclosed $1.00 to:
POD'S AQUATIC ZOO SUPPLY CO.
85 Algae Ave., Suite 900, The Pond
NAME
ADDRESS
CITY
STATE
ZIP
ONLY $1.00!

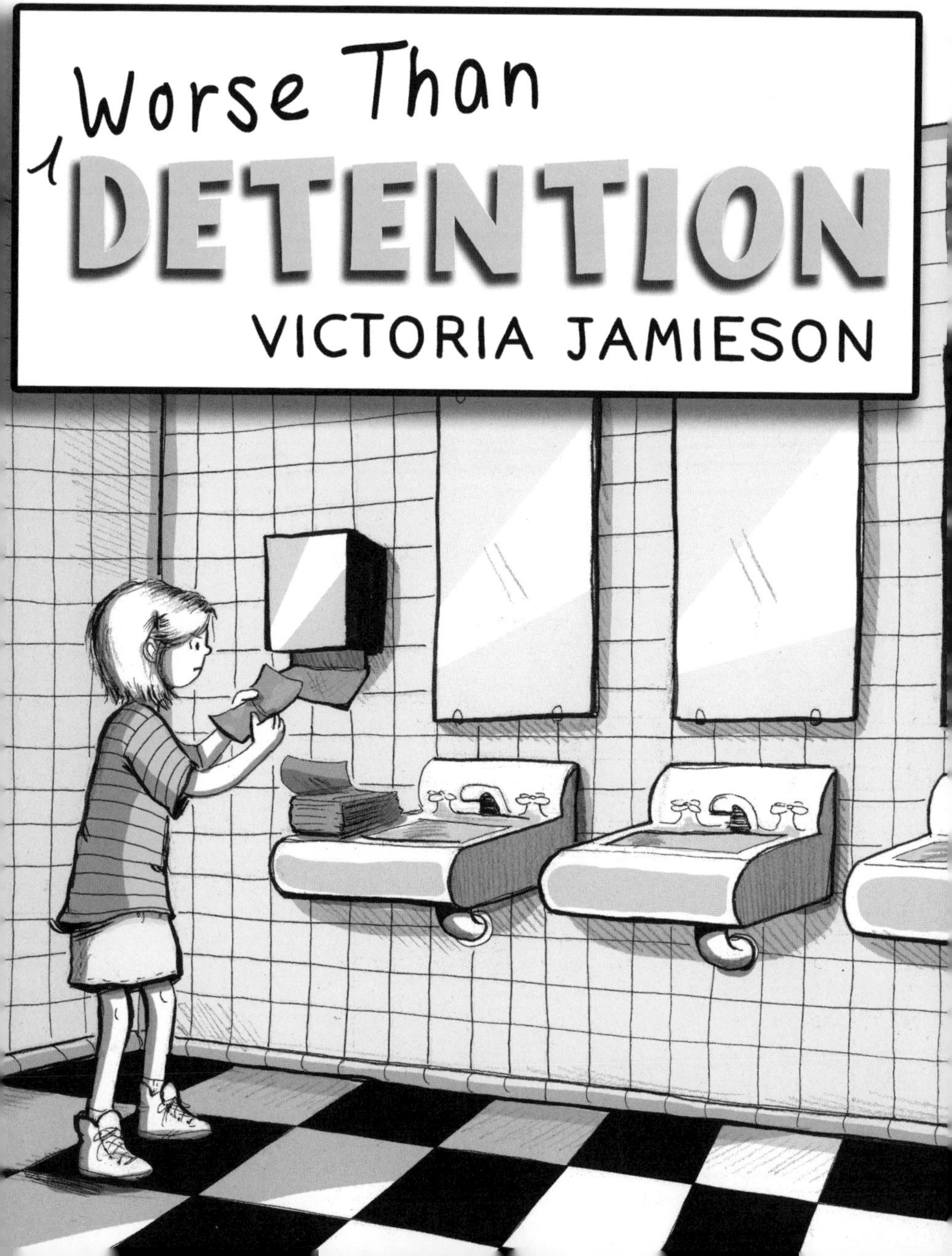
Worse Than
DETENTION
VICTORIA JAMIESON

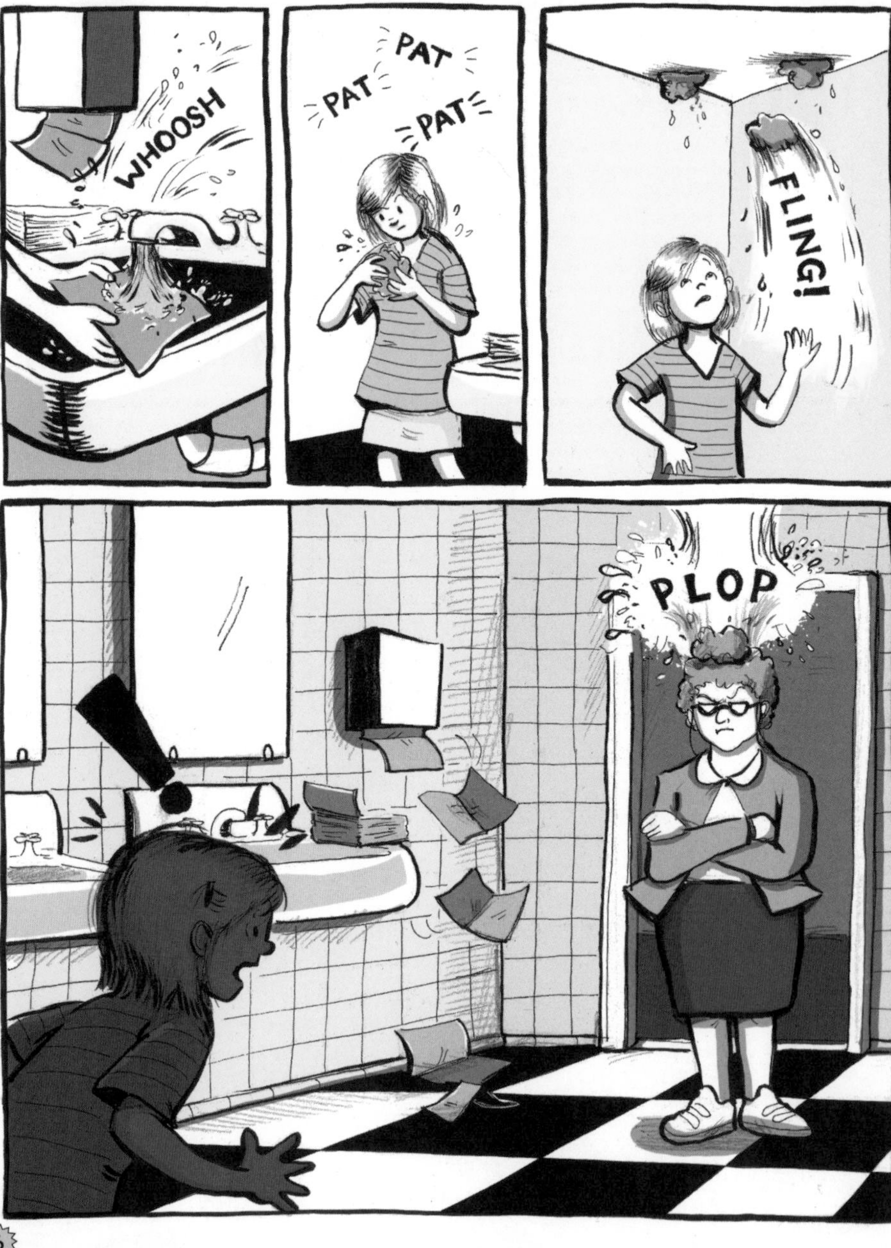
WHOOSH
PAT
PAT
PAT
FLING!
PLOP

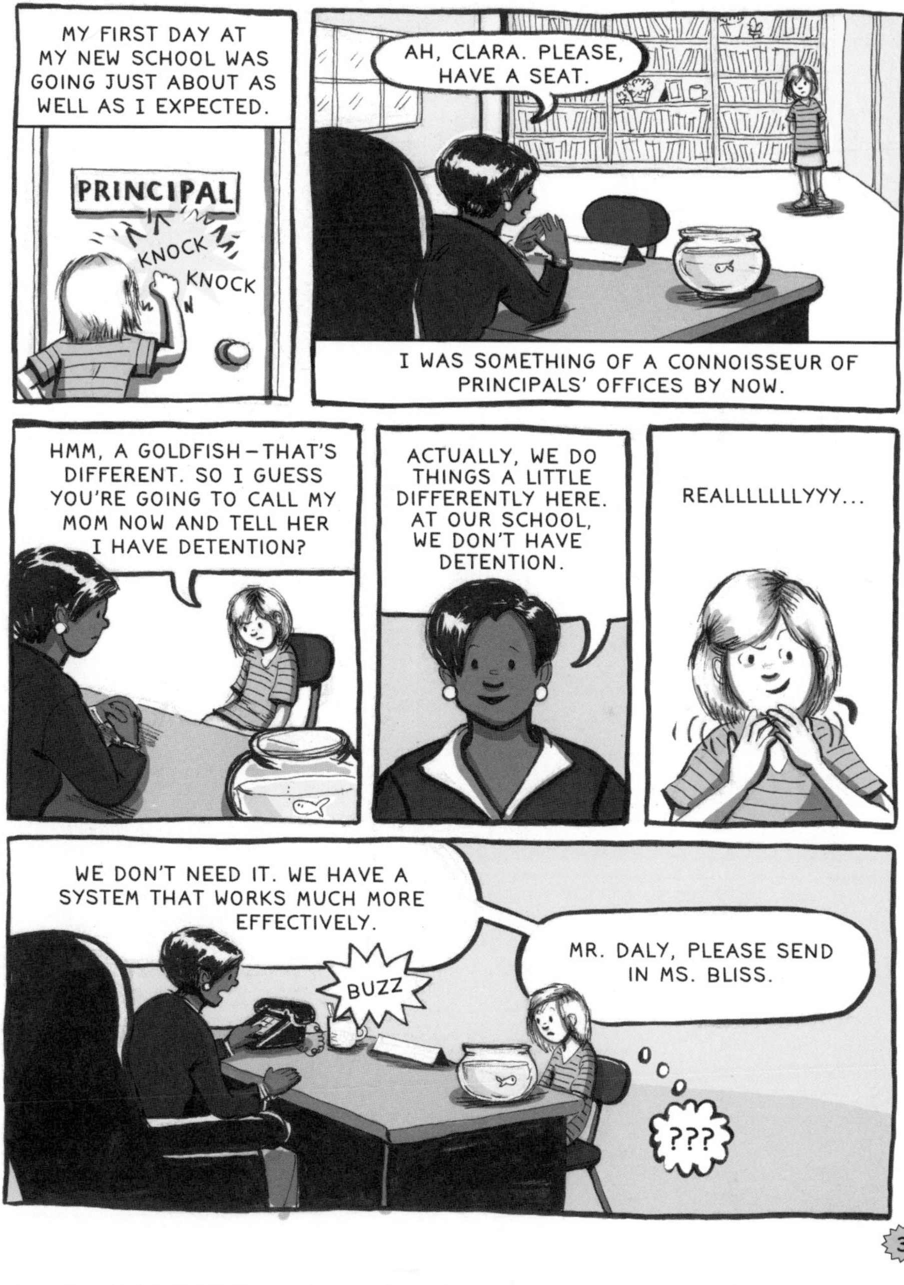
MY FIRST DAY AT MY NEW SCHOOL WAS GOING JUST ABOUT AS WELL AS I EXPECTED.
PRINCIPAL
KNOCK
KNOCK
AH, CLARA. PLEASE, HAVE A SEAT.
I WAS SOMETHING OF A CONNOISSEUR OF PRINCIPALS' OFFICES BY NOW.
HMM, A GOLDFISH—THAT'S DIFFERENT. SO I GUESS YOU'RE GOING TO CALL MY MOM NOW AND TELL HER I HAVE DETENTION?
ACTUALLY, WE DO THINGS A LITTLE DIFFERENTLY HERE. AT OUR SCHOOL, WE DON'T HAVE DETENTION.
REALLLLLLLYYY...
WE DON'T NEED IT. WE HAVE A SYSTEM THAT WORKS MUCH MORE EFFECTIVELY.
BUZZ
MR. DALY, PLEASE SEND IN MS. BLISS.
???

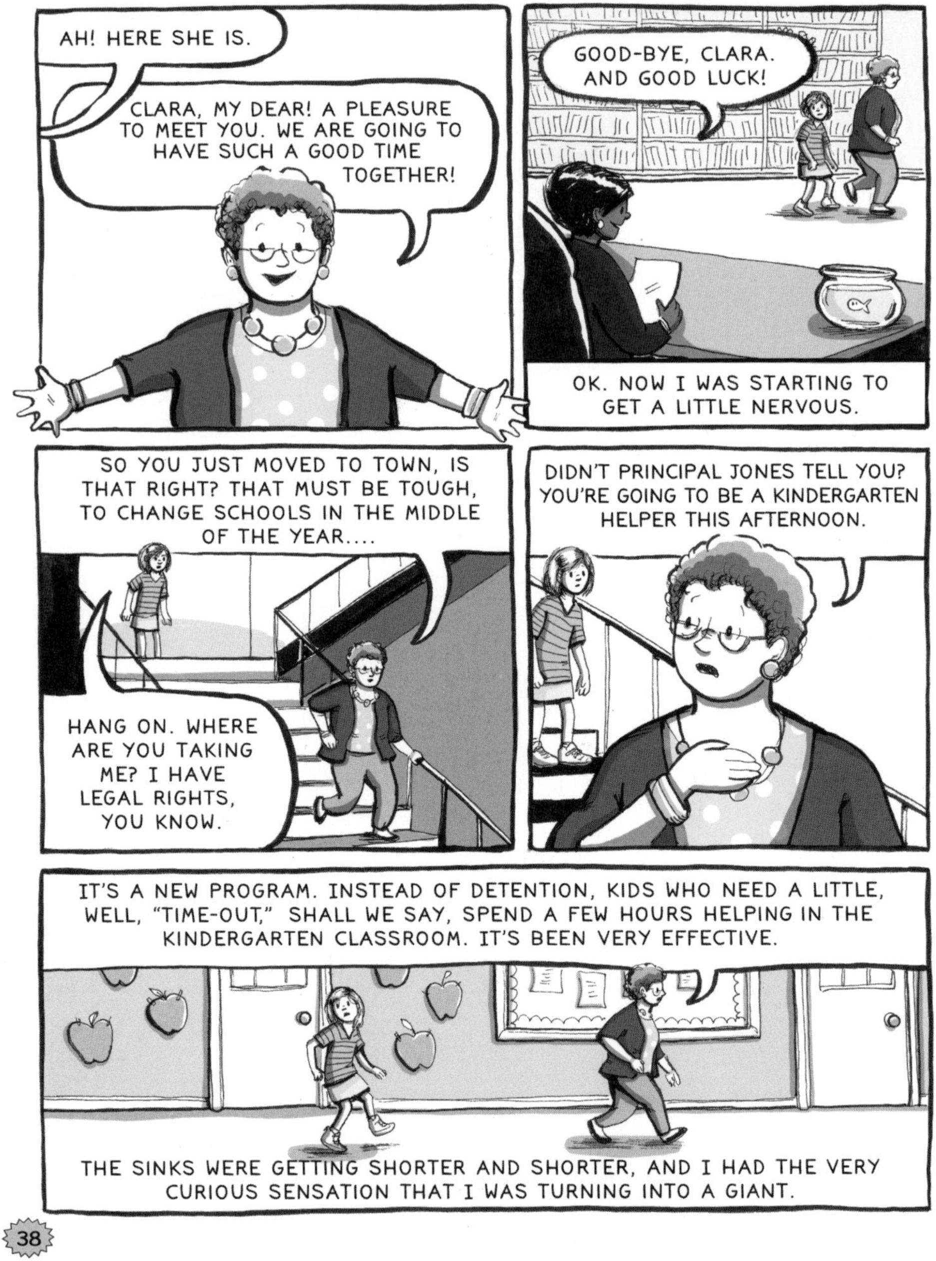
AH! HERE SHE IS.
CLARA, MY DEAR! A PLEASURE TO MEET YOU. WE ARE GOING TO HAVE SUCH A GOOD TIME TOGETHER!
GOOD-BYE, CLARA. AND GOOD LUCK!
OK. NOW I WAS STARTING TO GET A LITTLE NERVOUS.
SO YOU JUST MOVED TO TOWN, IS THAT RIGHT? THAT MUST BE TOUGH, TO CHANGE SCHOOLS IN THE MIDDLE OF THE YEAR....
HANG ON. WHERE ARE YOU TAKING ME? I HAVE LEGAL RIGHTS, YOU KNOW.
DIDN'T PRINCIPAL JONES TELL YOU? YOU'RE GOING TO BE A KINDERGARTEN HELPER THIS AFTERNOON.
IT'S A NEW PROGRAM. INSTEAD OF DETENTION, KIDS WHO NEED A LITTLE, WELL, "TIME-OUT," SHALL WE SAY, SPEND A FEW HOURS HELPING IN THE KINDERGARTEN CLASSROOM. IT'S BEEN VERY EFFECTIVE.
THE SINKS WERE GETTING SHORTER AND SHORTER, AND I HAD THE VERY CURIOUS SENSATION THAT I WAS TURNING INTO A GIANT.

41

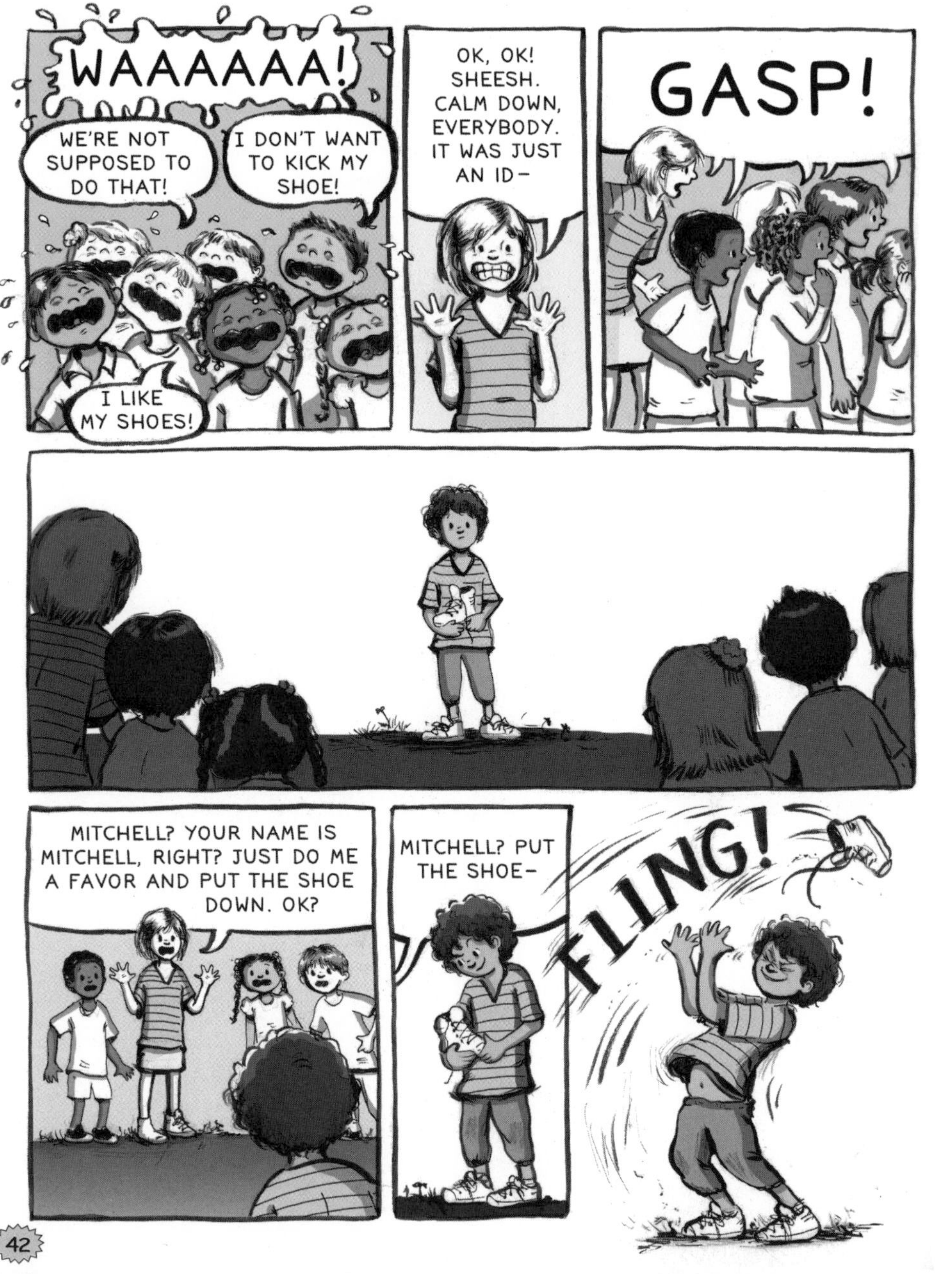
WAAAAAA!
WE'RE NOT SUPPOSED TO DO THAT!
I DON'T WANT TO KICK MY SHOE!
I LIKE MY SHOES!
OK, OK! SHEESH. CALM DOWN, EVERYBODY. IT WAS JUST AN ID–
GASP!
MITCHELL? YOUR NAME IS MITCHELL, RIGHT? JUST DO ME A FAVOR AND PUT THE SHOE DOWN. OK?
MITCHELL? PUT THE SHOE–
FLING!

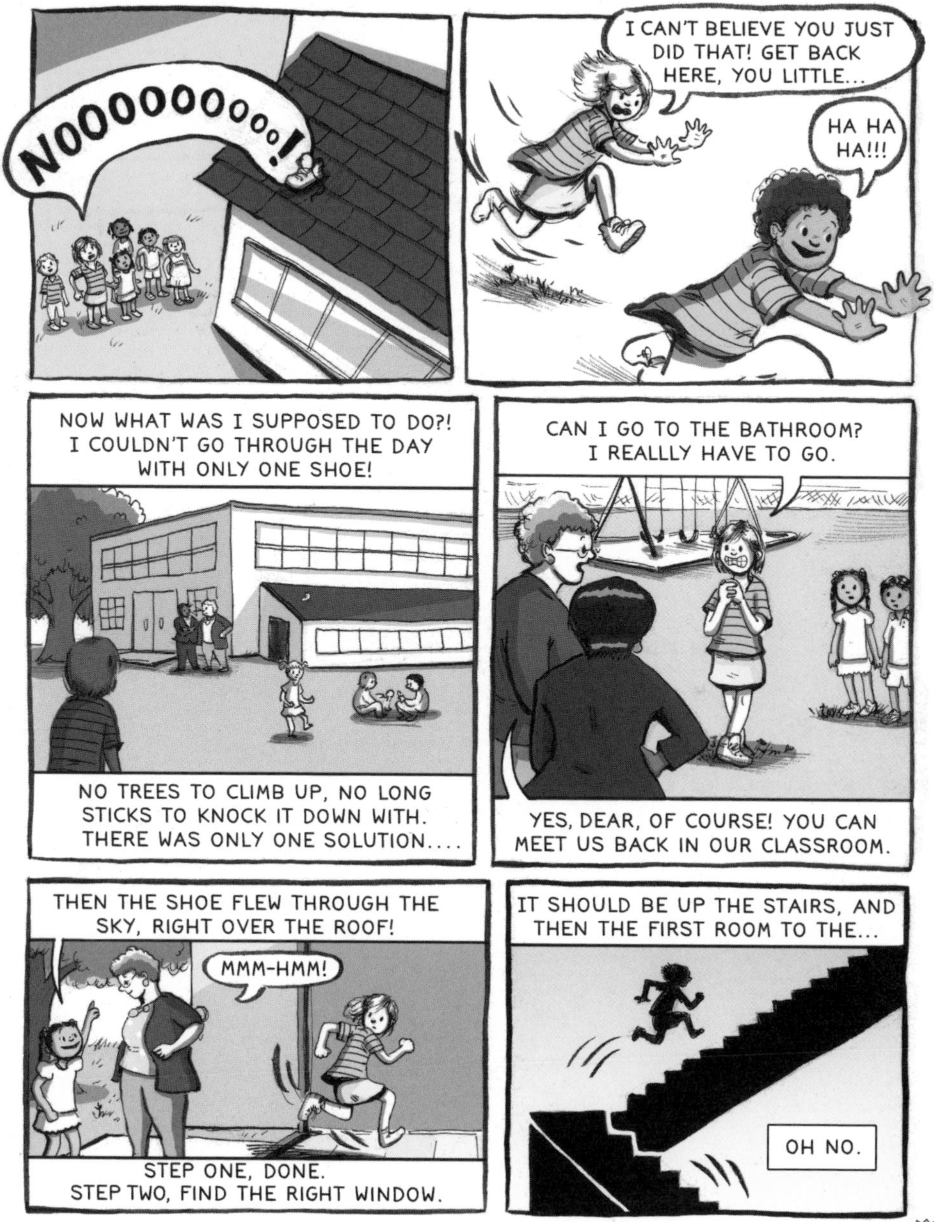

NOOOOOOooo!
I CAN'T BELIEVE YOU JUST DID THAT! GET BACK HERE, YOU LITTLE...
HA HA HA!!!
NOW WHAT WAS I SUPPOSED TO DO?! I COULDN'T GO THROUGH THE DAY WITH ONLY ONE SHOE!
NO TREES TO CLIMB UP, NO LONG STICKS TO KNOCK IT DOWN WITH. THERE WAS ONLY ONE SOLUTION....
CAN I GO TO THE BATHROOM? I REALLLY HAVE TO GO.
YES, DEAR, OF COURSE! YOU CAN MEET US BACK IN OUR CLASSROOM.
THEN THE SHOE FLEW THROUGH THE SKY, RIGHT OVER THE ROOF!
MMM-HMM!
STEP ONE, DONE.
STEP TWO, FIND THE RIGHT WINDOW.
IT SHOULD BE UP THE STAIRS, AND THEN THE FIRST ROOM TO THE...
OH NO.

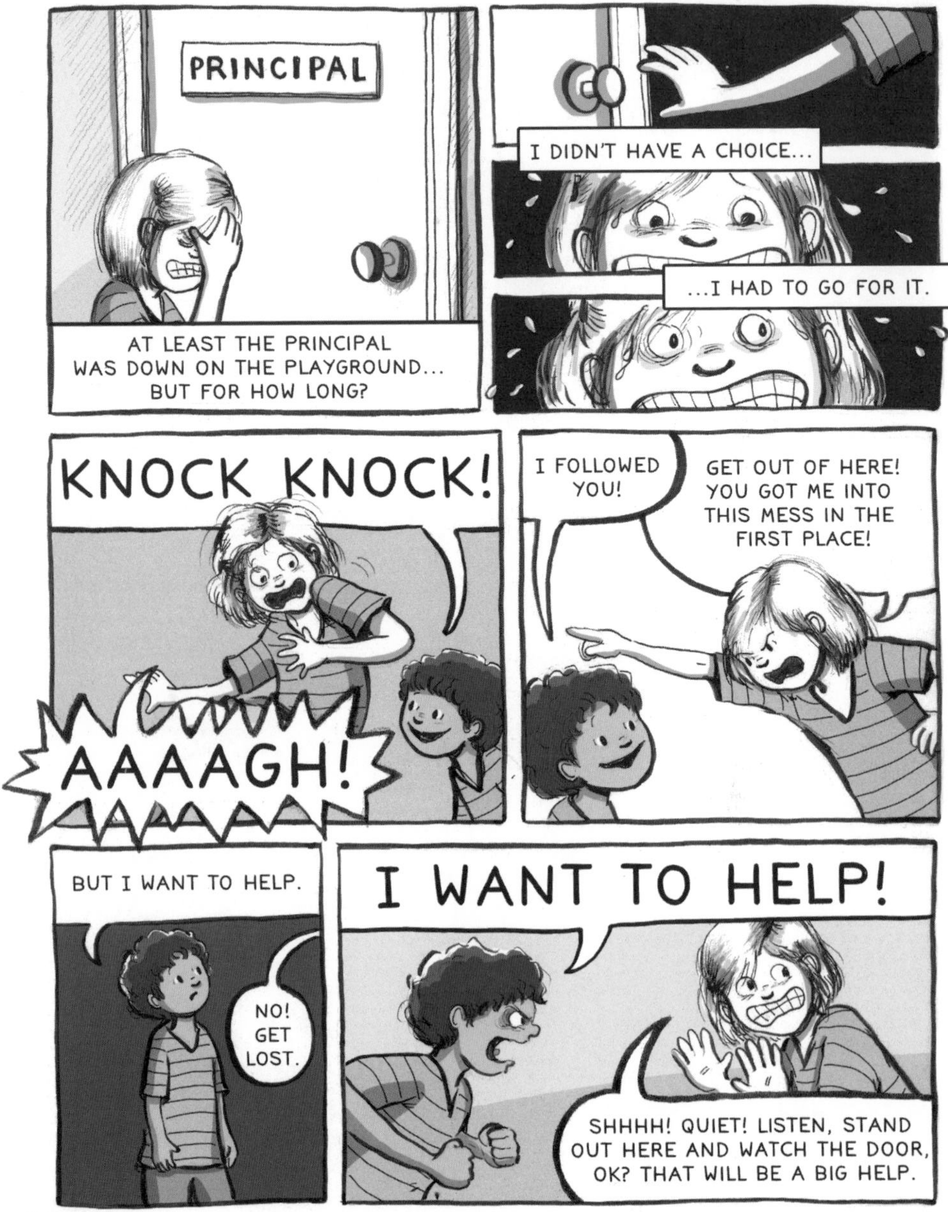
PRINCIPAL
AT LEAST THE PRINCIPAL WAS DOWN ON THE PLAYGROUND... BUT FOR HOW LONG?
I DIDN'T HAVE A CHOICE...
...I HAD TO GO FOR IT.
KNOCK KNOCK!
AAAAGH!
I FOLLOWED YOU!
GET OUT OF HERE! YOU GOT ME INTO THIS MESS IN THE FIRST PLACE!
BUT I WANT TO HELP.
NO! GET LOST.
I WANT TO HELP!
SHHHH! QUIET! LISTEN, STAND OUT HERE AND WATCH THE DOOR, OK? THAT WILL BE A BIG HELP.

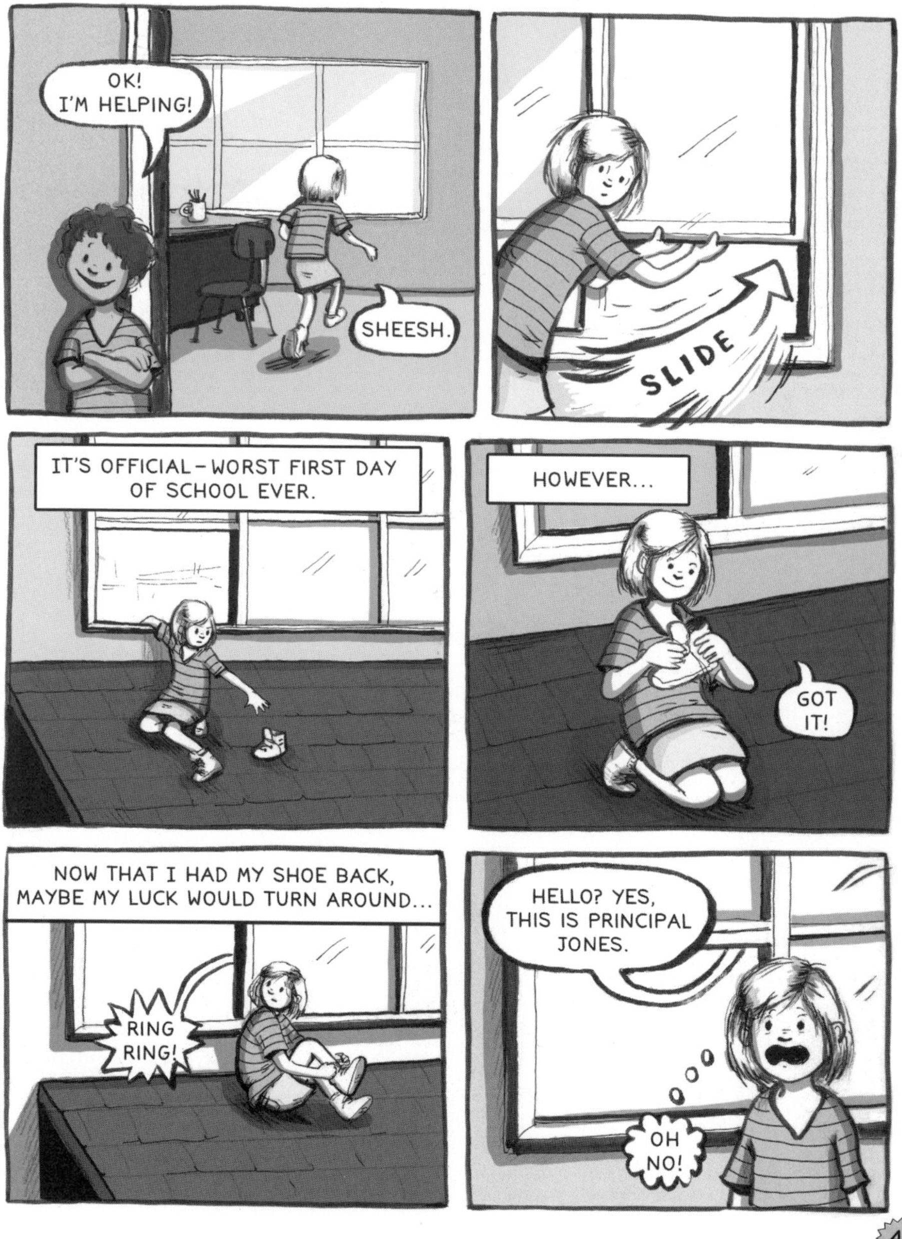
OK! I'M HELPING!
SHEESH.
SLIDE
IT'S OFFICIAL – WORST FIRST DAY OF SCHOOL EVER.
HOWEVER...
GOT IT!
NOW THAT I HAD MY SHOE BACK, MAYBE MY LUCK WOULD TURN AROUND...
RING RING!
HELLO? YES, THIS IS PRINCIPAL JONES.
OH NO!

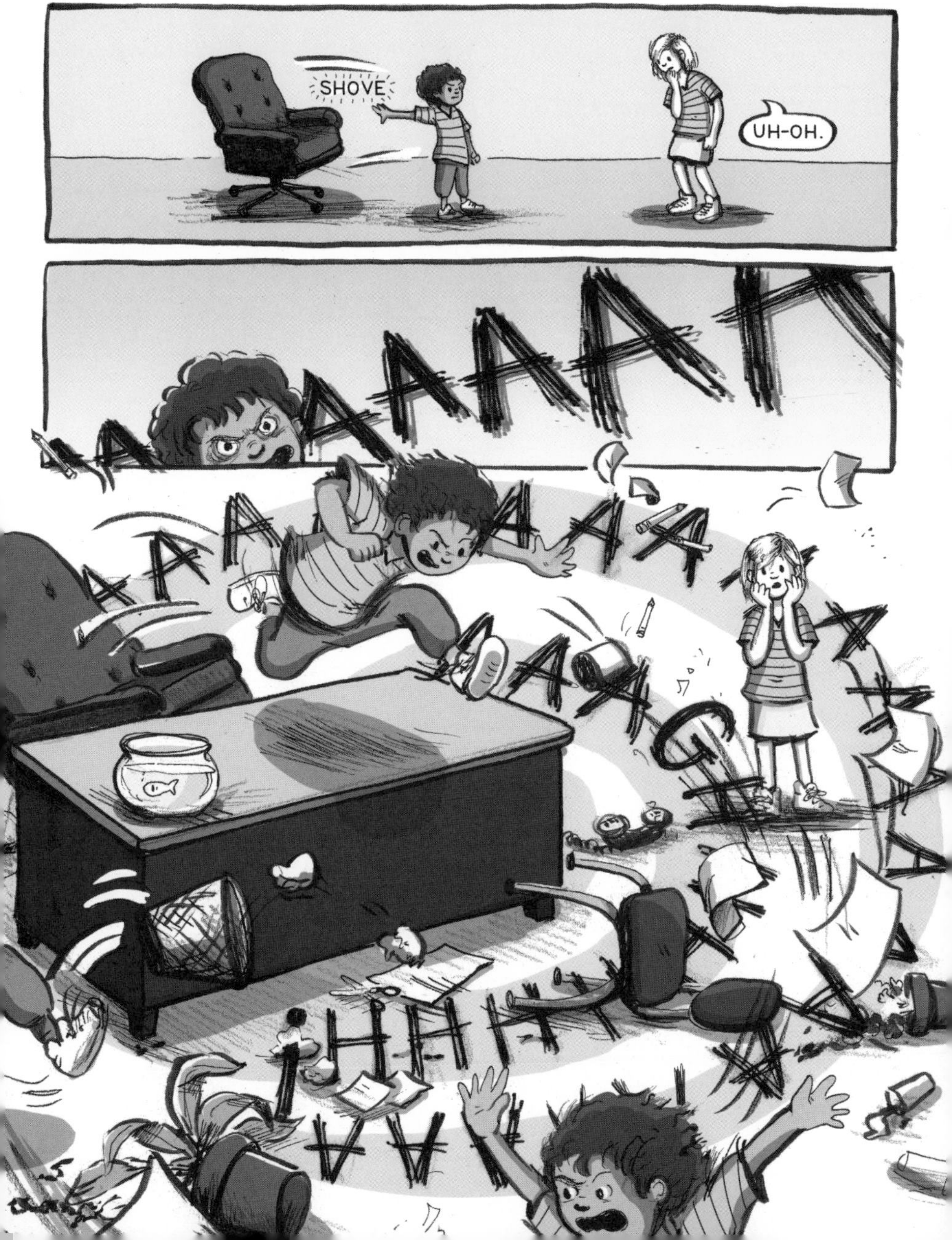
SHOVE
UH-OH.

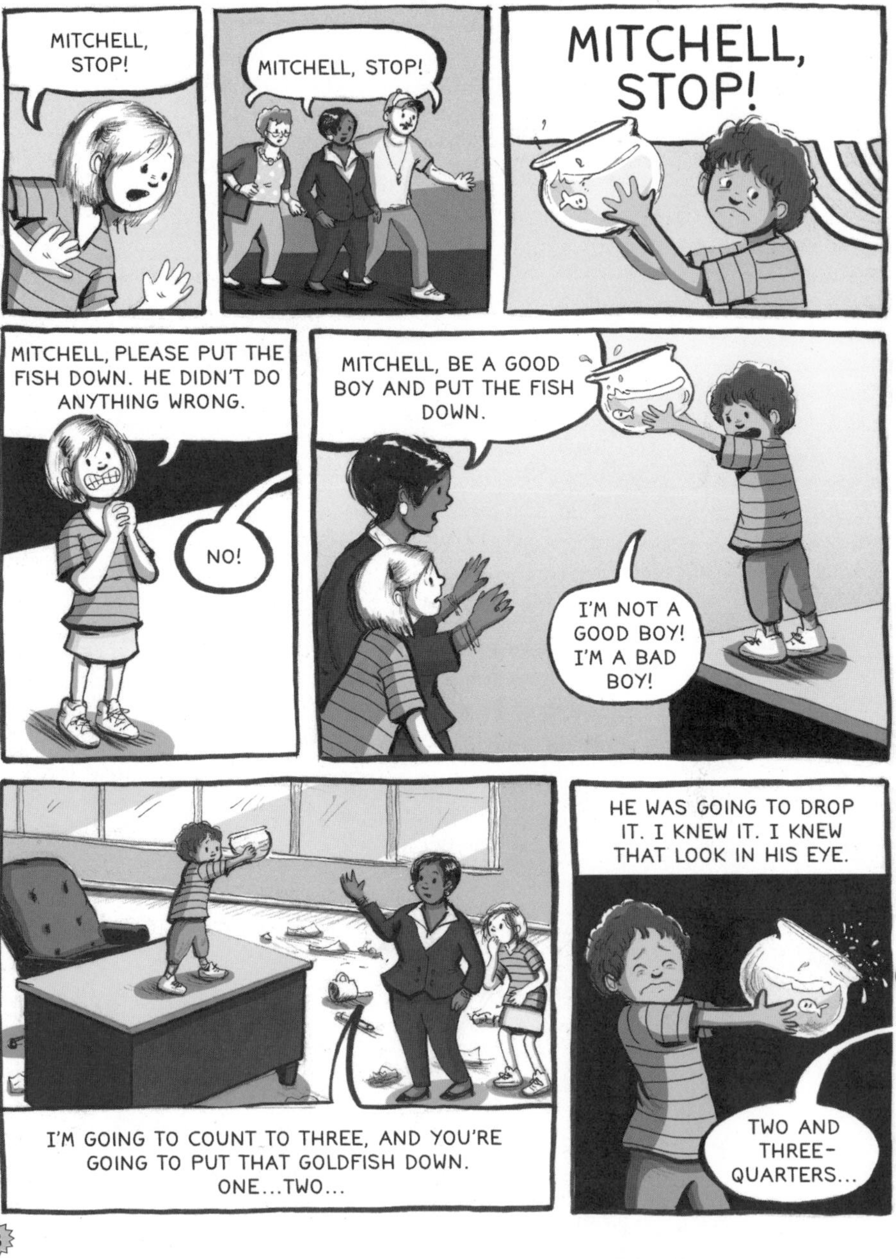

MITCHELL, STOP!
MITCHELL, STOP!
MITCHELL, STOP!
MITCHELL, PLEASE PUT THE FISH DOWN. HE DIDN'T DO ANYTHING WRONG.
NO!
MITCHELL, BE A GOOD BOY AND PUT THE FISH DOWN.
I'M NOT A GOOD BOY! I'M A BAD BOY!
I'M GOING TO COUNT TO THREE, AND YOU'RE GOING TO PUT THAT GOLDFISH DOWN. ONE...TWO...
HE WAS GOING TO DROP IT. I KNEW IT. I KNEW THAT LOOK IN HIS EYE.
TWO AND THREE-QUARTERS...

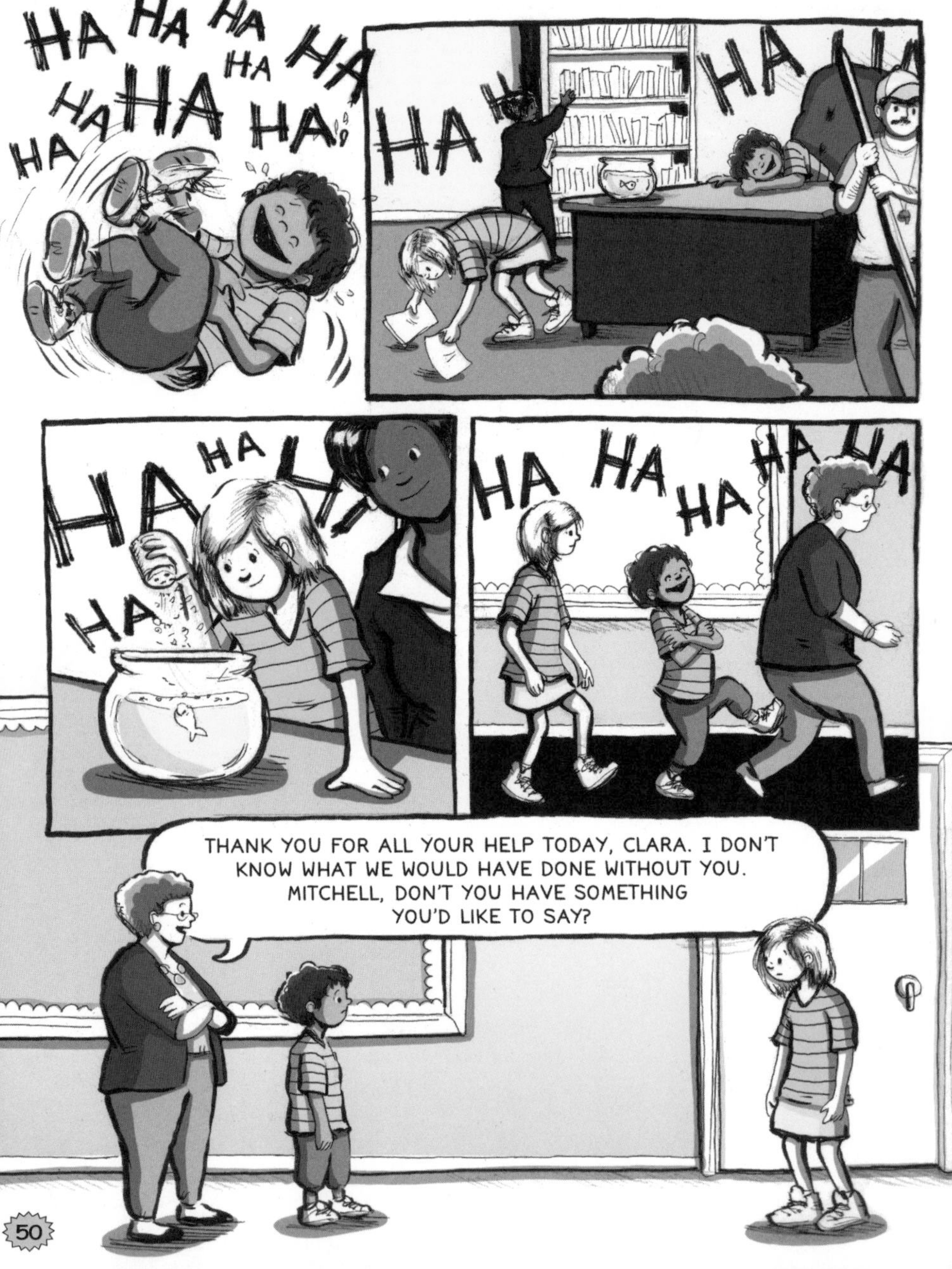
HA HA HA HA HA HA HA HA HA HA
HA HA
HA HA HA
HA HA
HA HA HA HA
THANK YOU FOR ALL YOUR HELP TODAY, CLARA. I DON'T KNOW WHAT WE WOULD HAVE DONE WITHOUT YOU. MITCHELL, DON'T YOU HAVE SOMETHING YOU'D LIKE TO SAY?

I GUESS THE SCHOOL HAD THE RIGHT IDEA, BECAUSE I DIDN'T GET INTO TOO MUCH TROUBLE AFTER THAT. ANYTIME I WANTED TO DO SOMETHING DRASTIC LIKE, SAY, JUMP OUT THE WINDOW DURING A MATH TEST...

SIGH

KNOCK KNOCK!

AAAAGH!

SOMETHING KEPT ME ON THE STRAIGHT AND NARROW.

YOU'RE MY BEST FRIEND, CLARA! YOU'RE MY BEST...AAAAGH! OK, OK, I'M COMING!

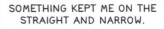

TEE HEE!

TEE HEE!

OK, CLASS, BACK TO YOUR TESTS.

THE END

MILO'S JOURNEY

BY BEN HATKE

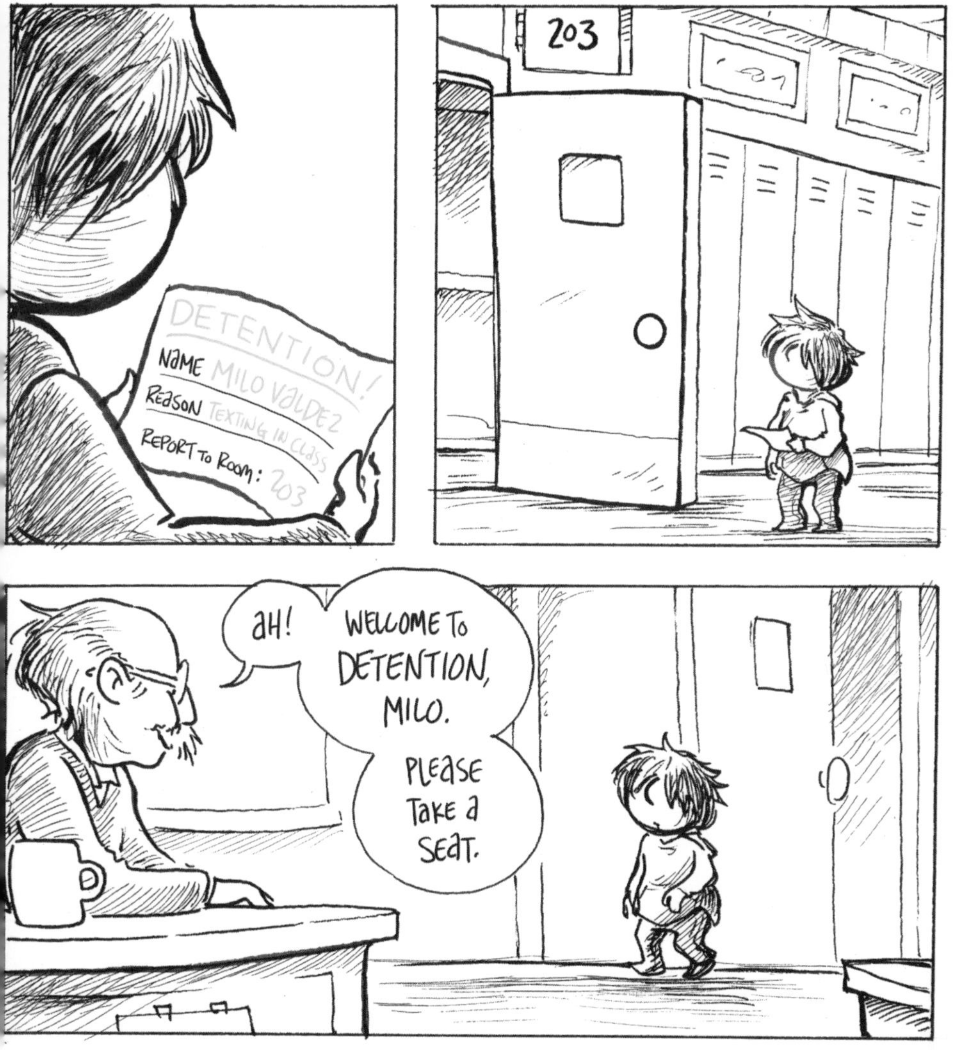
DETENTION!
NAME MILO VALDEZ
REASON TEXTING IN CLASS
REPORT TO ROOM: 203
203
AH!
WELCOME TO DETENTION, MILO.
PLEASE TAKE A SEAT.

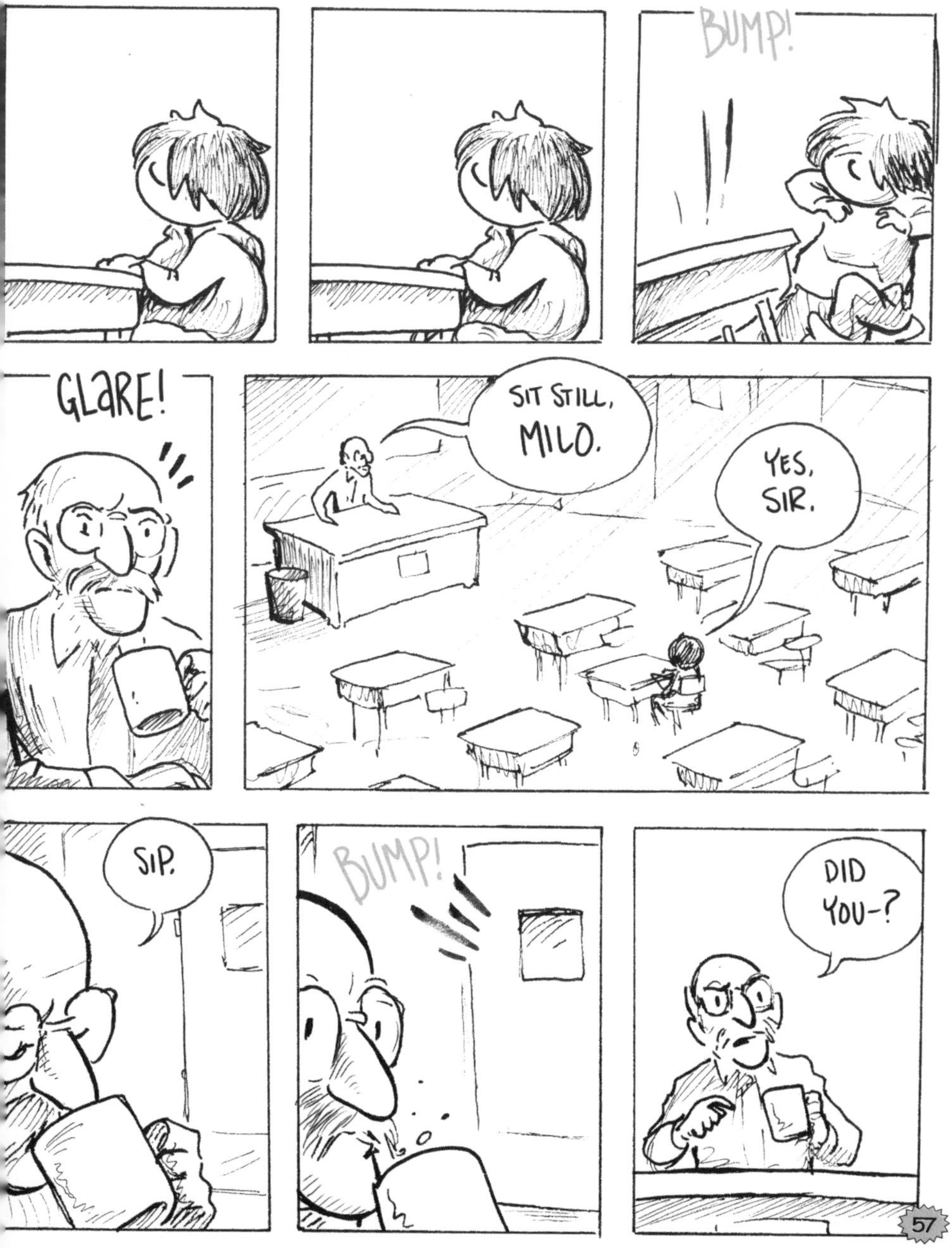
BUMP!
GLARE!
SIT STILL, MILO.
YES, SIR.
SIP.
BUMP!
DID YOU-?

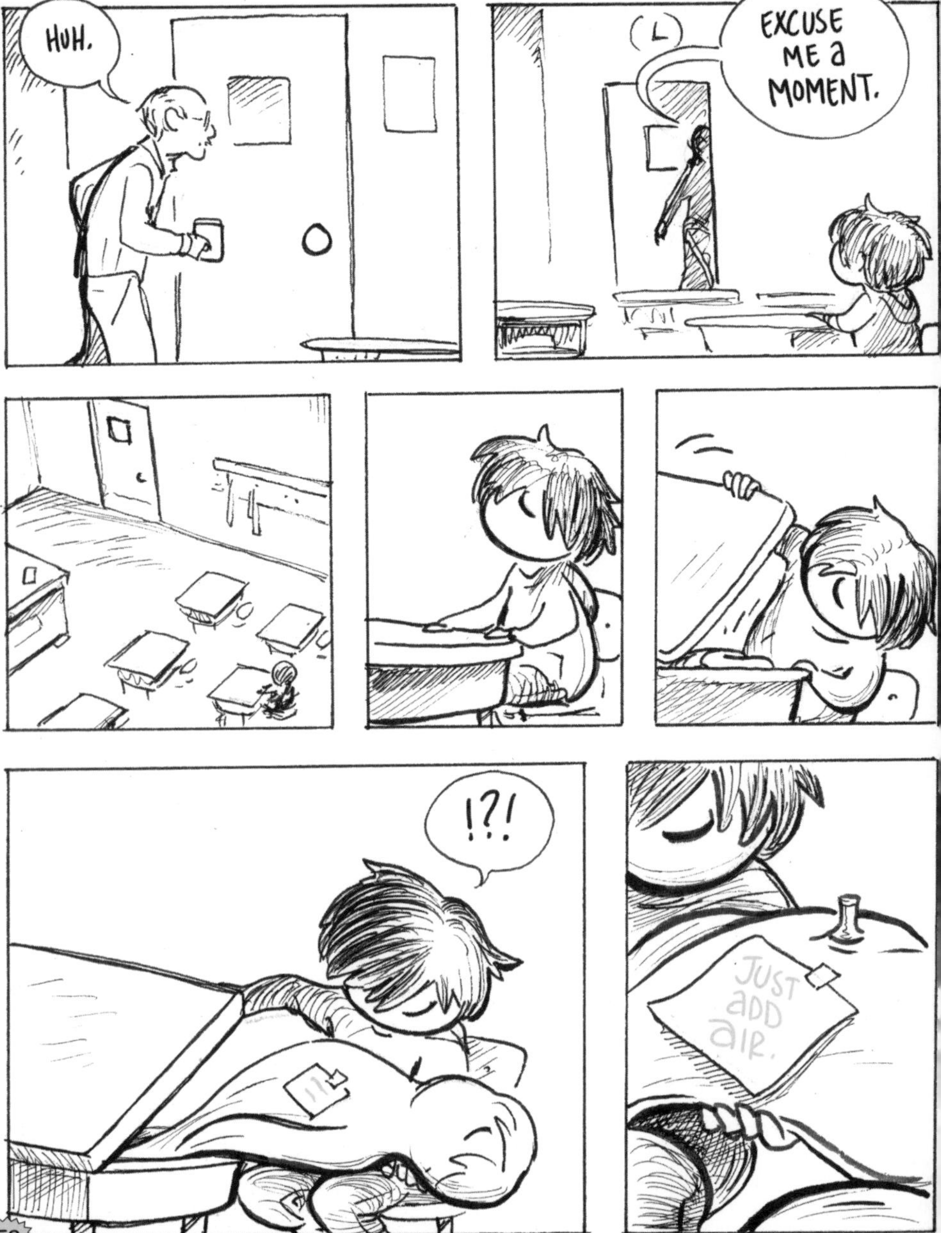
HUH.
EXCUSE ME a MOMENT.
!?!
JUST add aIR.

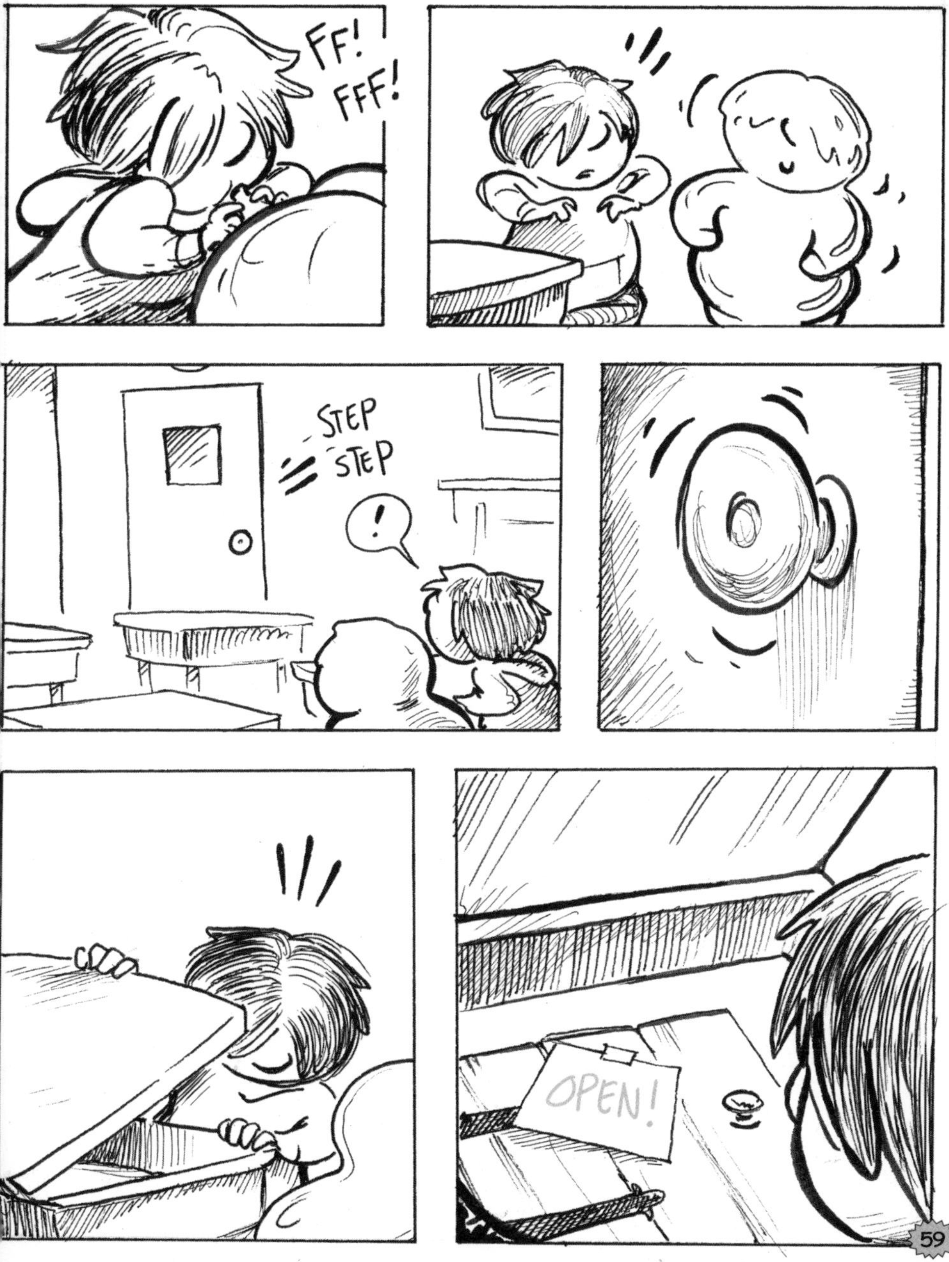
FF!
FFF!
STEP
STEP
!
OPEN!

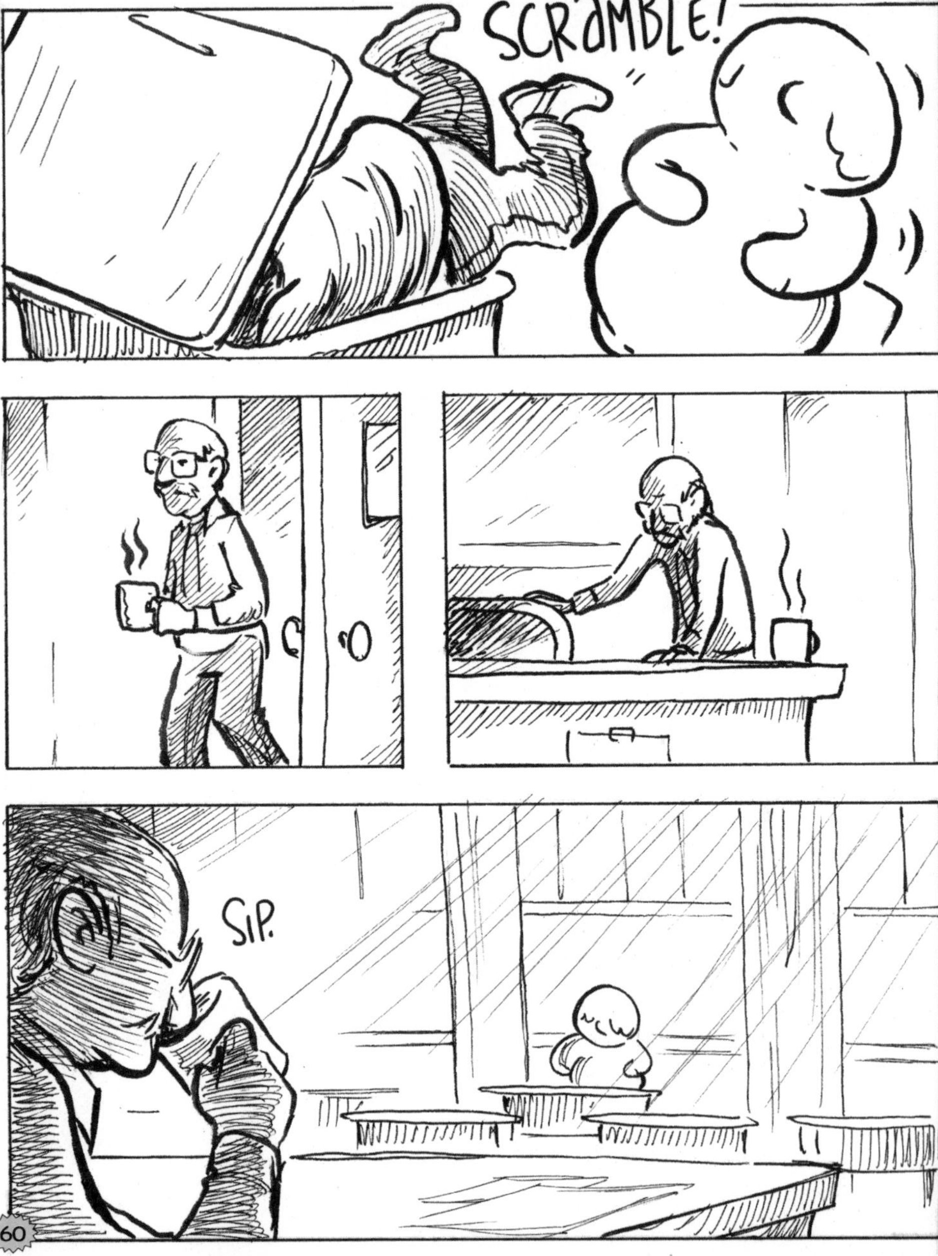
SCRAMBLE!
SIP.

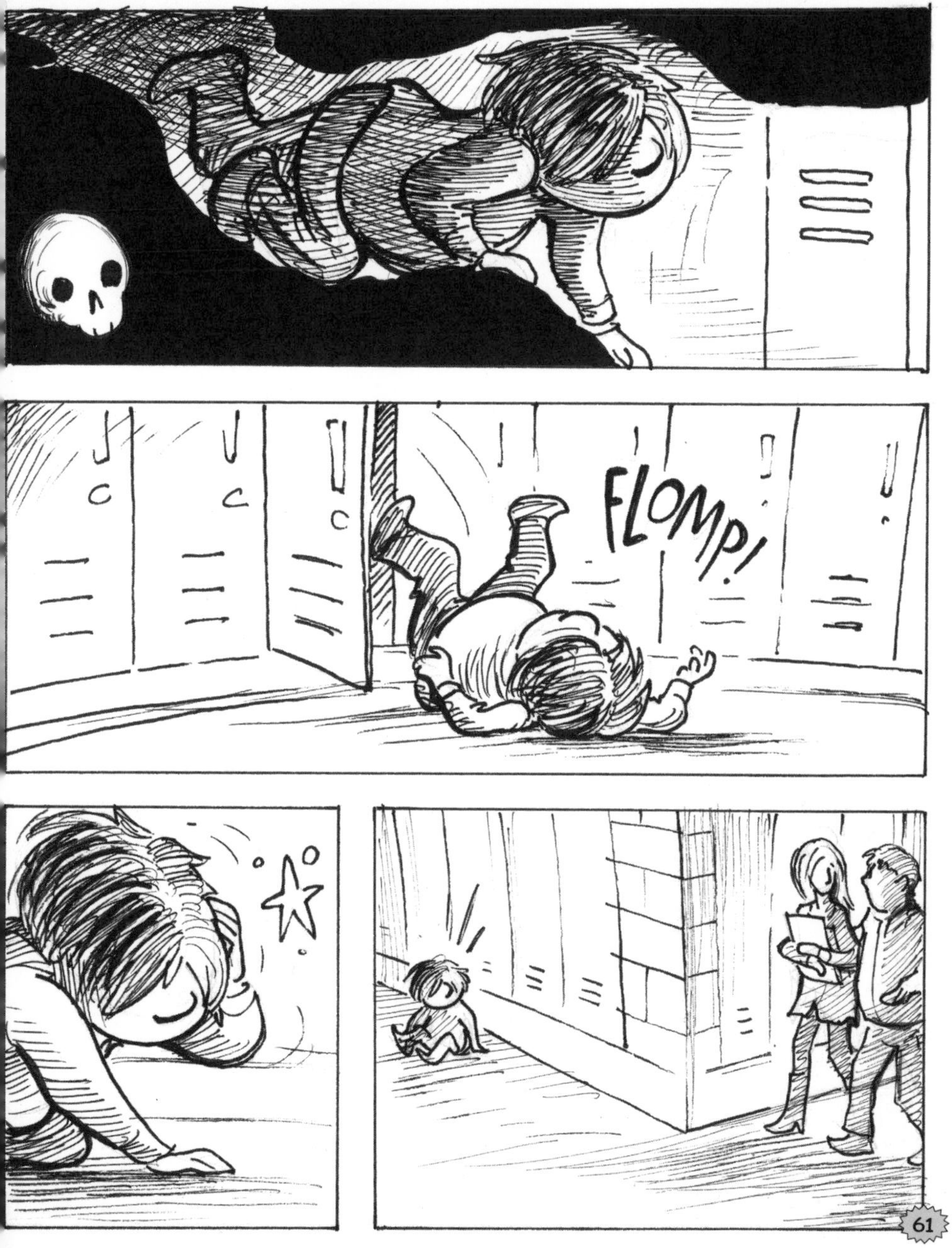
FLOMP!

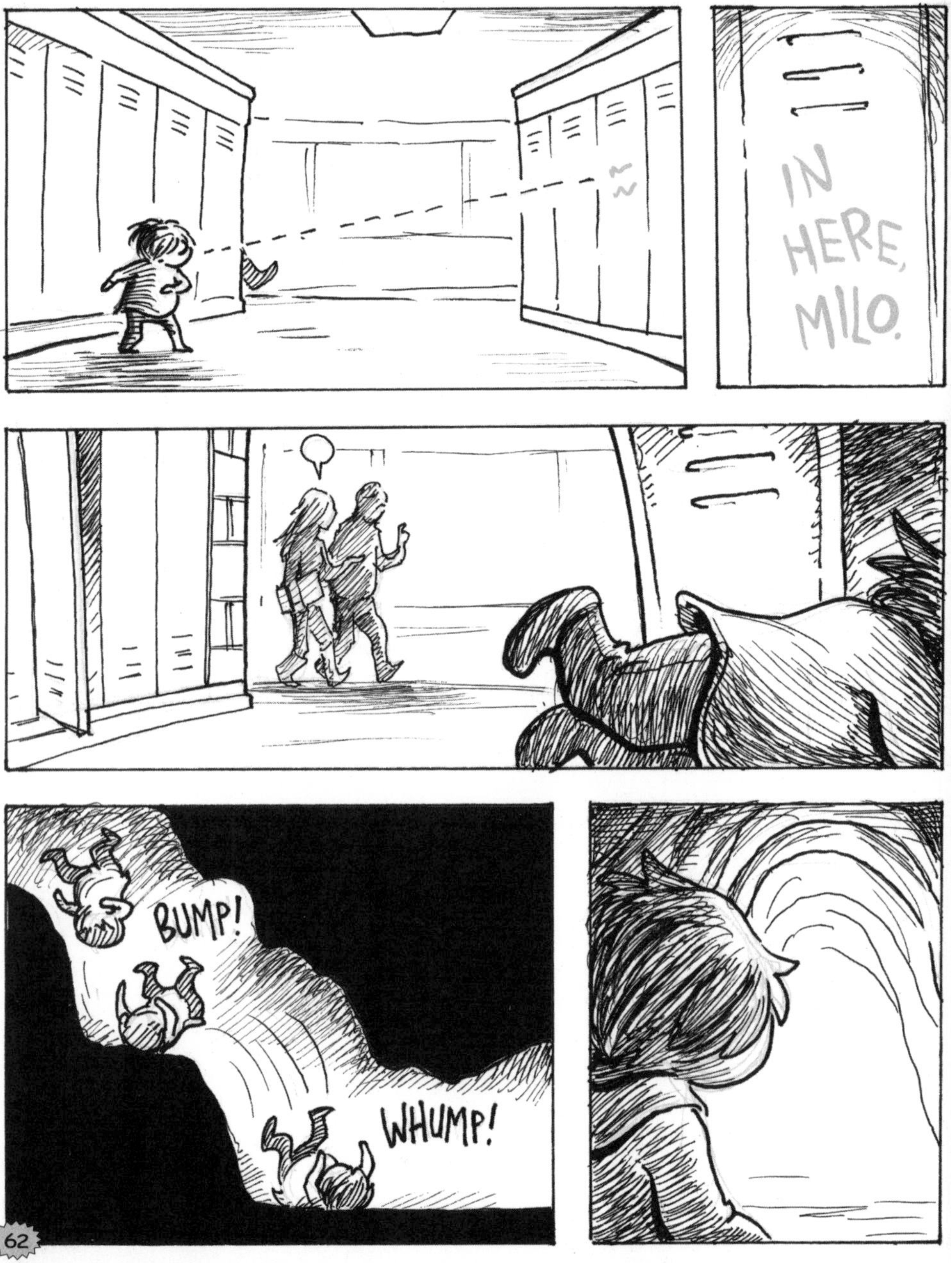
IN HERE, MILO.
BUMP!
WHUMP!

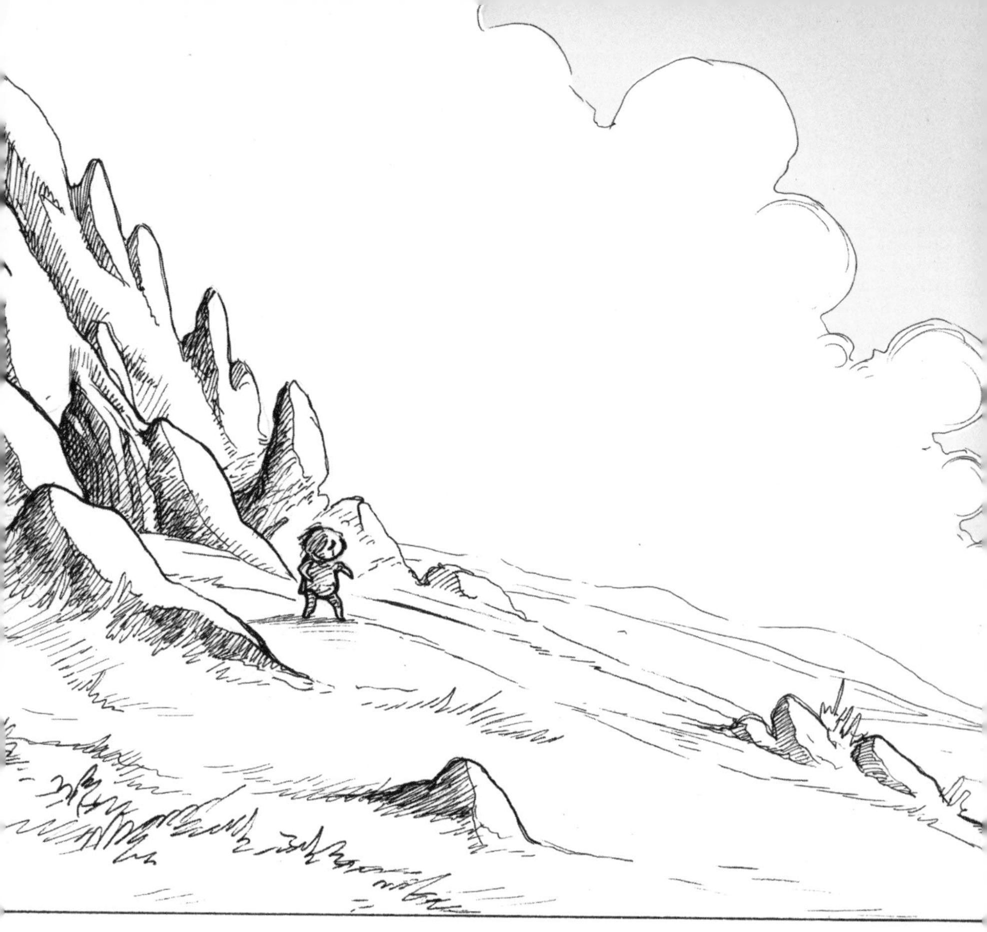

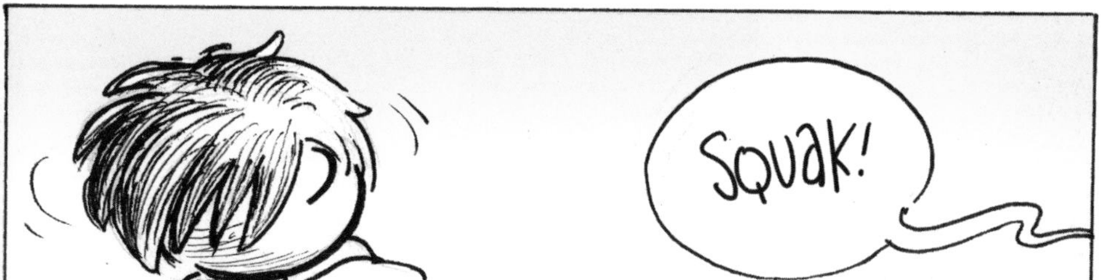
SQUAK!

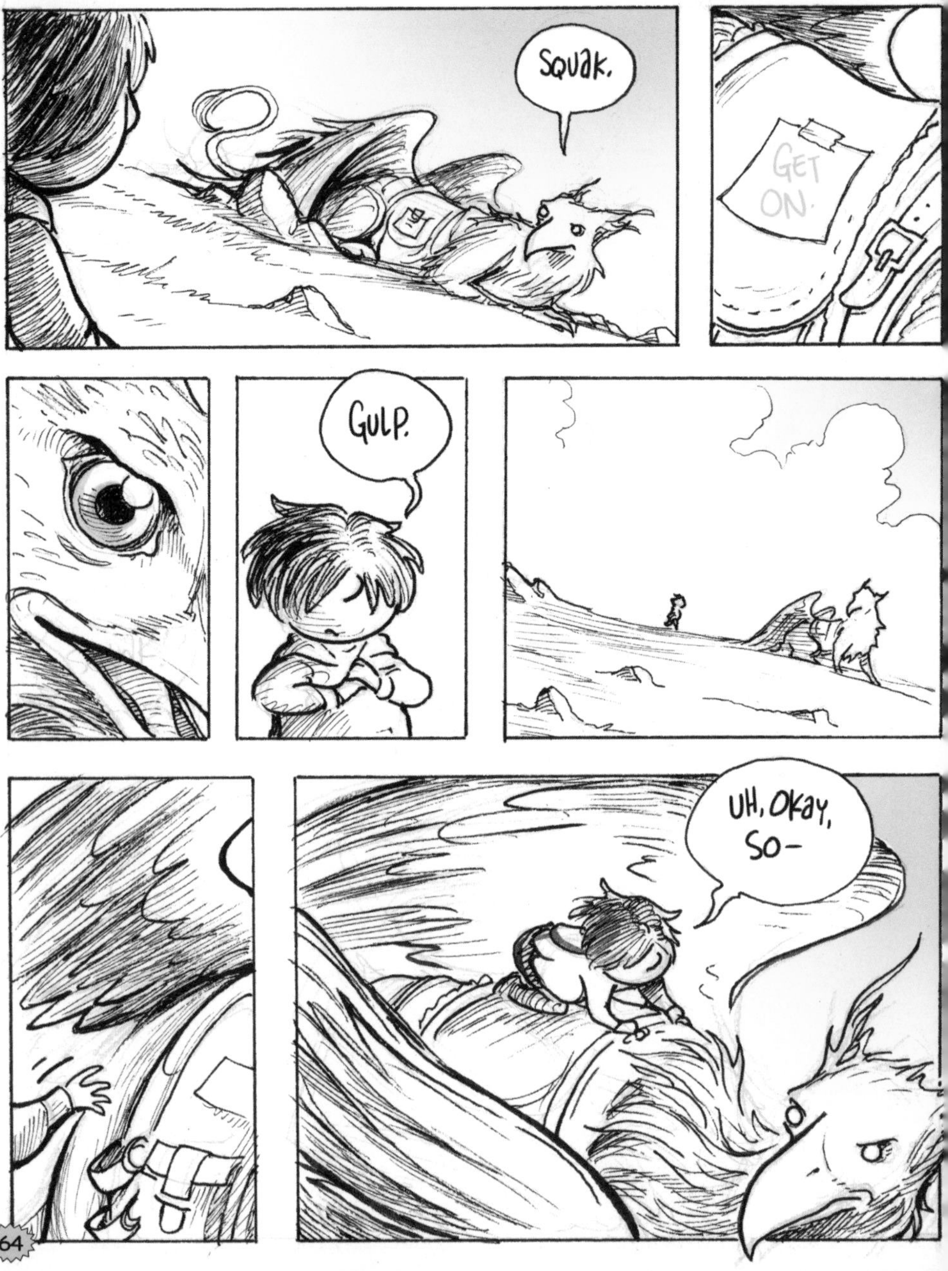
SQUAK.
GET ON.
GULP.
UH, OKAY, SO-

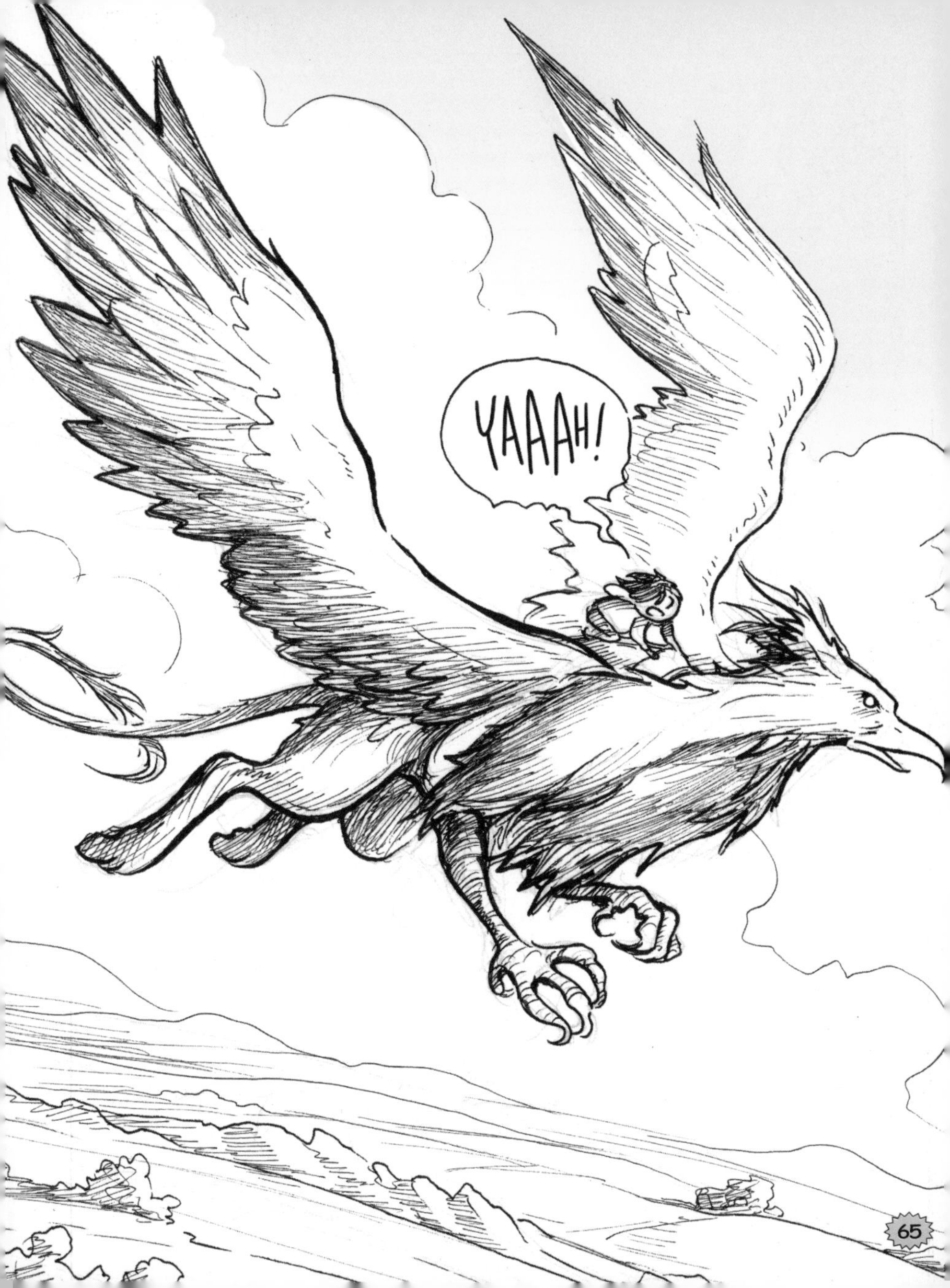
YAAAH!

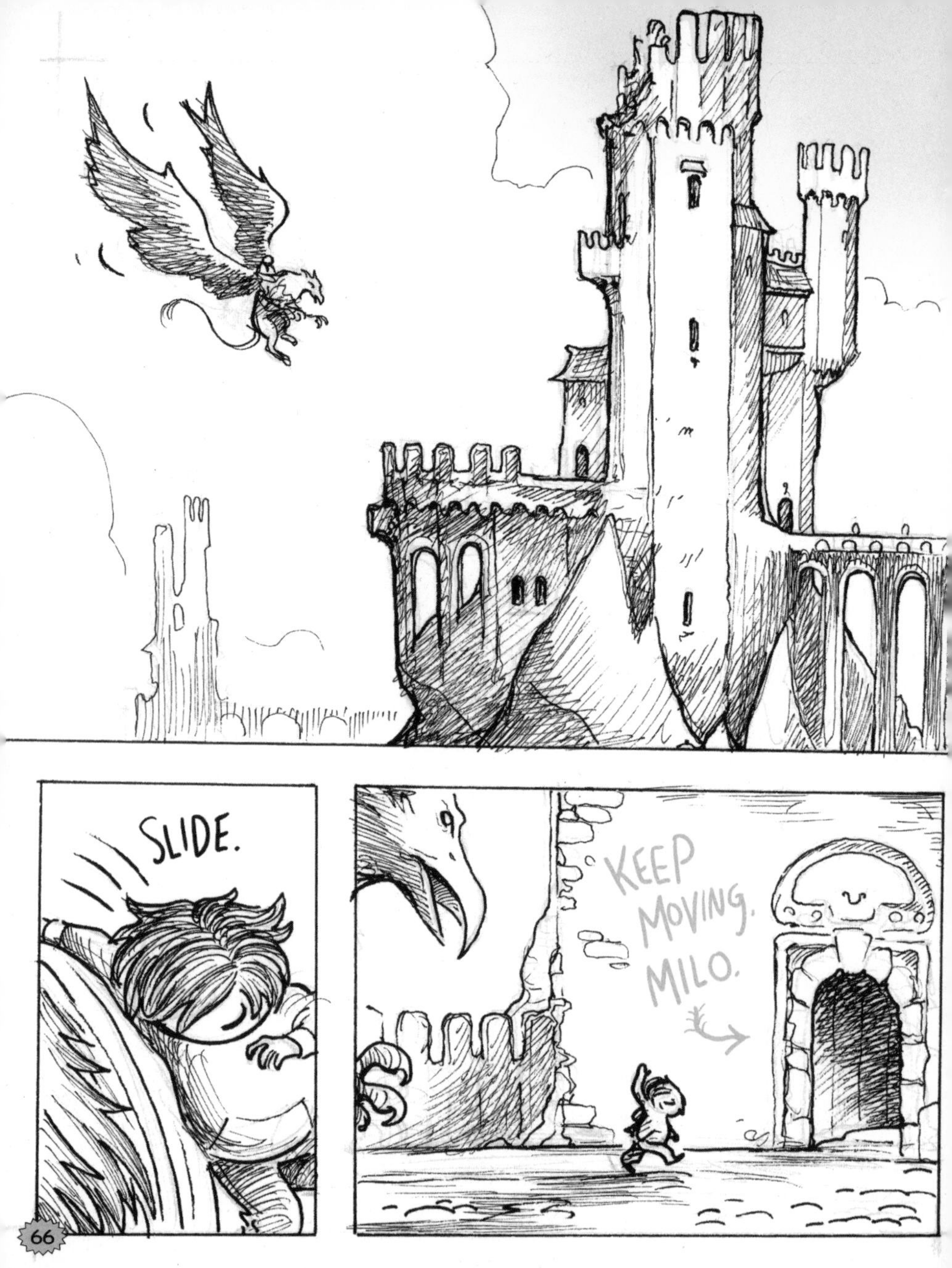
SLIDE.
KEEP MOVING. MILO.

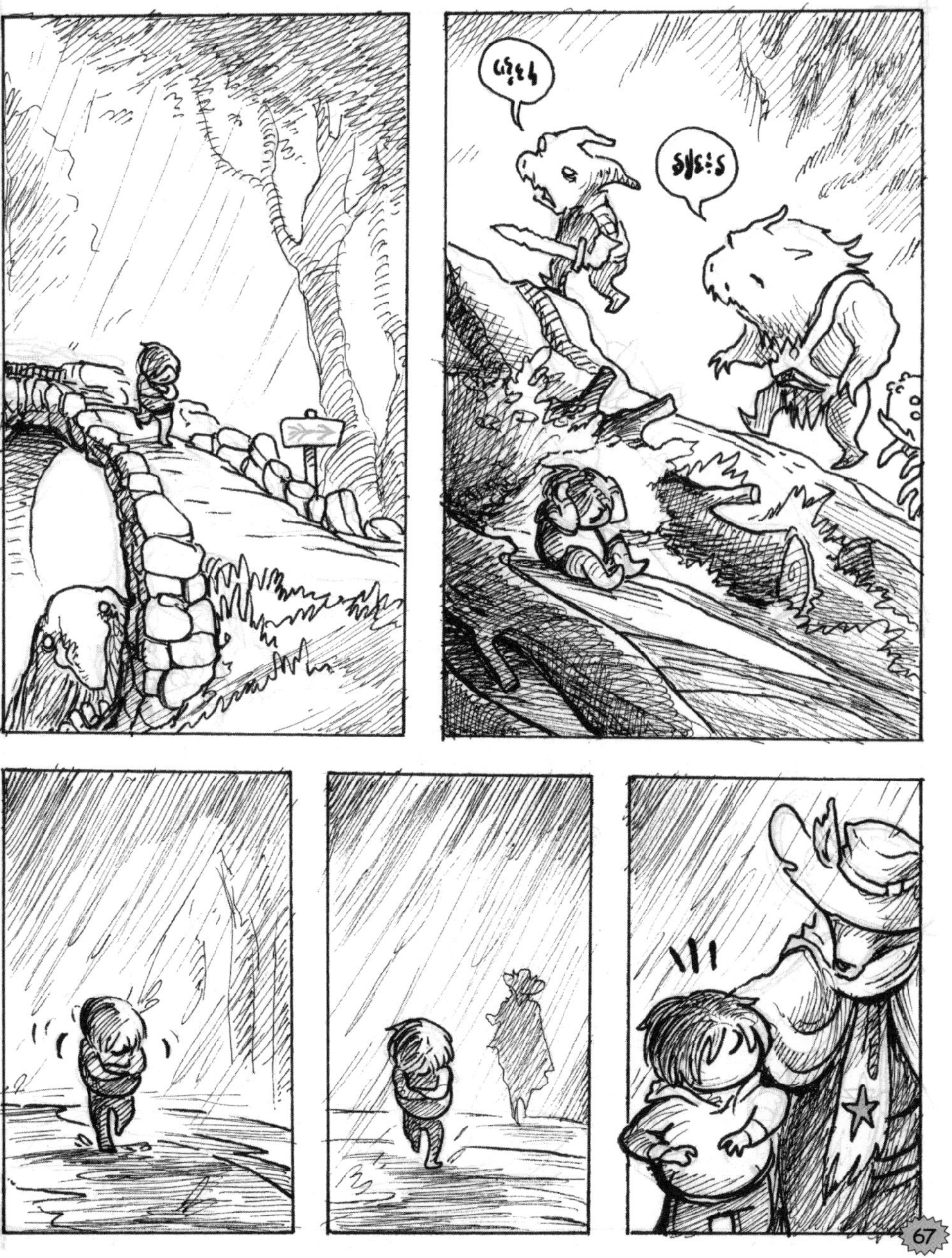

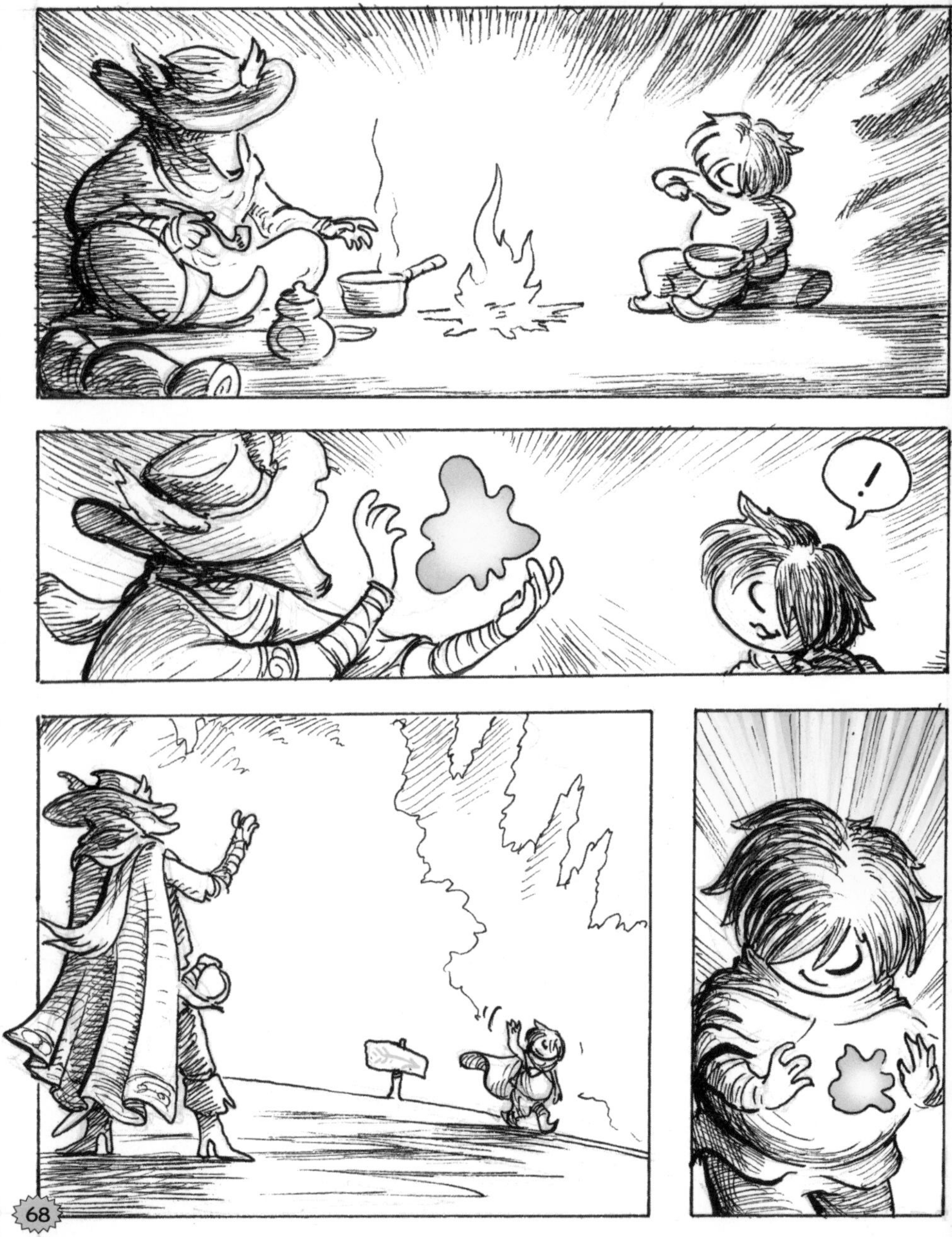
!

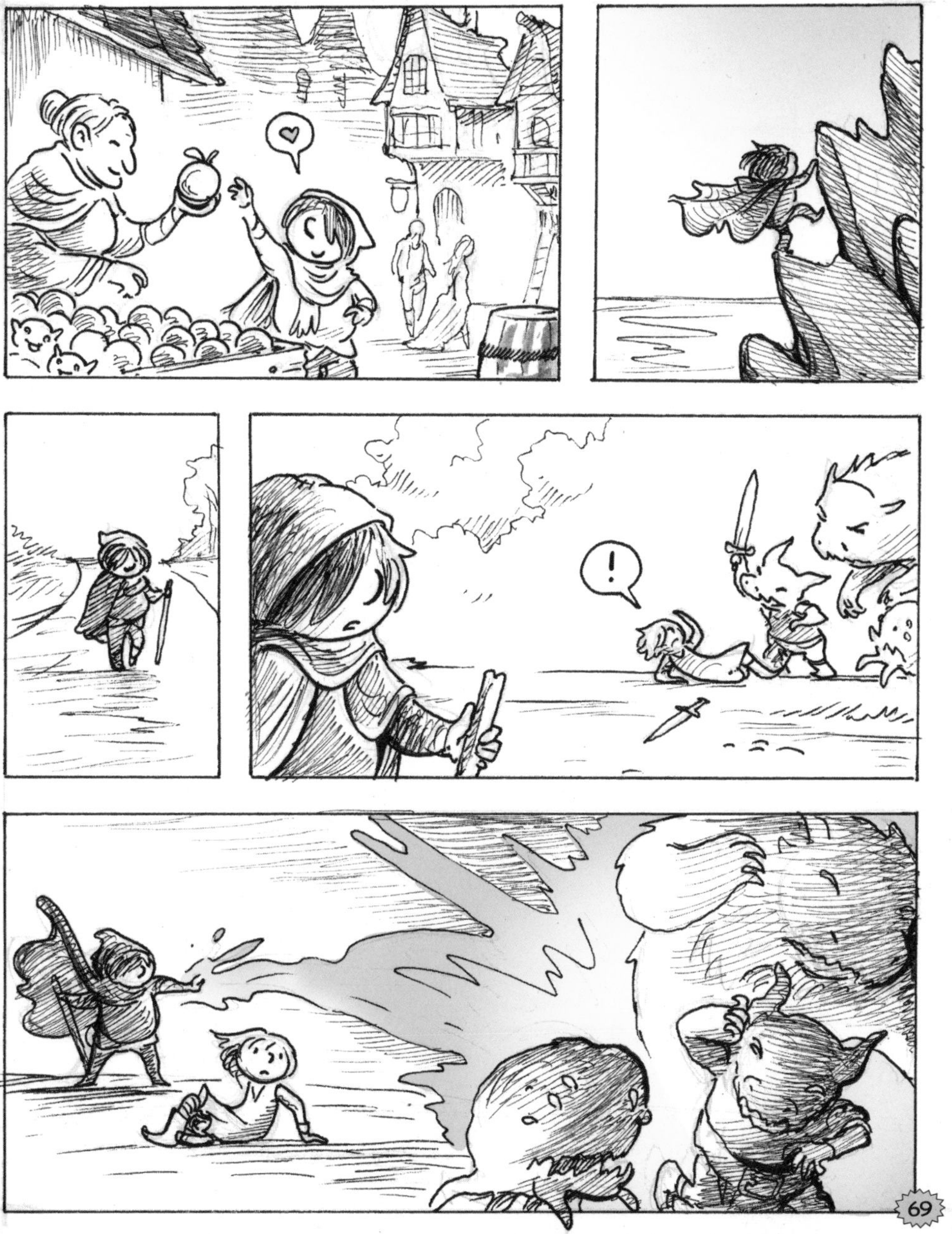
!

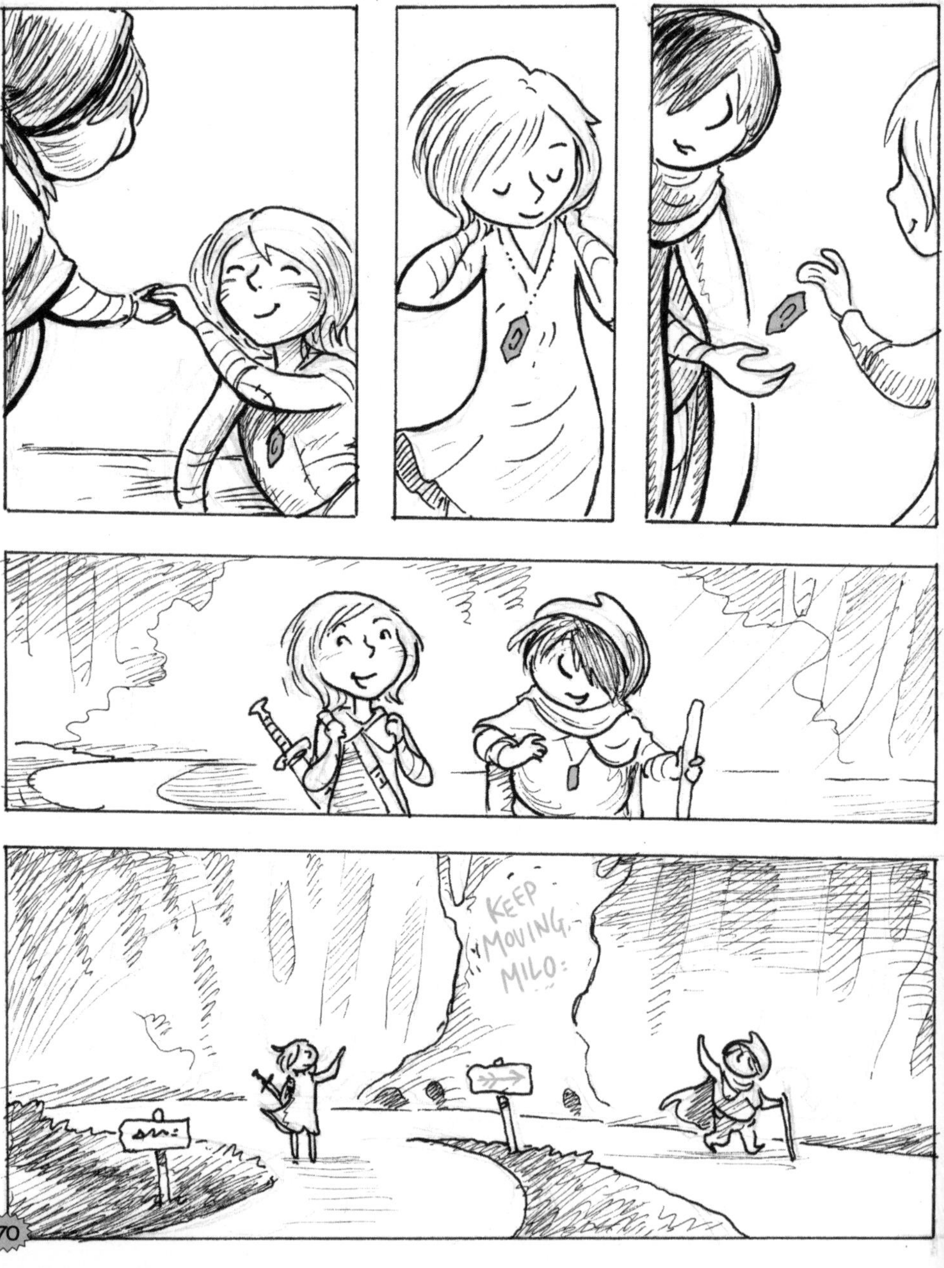
KEEP MOVING, MILO:

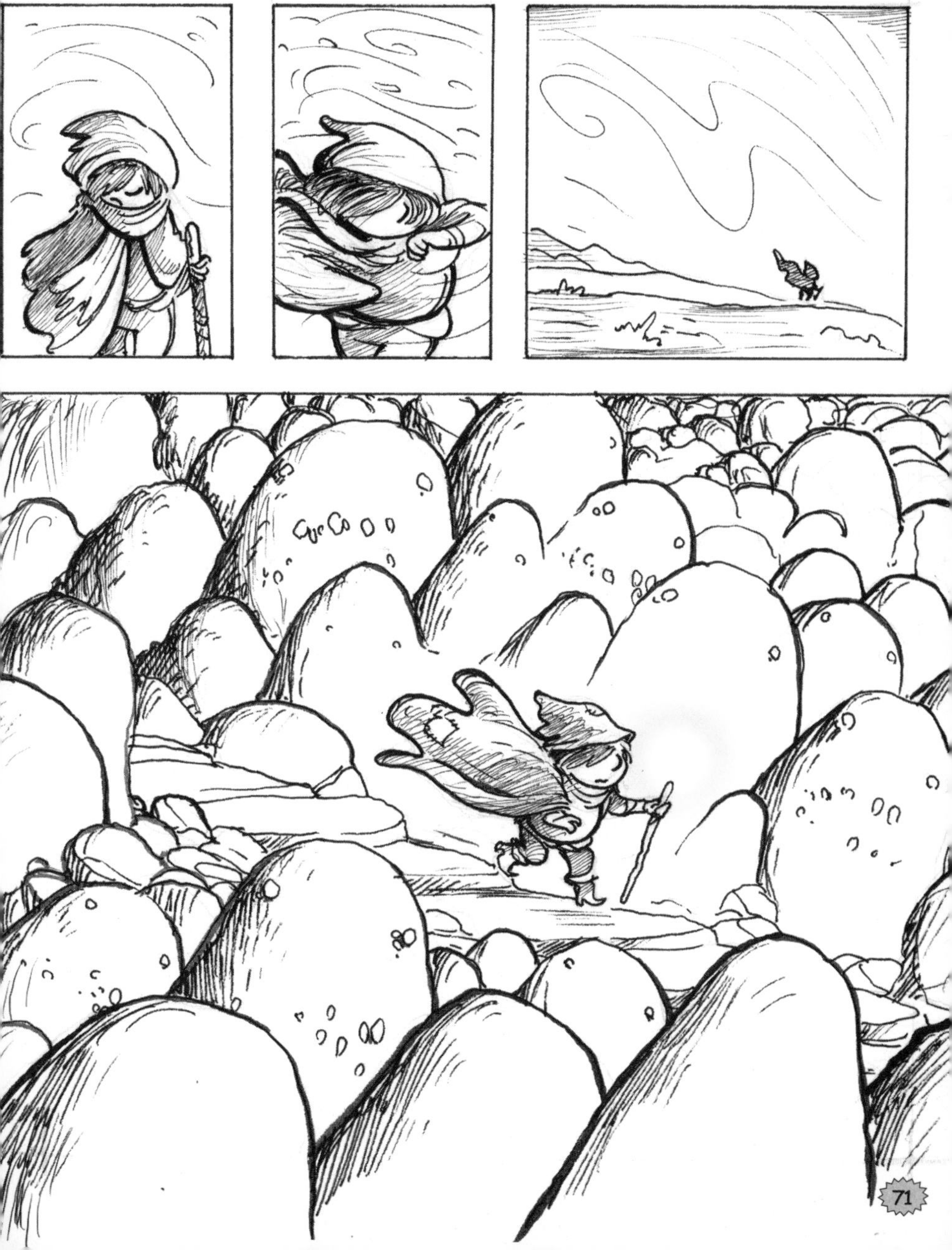

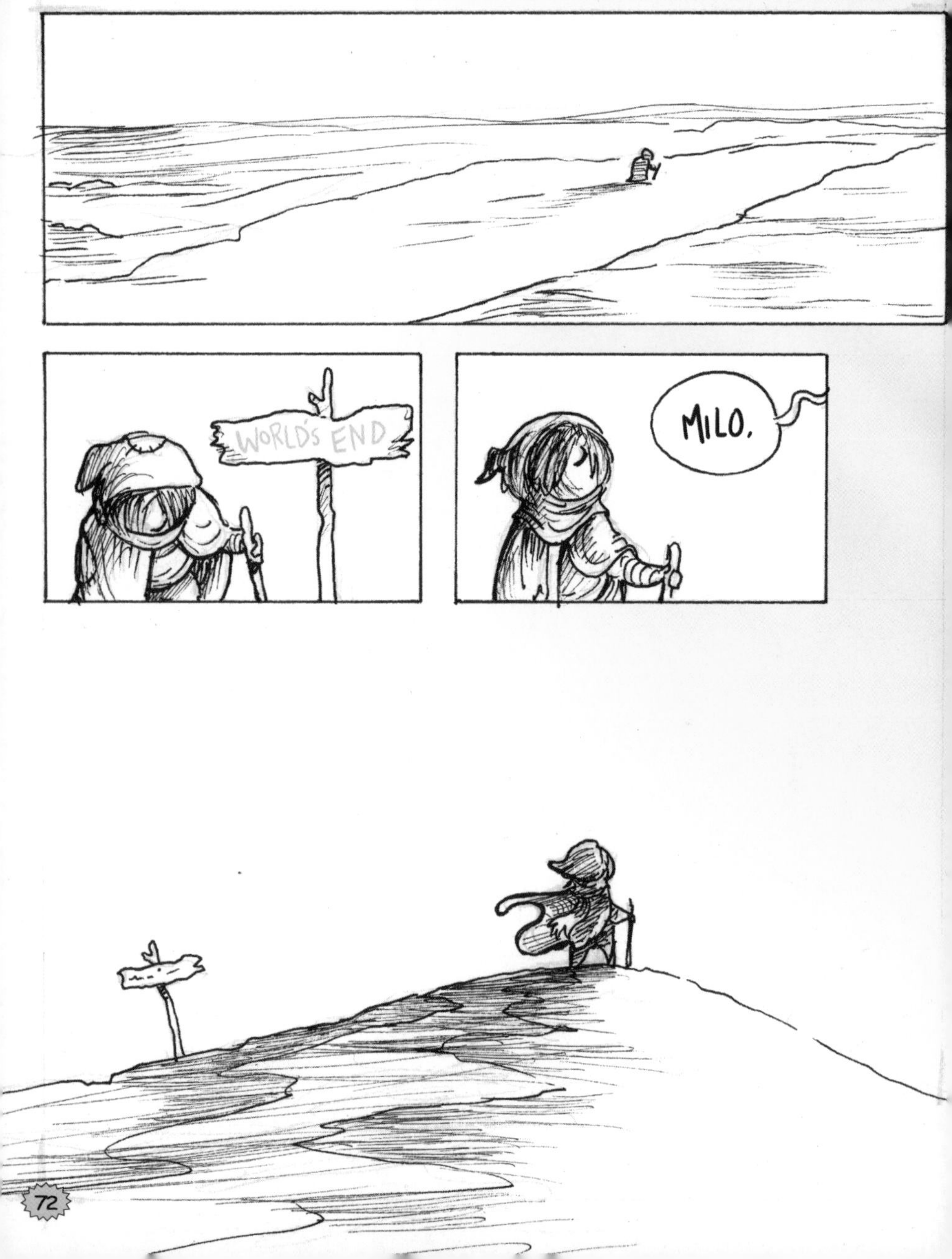
WORLD'S END
MILO.

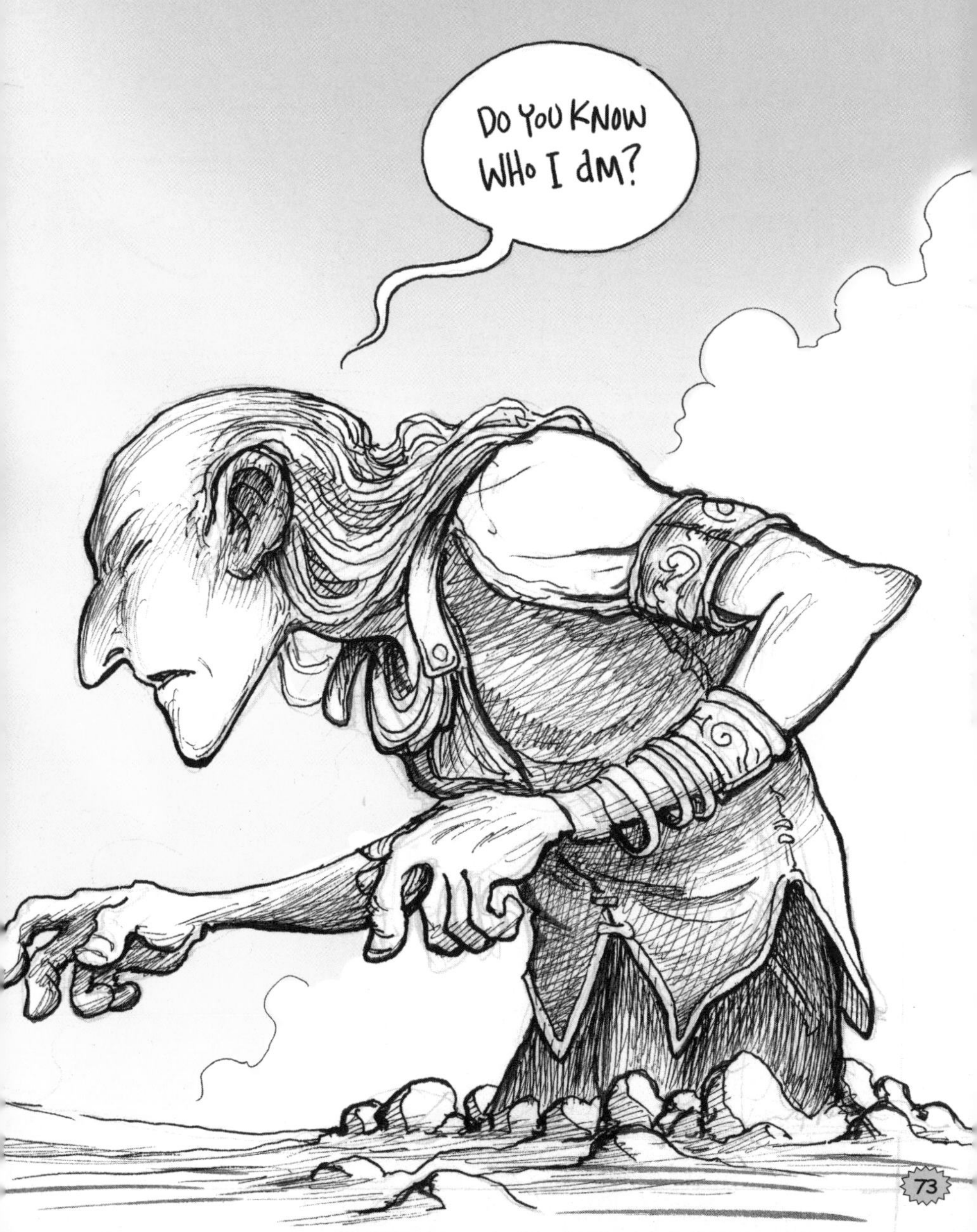
DO YOU KNOW WHO I AM?

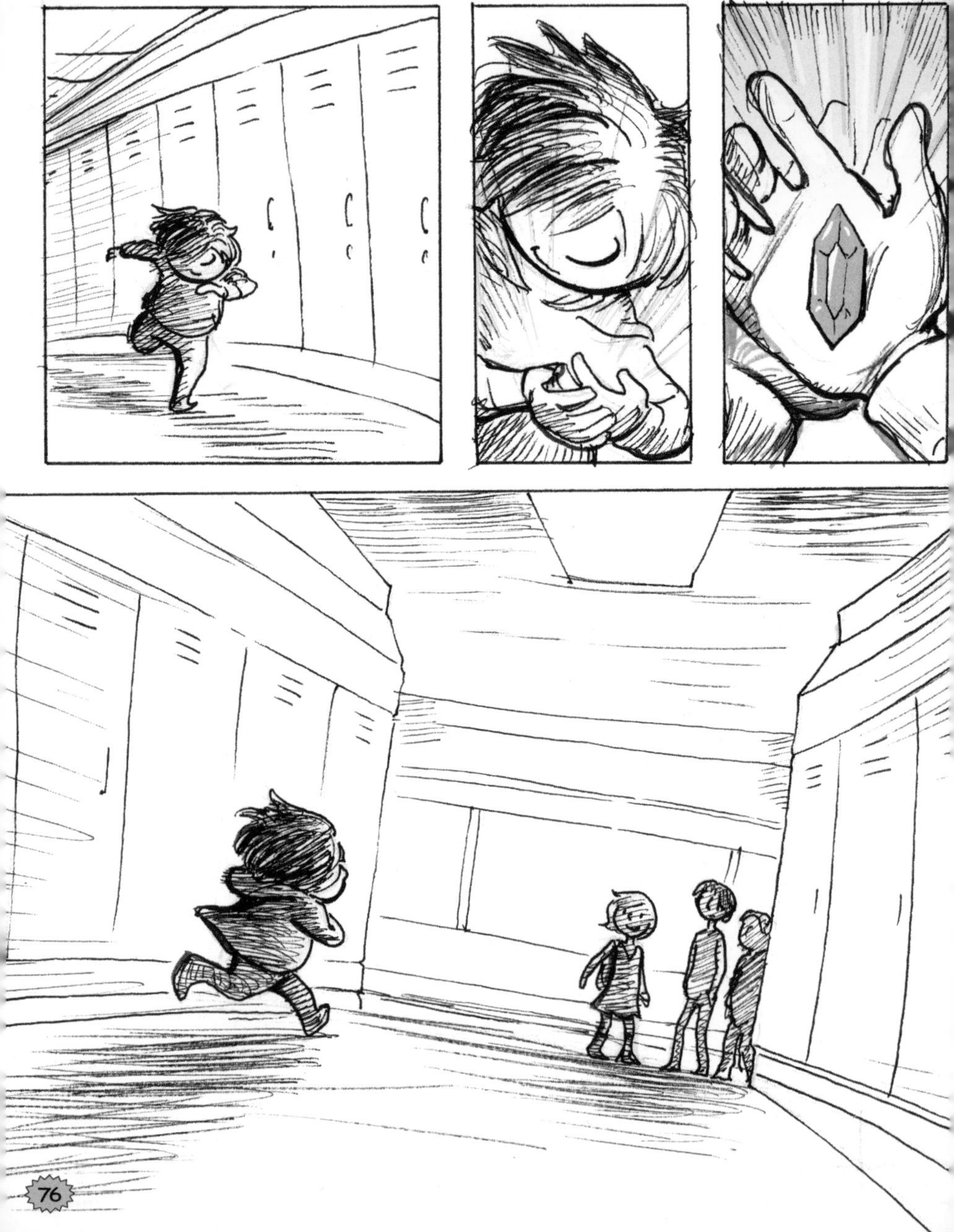

84

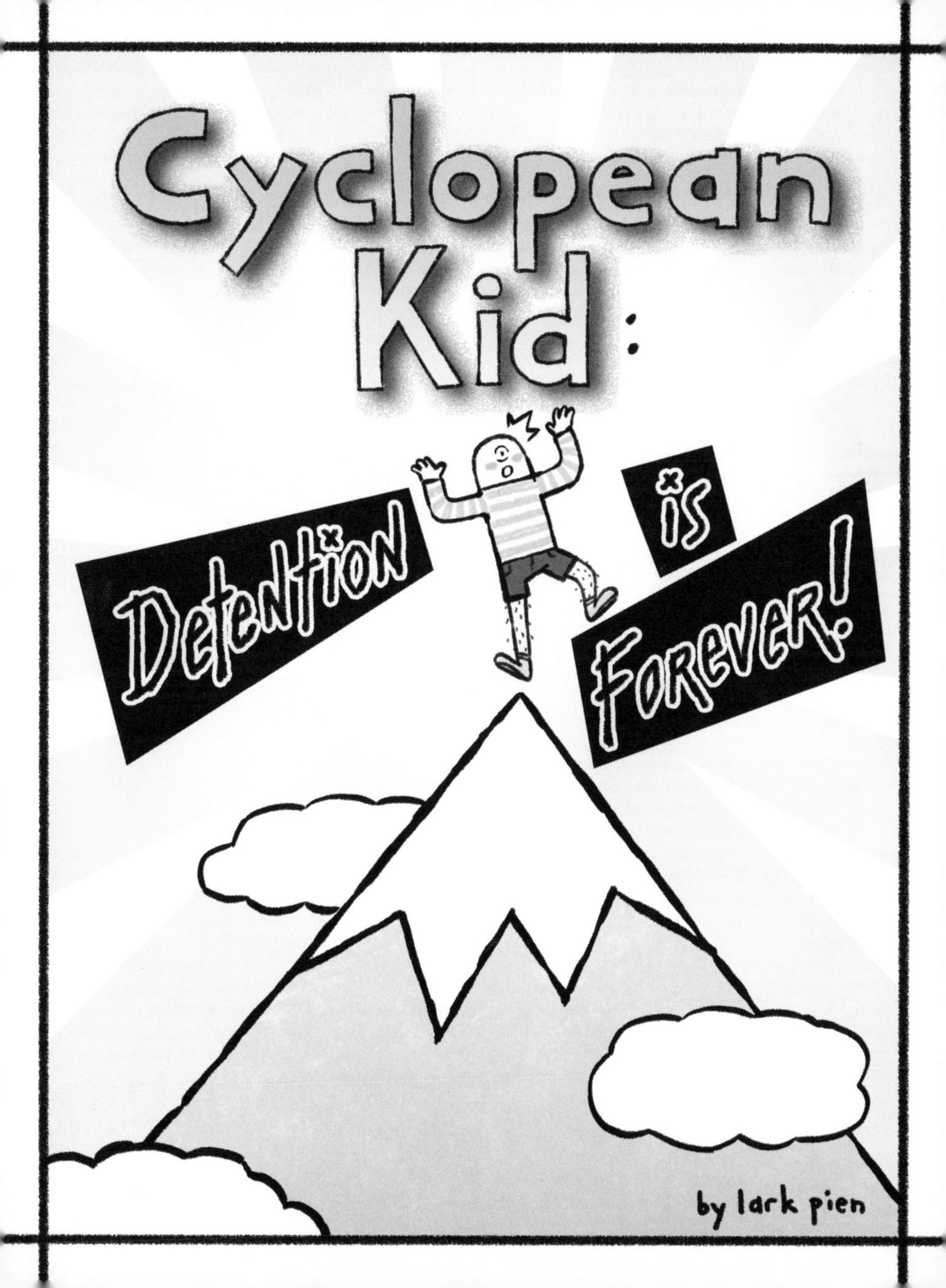

Cyclopean Kid:
Detention is Forever!
by lark pien

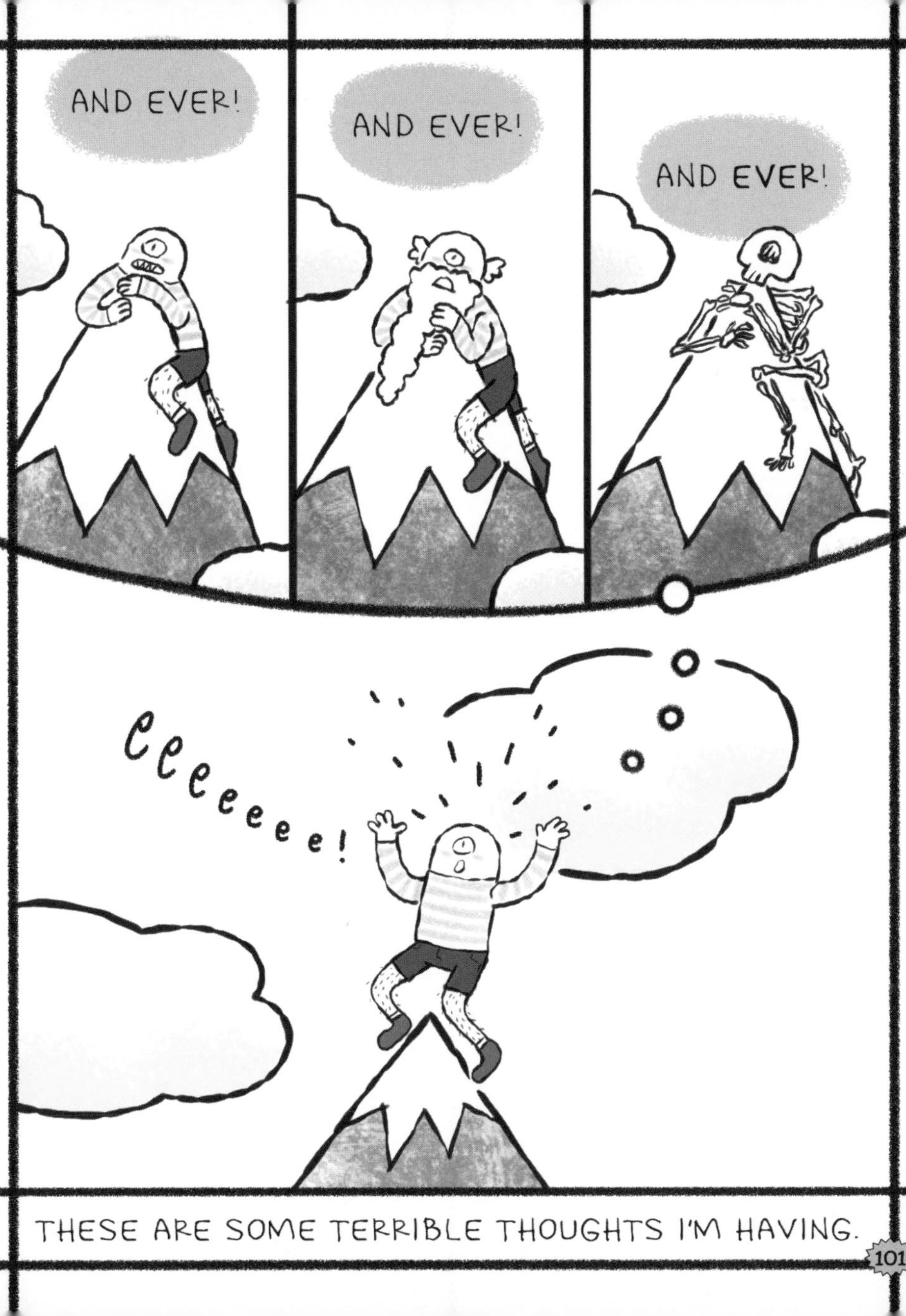
AND EVER!
AND EVER!
AND EVER!
eeeeeeee!
THESE ARE SOME TERRIBLE THOUGHTS I'M HAVING.

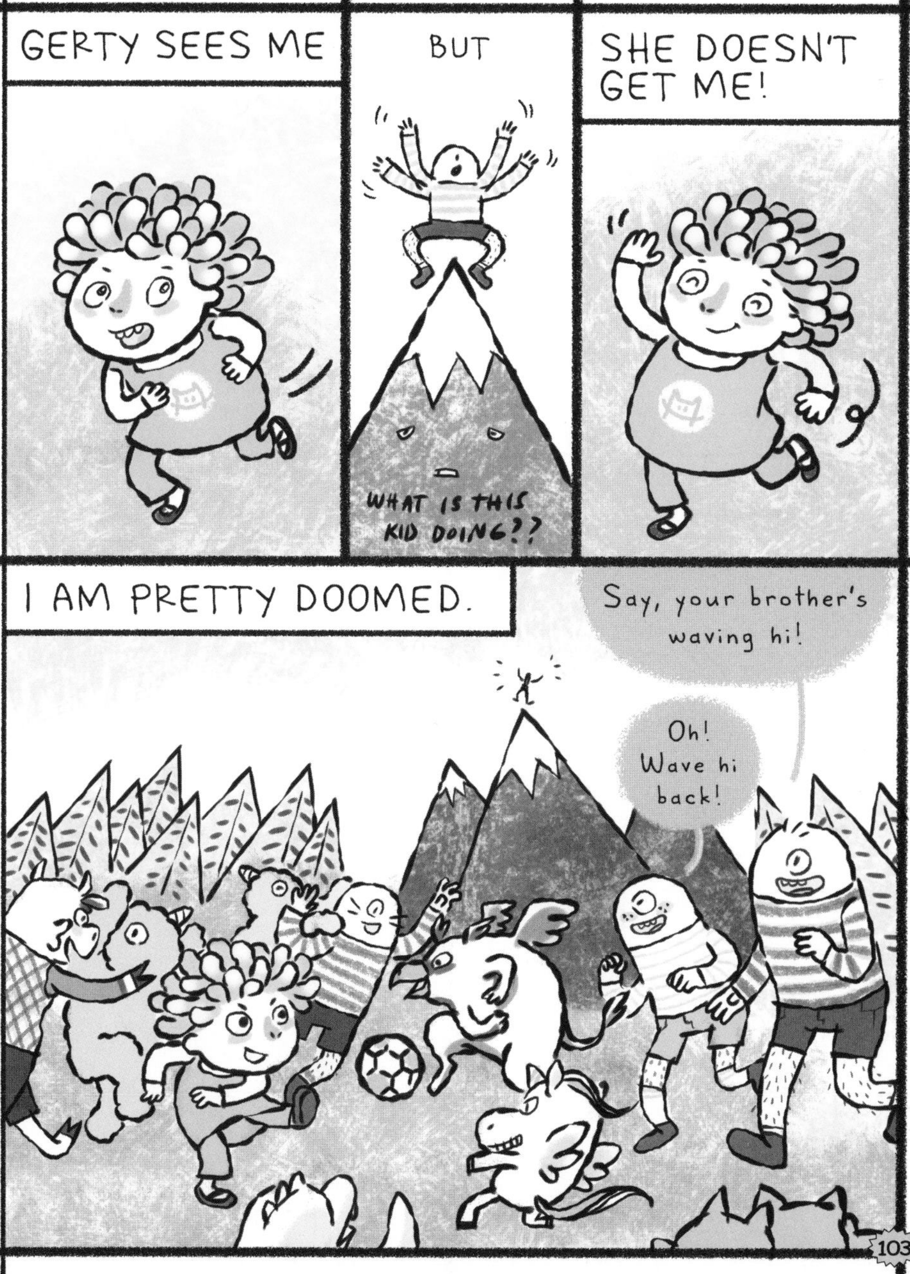
GERTY SEES ME
BUT
WHAT IS THIS KID DOING??
SHE DOESN'T GET ME!
I AM PRETTY DOOMED.
Say, your brother's waving hi!
Oh! Wave hi back!

Finally free!
Mandy! You kept your word! I **lurve** you!
HOOPLAH!
I would've come sooner...only I got into trouble at school!
You too? Wait... What???
I was late to class, and so the teacher gave me **detention**!
Huh?!
My brain's exploding! Please explain.

I'm a student there...
(college)→
and a teacher here!
Gee, that's bananas!
(monstergarten)
Nope! Anyhoo, time to join in on the fun.
I guess there is no end to learning, is there?
(heard an adult say this once)
Nice play!
Good game!
woot!
DETENTION: NEVER AGAIN! THERE ARE TOO MANY THINGS IN LIFE (like soccer!) I JUST DON'T WANT TO MISS!
GOOOOAAALL!!!
boot!
Uh...
Please don't kick the ball off the page.
end

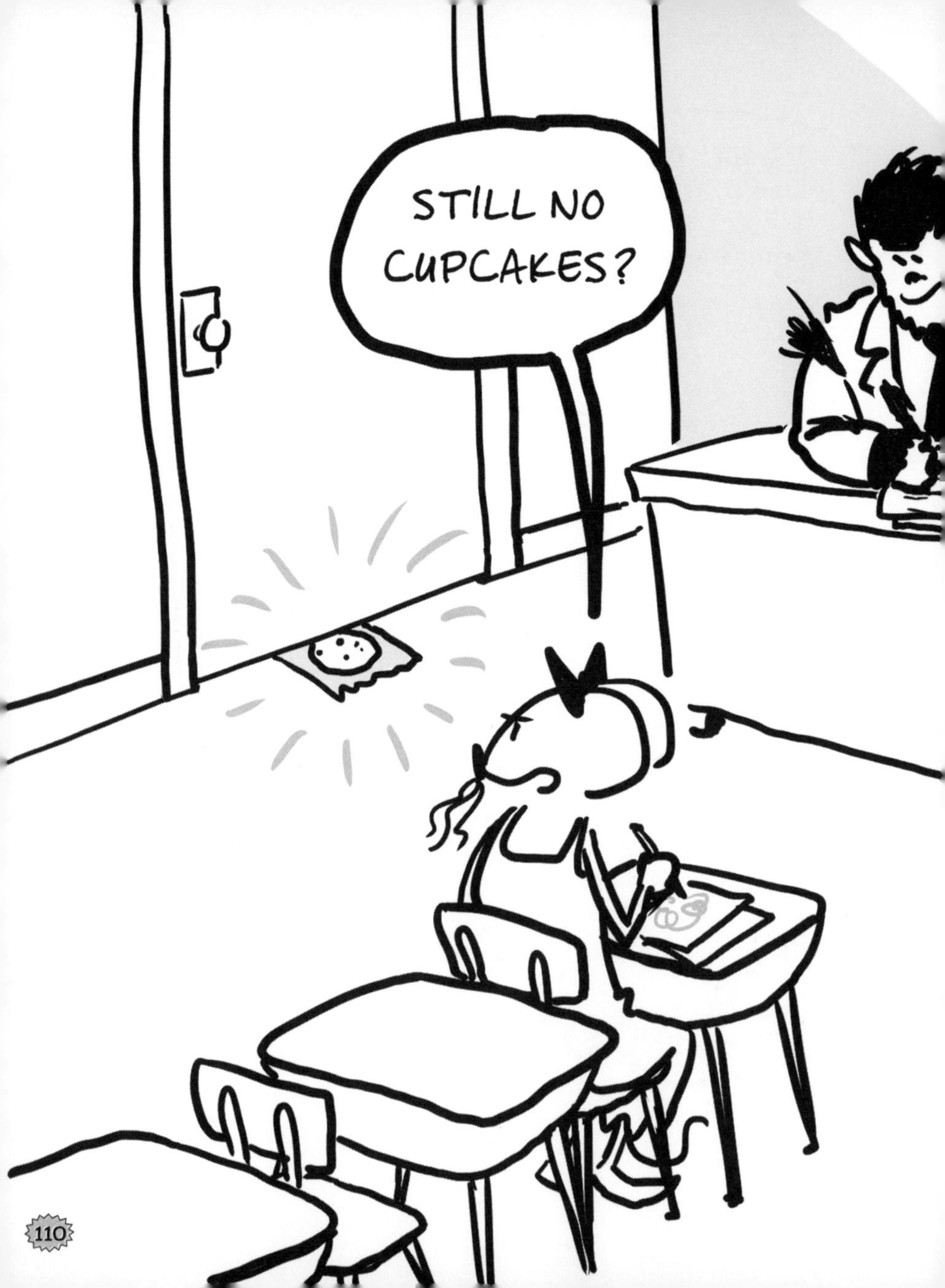
STILL NO
CUPCAKES?

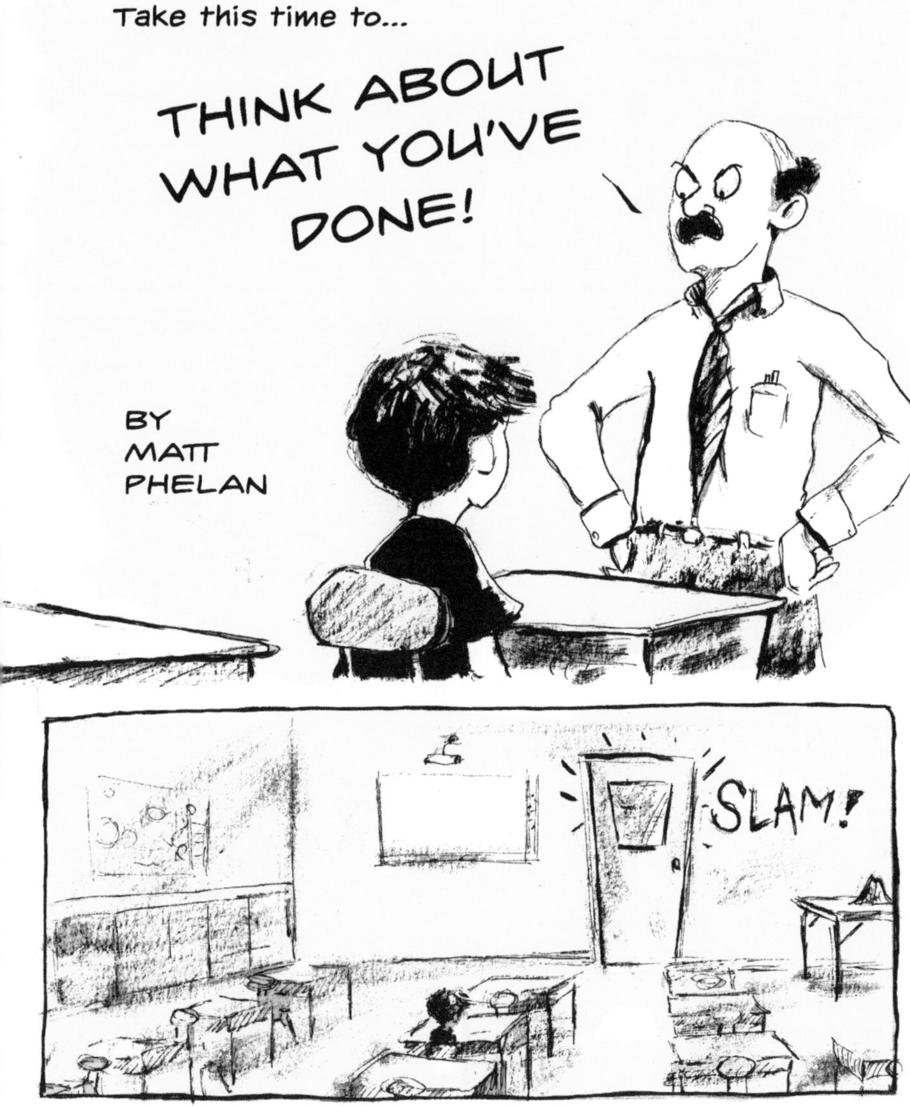
Take this time to...
THINK ABOUT WHAT YOU'VE DONE!
BY MATT PHELAN
SLAM!

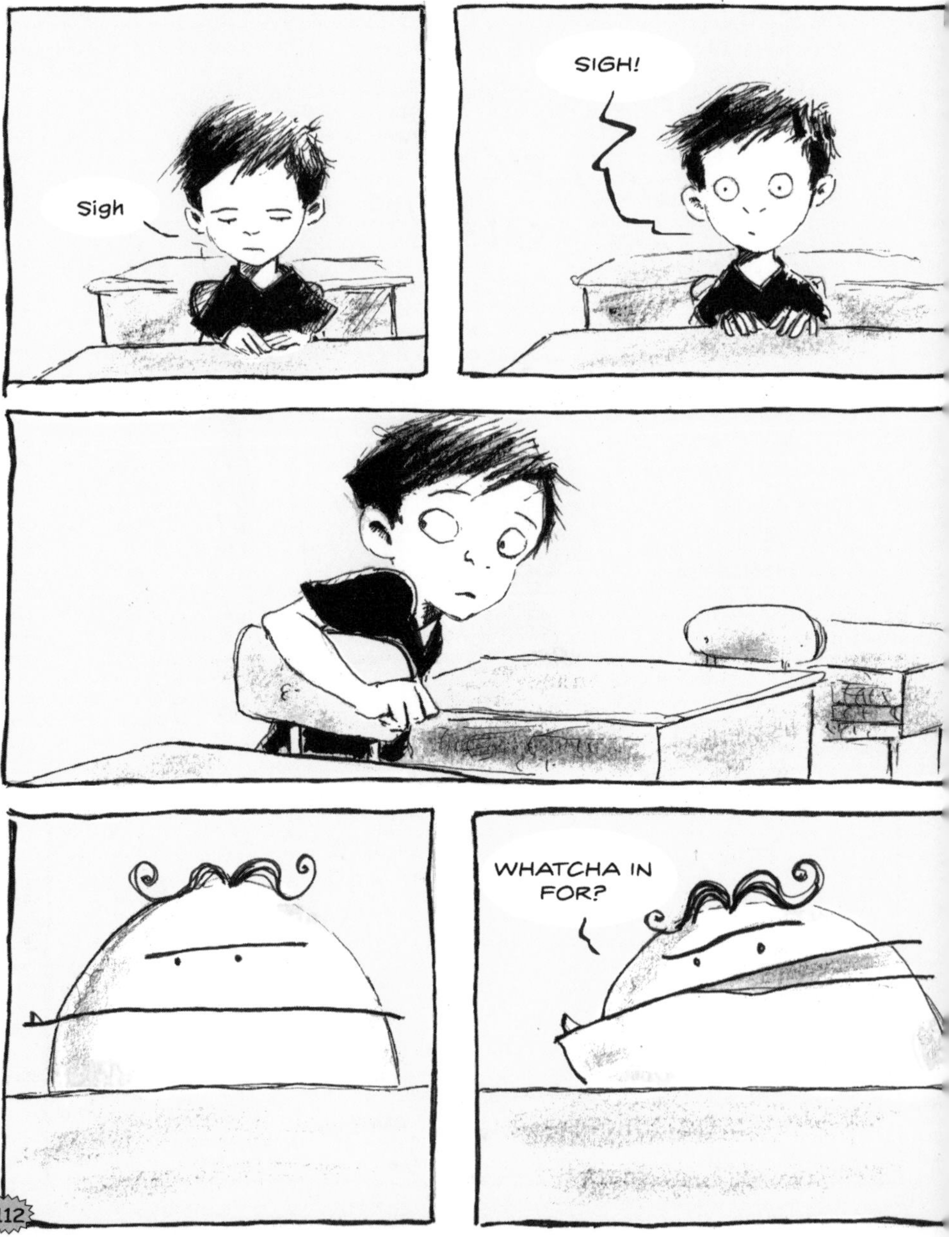
Sigh
SIGH!
WHATCHA IN FOR?

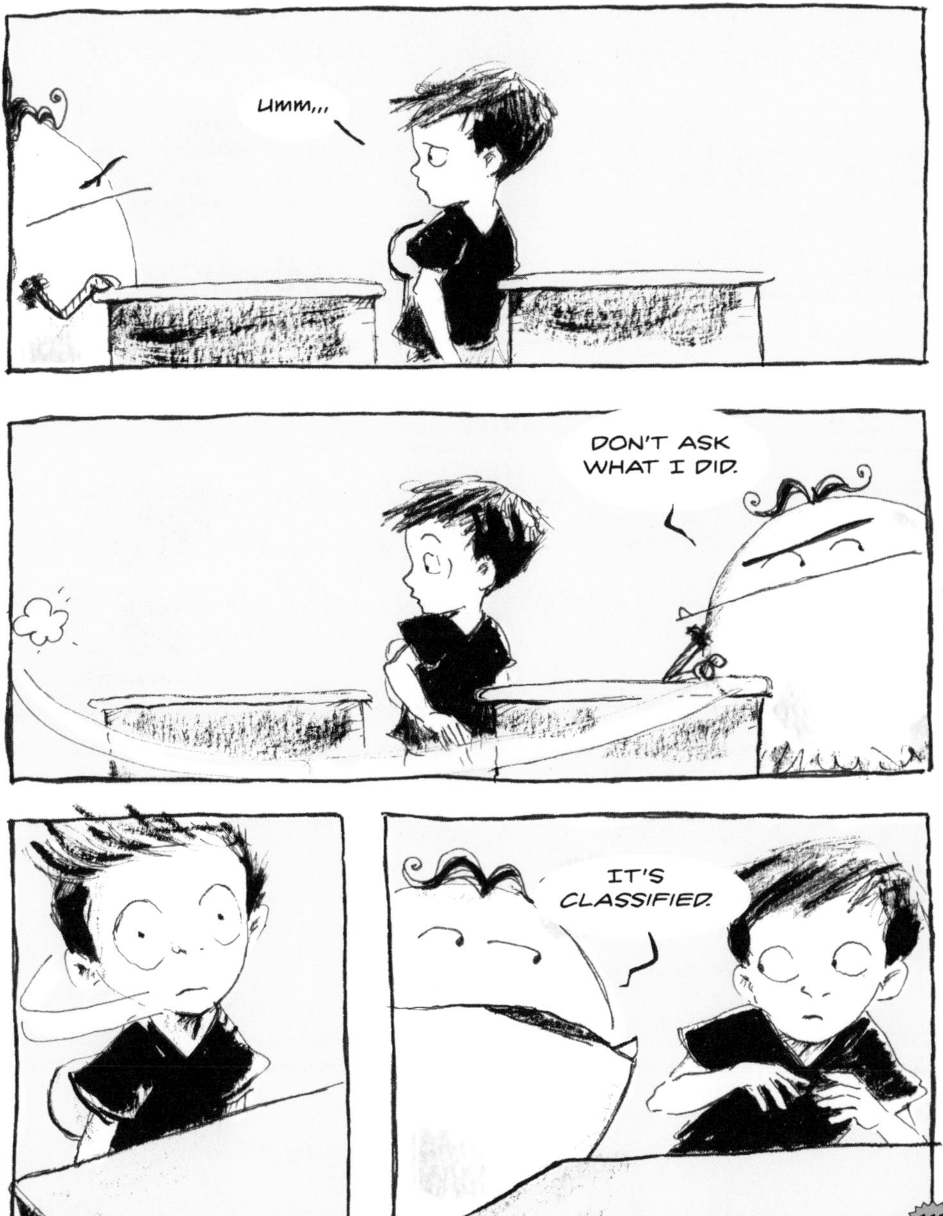
Umm...
DON'T ASK WHAT I DID.
IT'S CLASSIFIED.

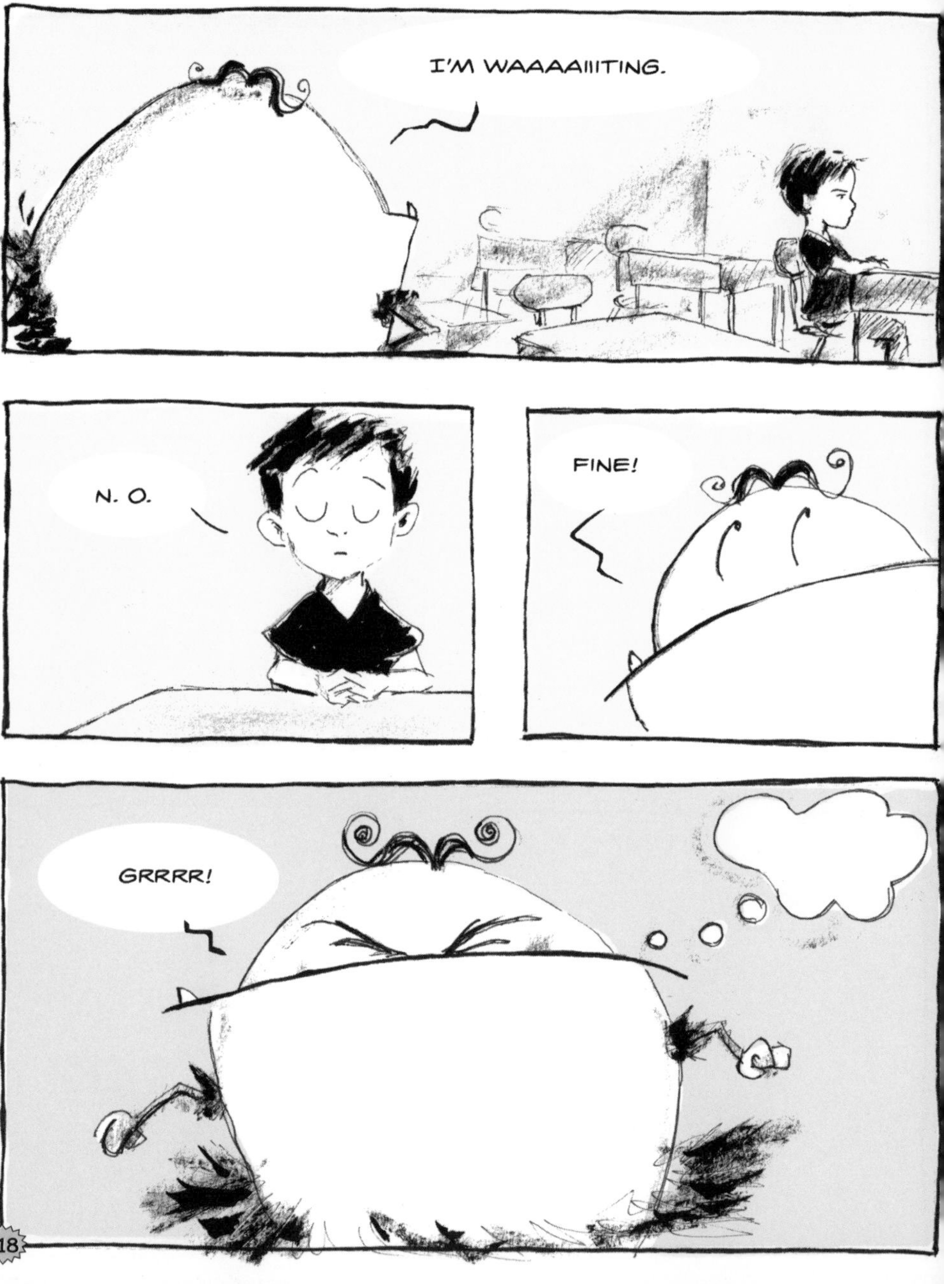
I'M WAAAAIIITING.
N. O.
FINE!
GRRRR!

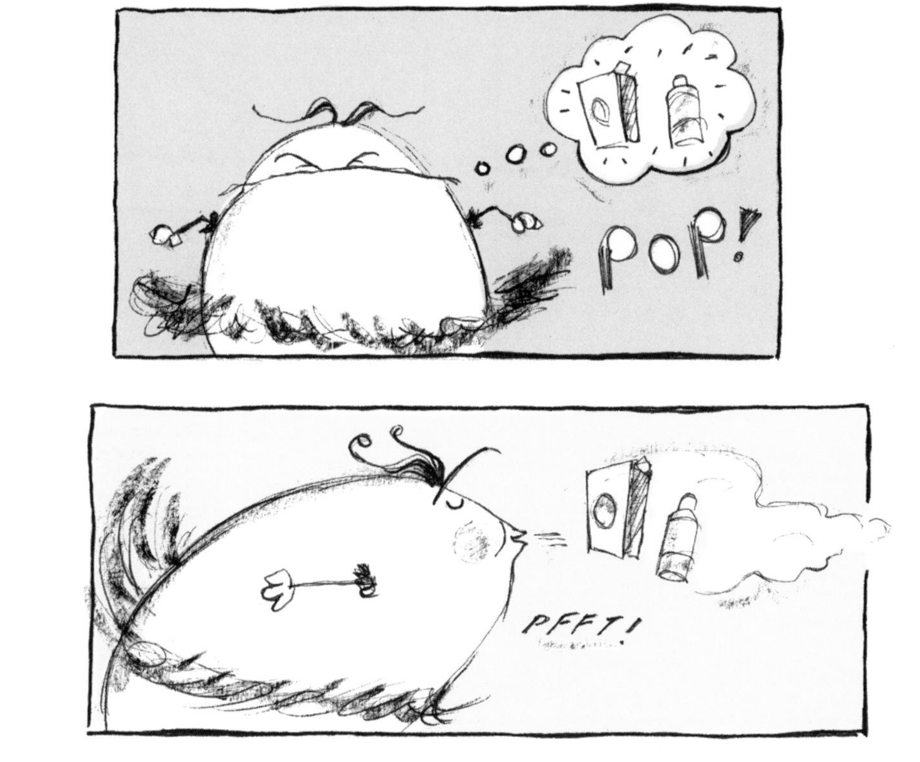
POP!
PFFT!
HA!

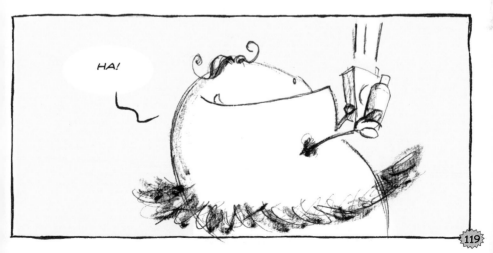

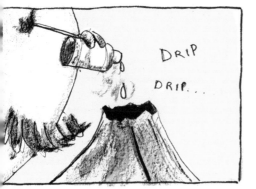

DRIP

DRIP. . .

BLOOP!

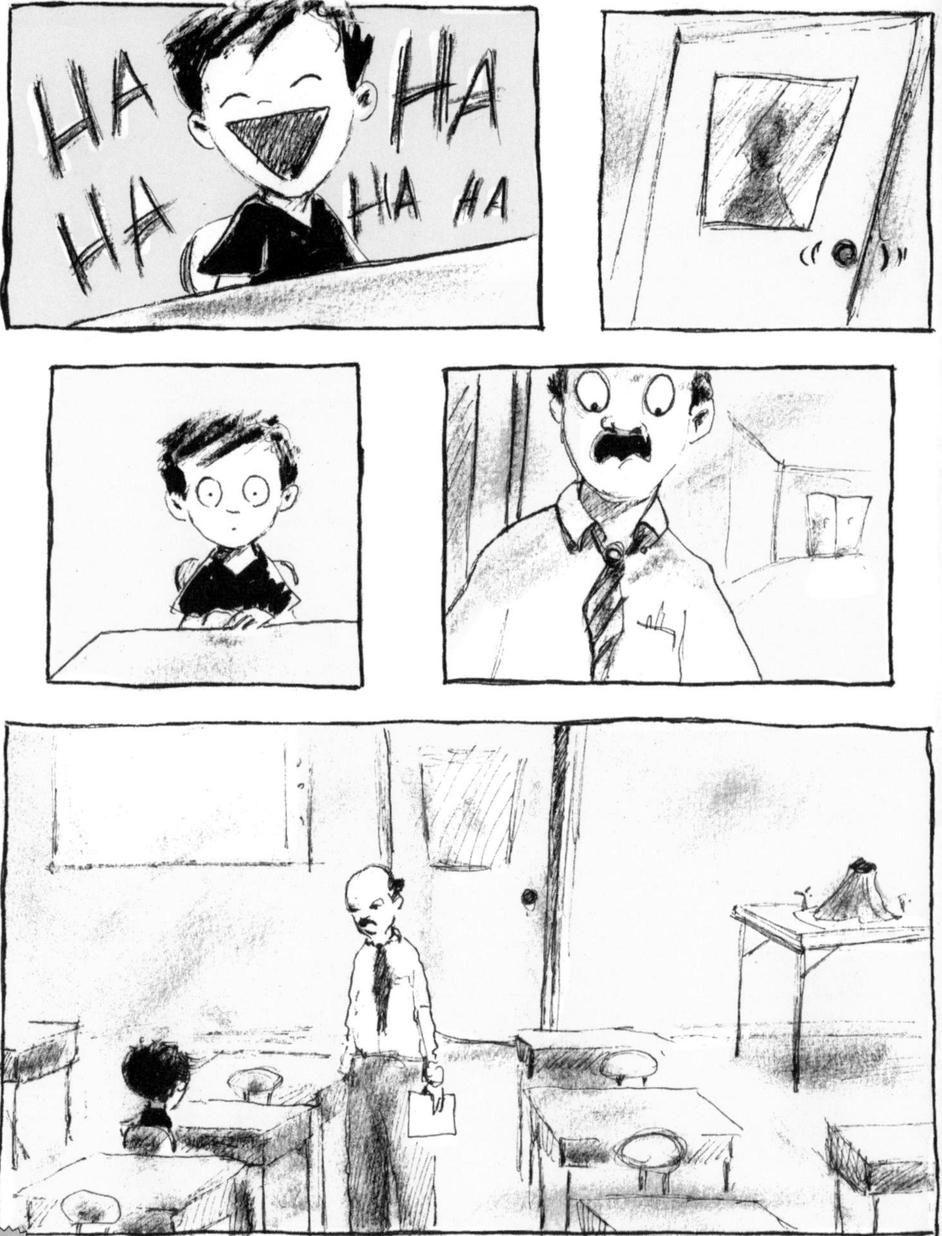
HA HA
HA HA HA HA

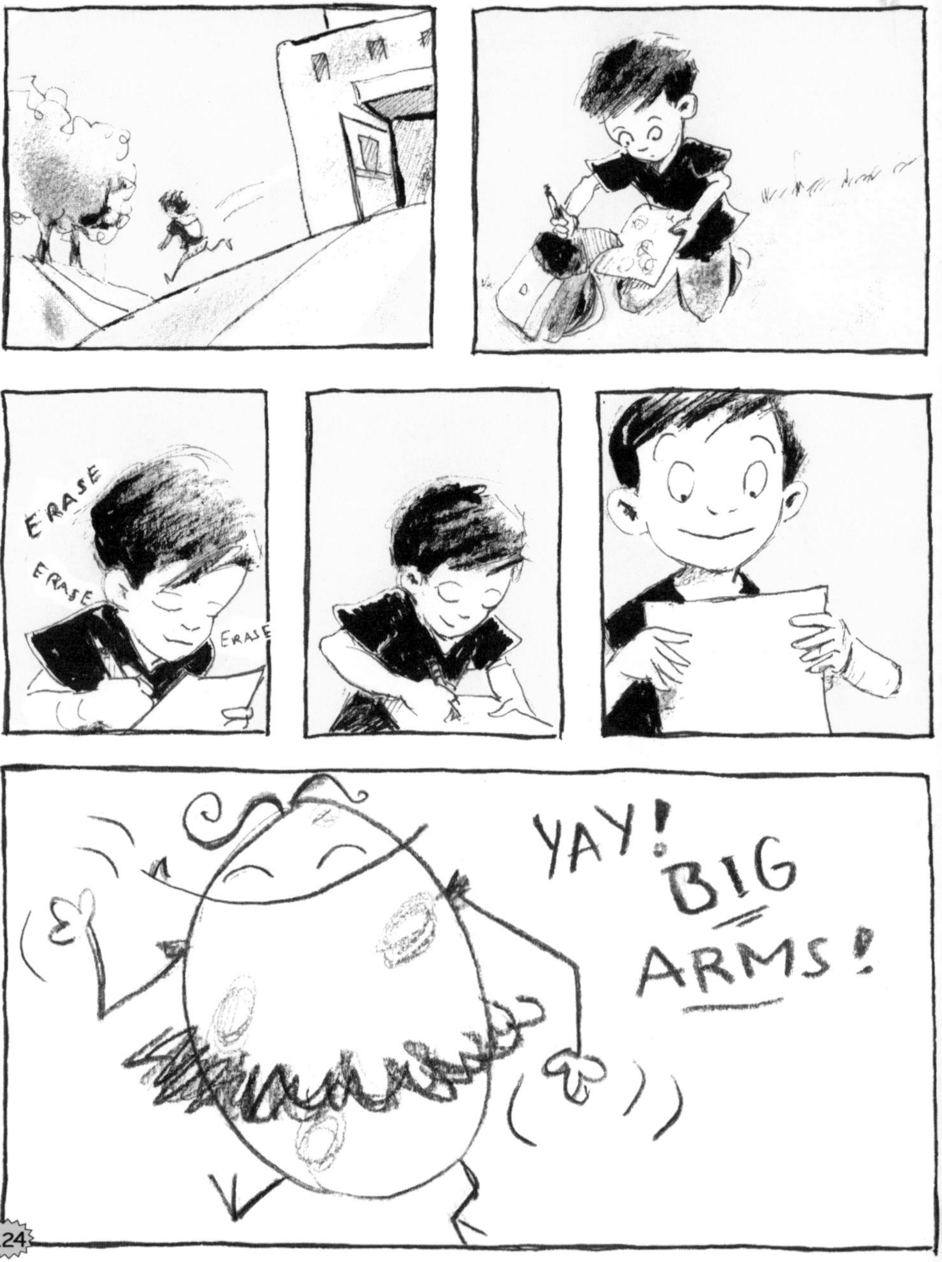
ERASE
ERASE
ERASE
YAY! BIG ARMS!

squish
LEAVE NO CELL BEHIND!

BY JENNIFER L. HOLM & MATTHEW HOLM

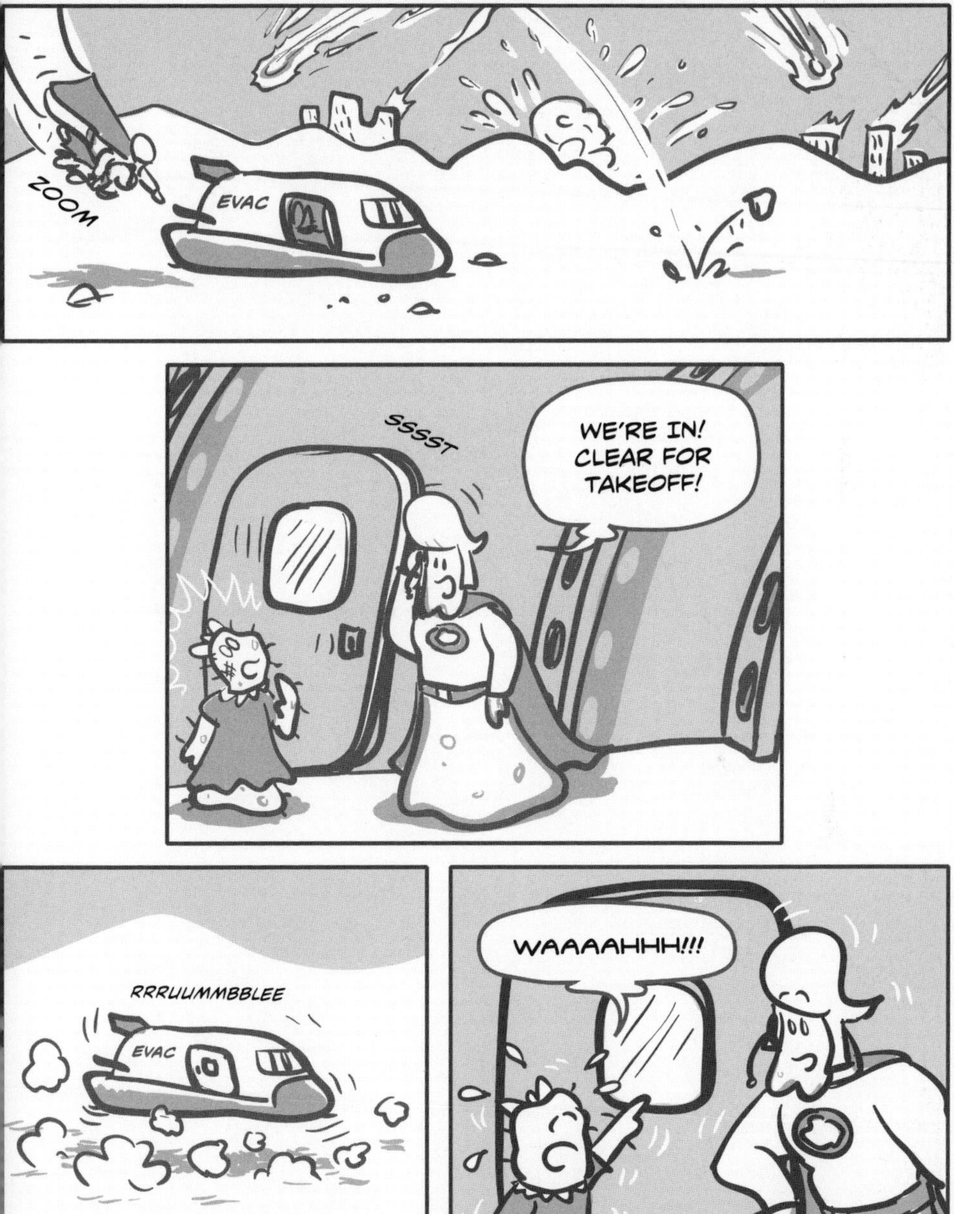
ZOOM
EVAC
SSSST
WE'RE IN! CLEAR FOR TAKEOFF!
RRRUUMMBBLEE
EVAC
WAAAAHHH!!!

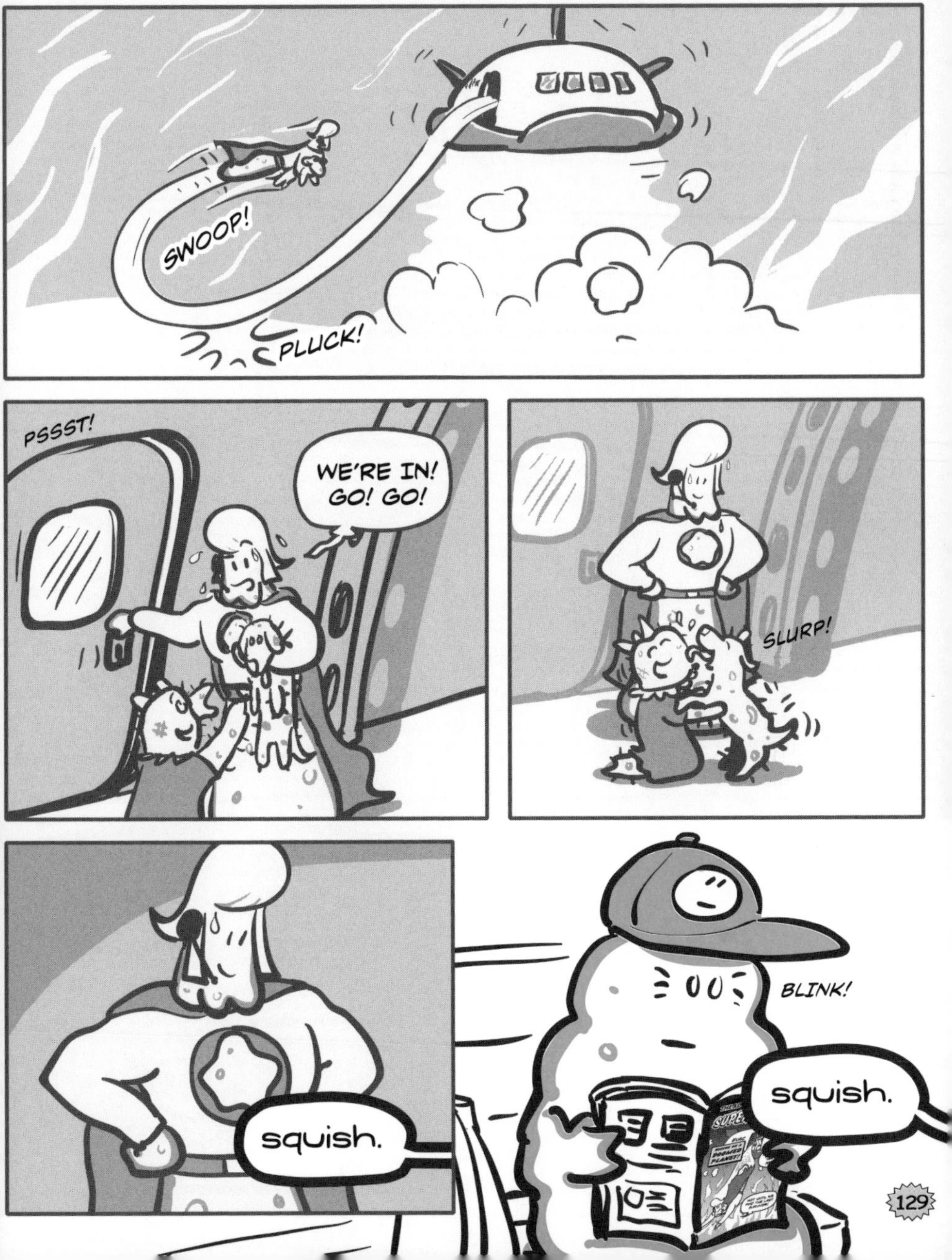
SWOOP!
PLUCK!
PSSST!
WE'RE IN! GO! GO!
SLURP!
squish.
BLINK!
squish.

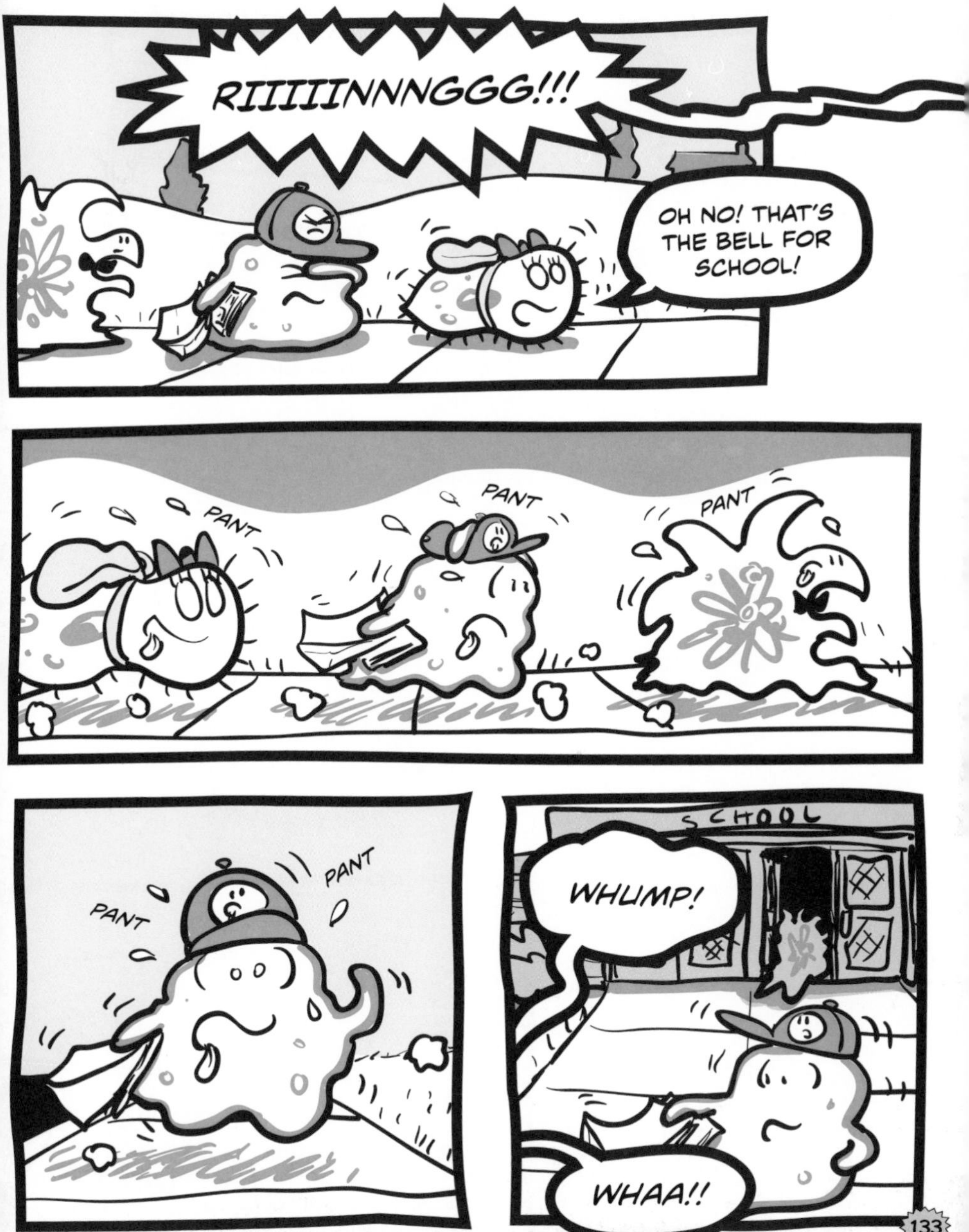
RIIIIINNNGGG!!!
OH NO! THAT'S THE BELL FOR SCHOOL!
PANT
PANT
PANT
PANT
PANT
SCHOOL
WHUMP!
WHAA!!

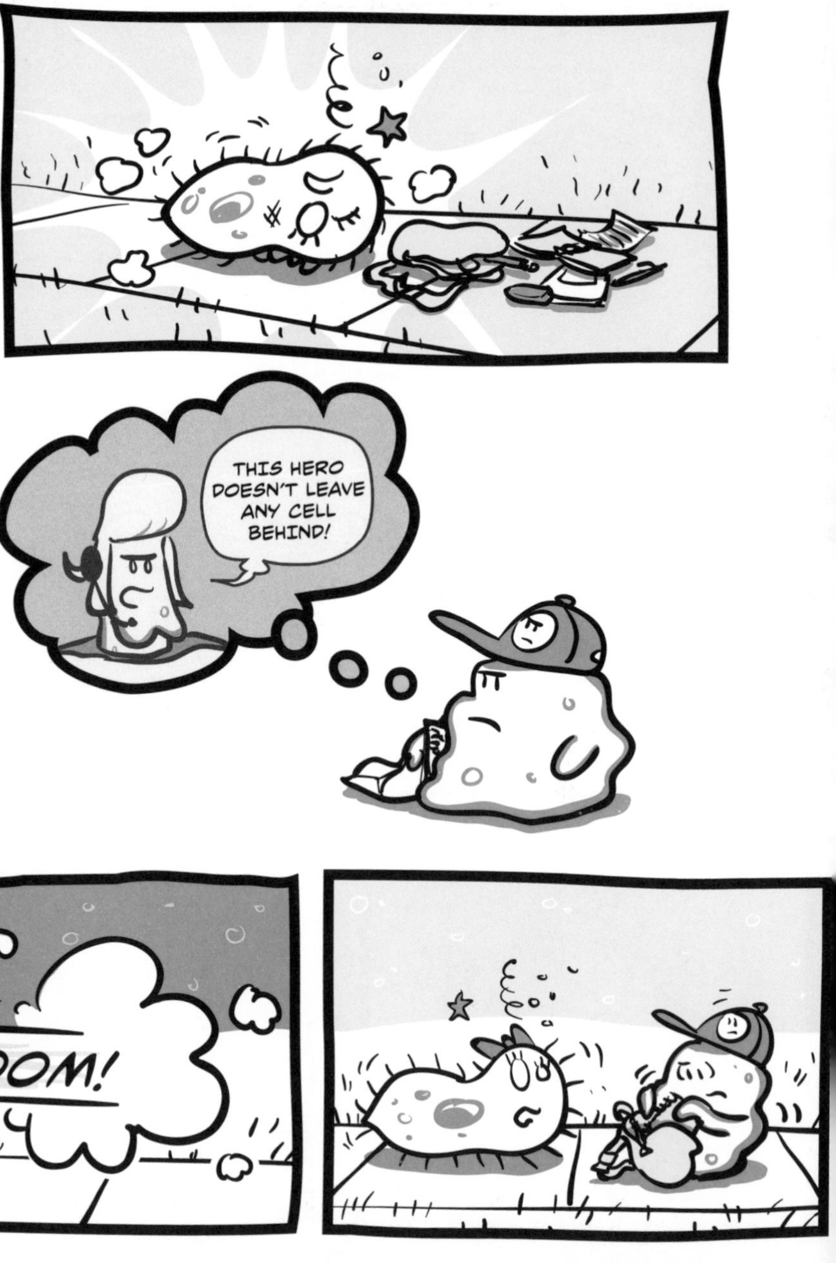
THIS HERO DOESN'T LEAVE ANY CELL BEHIND!
ZOOM!

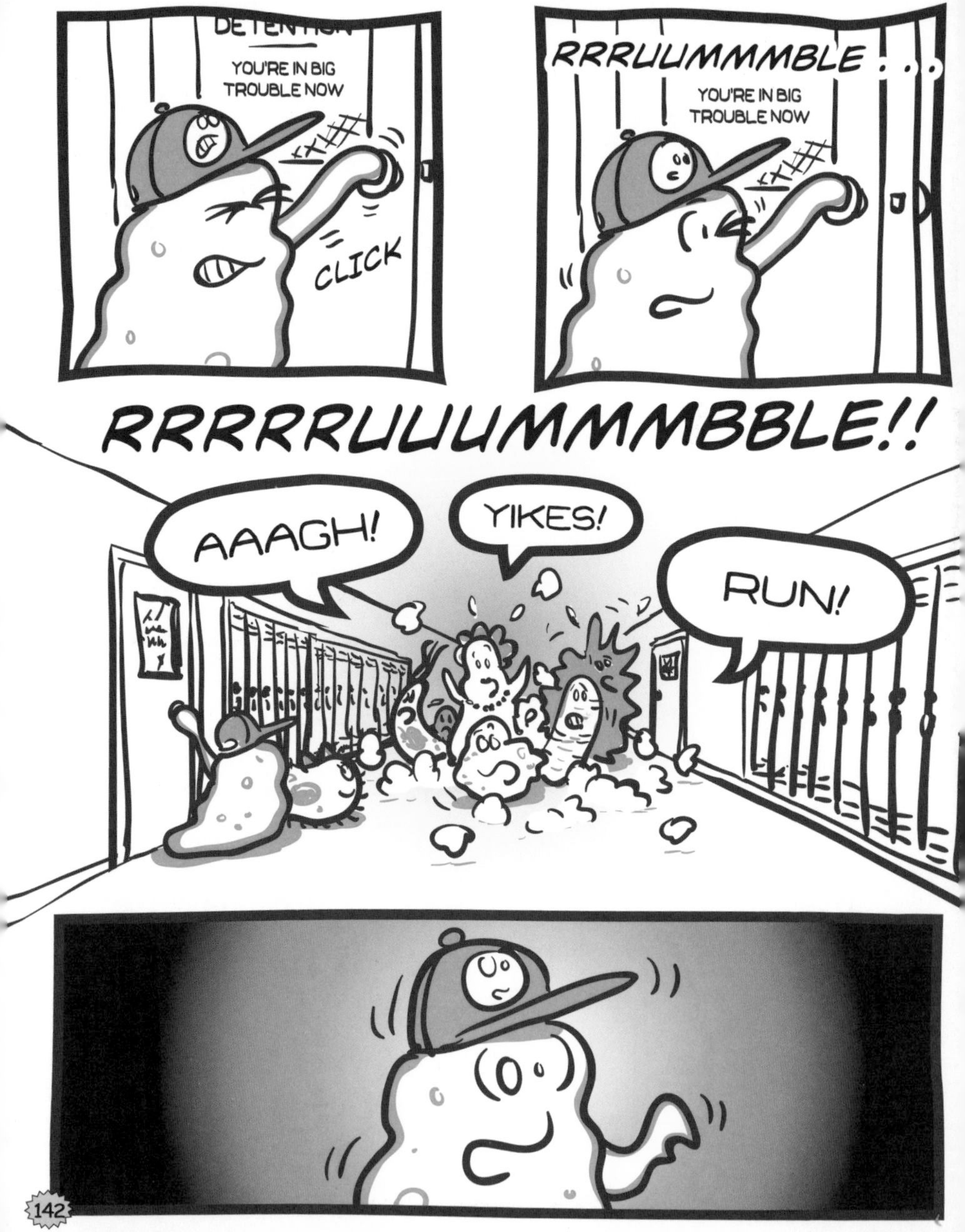
DETENTION
YOU'RE IN BIG TROUBLE NOW
CLICK
RRRUUMMMMBLE . . .
YOU'RE IN BIG TROUBLE NOW
RRRRRRUUUMMMMBBLE!!
AAAGH!
YIKES!
RUN!

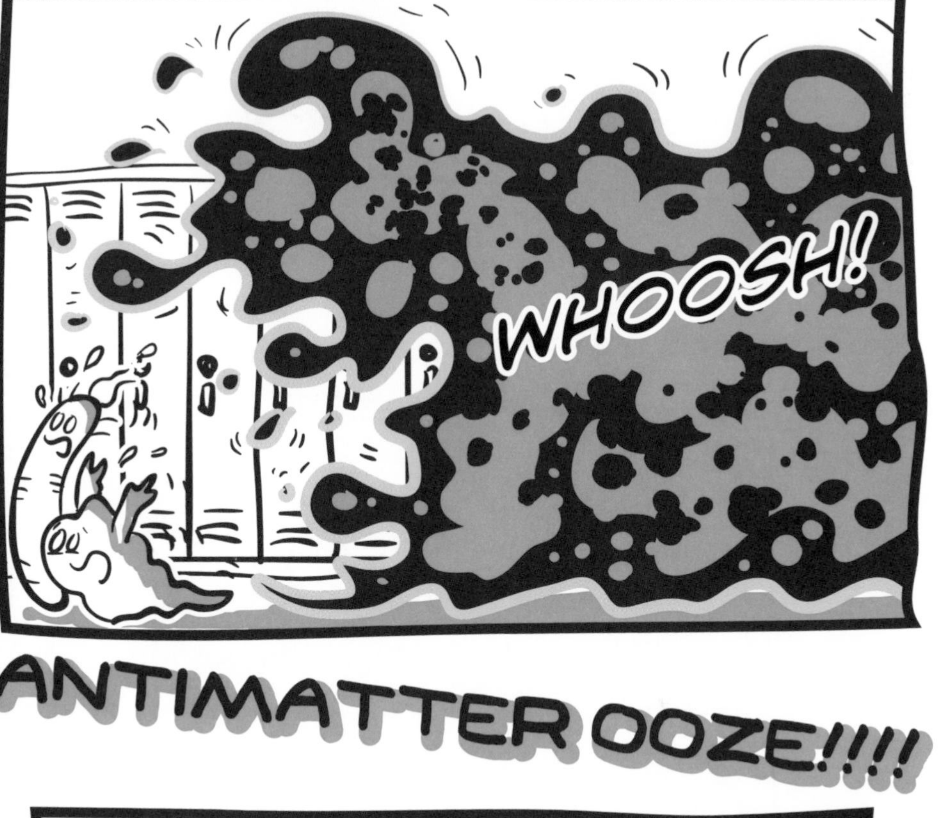
WHOOSH!

ANTIMATTER OOZE!!!!

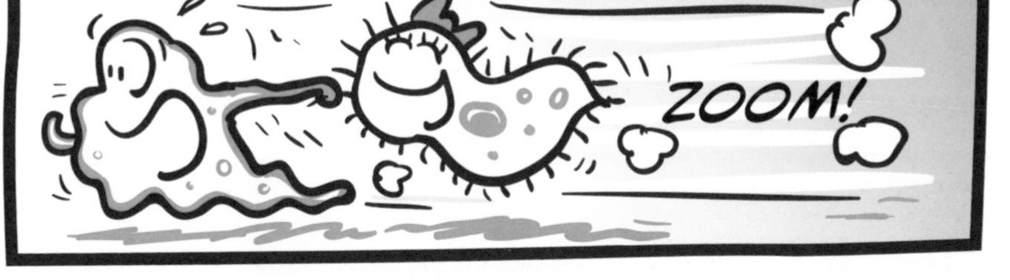
Run, Peggy!!
WHEEEEEE!!!
ZOOM!

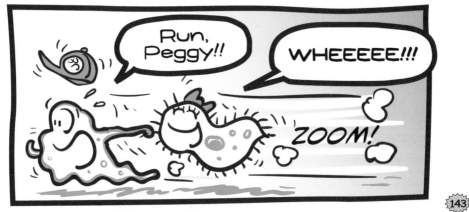

145

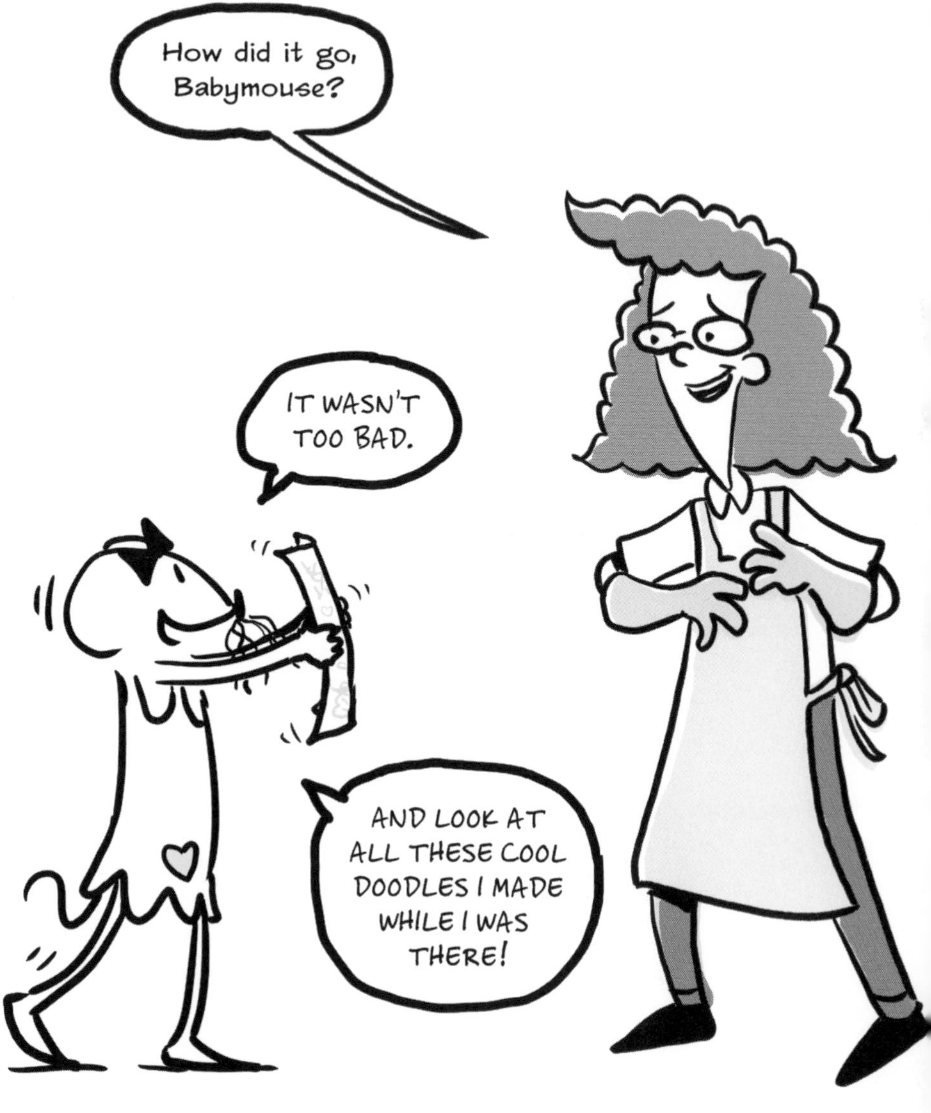
How did it go, Babymouse?
IT WASN'T TOO BAD.
AND LOOK AT ALL THESE COOL DOODLES I MADE WHILE I WAS THERE!

★ ABOUT THE AUTHORS ★

JARRETT J. KROSOCZKA

is the author and illustrator of more than thirty books, including the popular Lunch Lady graphic novels. He's delivered two TED Talks and can be heard weekly on SiriusXM's Kids Place Live. Jarrett is well-behaved; his pugs are not. (studiojjk.com)

GEORGE O'CONNOR

is the cartoonist behind the Olympians series of graphic novels. He never, ever had detention because he was always a very, very good boy. Totally. (olympiansrule.com)

VICTORIA JAMIESON

is the author and illustrator of the graphic novel *Roller Girl,* which won a Newbery Honor award. She lives in Portland, Oregon, with her family. She has only had one detention in her life, in driver's ed class in high school. Cause for the detention is still undetermined. (victoriajamieson.com)

BEN HATKE

draws and writes both comics and picture books. He's particularly known for the Zita the Spacegirl trilogy. Ben dressed up as an eyeball once for Halloween. It was awesome. (benhatke.com)

RAFAEL ROSADO & JORGE AGUIRRE

are the team behind the pint-sized hero Claudette (*Giants Beware*, *Dragons Beware*, and an upcoming third book). They became friends while at the Ohio State University. They have never been sent to detention together, but if they ever were, they'd probably spend the time making more comics. (dragonsbeware.com)

LARK PIEN

is the author of *Long Tail Kitty* and *Mr. Elephanter*, and the colorist of *American Born Chinese*, *Boxers and Saints*, and *Sunny Side Up*. Sometimes she is also a troublemaker!

MATT PHELAN

is the author-illustrator of *Bluffton* and three other graphic novels. This is the first comic he has set in the present day. Huh. Weird. (mattphelan.com)

JENNIFER L. HOLM & MATTHEW HOLM

are the brother-sister team behind two graphic novel series, Babymouse and Squish. They grew up reading lots of comics, and they turned out just fine. (babymouse.com)

LUNCH LADY

Serving justice! And serving lunch!